Praise for DeWanna Pace's previous novels:

"A fervent novel that places the importance of honor high on the list to keep a friendship genuine and alive. The entire ensemble of this book is dazzlingly developed . . . *A Taste of Honey* is a sweet-tasting appetizer in what appears to have the makings of a fabulous collection."
—Harriet Klausner, *Under the Covers*

"Ms. Pace's brilliant use of words and smooth storytelling make this a must-read. SWEET."
—*Romantic Times*

"Three little imps, a cast of colorful characters, a caring heroine, and a hero afraid to trust in love, plus the intrigue and the alluring power of the ocean make this a tale you won't put down till the last word. You'll be wanting the story to go on. I loved every page of it."
—*Rendezvous*

Jove titles by DeWanna Pace

SUGAR AND SPICE
BECKONING SHORE
A TASTE OF HONEY
WHERE HEROES SLEEP

Where Heroes Sleep

DeWanna Pace

JOVE BOOKS, NEW YORK

This is a work of fiction. Names, characters, places, and incidents are
either the product of the author's imagination or are used fictitiously,
and any resemblance to actual persons, living or dead, business
establishments, events or locales is entirely coincidental.

FRIENDS is a trademark of Penguin Putnam Inc.

WHERE HEROES SLEEP

A Jove Book / published by arrangement with
the author

PRINTING HISTORY
Jove edition / December 1999

The Penguin Putnam Inc. World Wide Web site address is
http://www.penguinputnam.com

ISBN: 0-515-12702-7

A JOVE BOOK®
Jove Books are published by The Berkley Publishing Group,
a division of Penguin Putnam Inc.,
375 Hudson Street, New York, New York 10014.
JOVE and the "J" design
are trademarks belonging to Penguin Putnam Inc.

PRINTED IN THE UNITED STATES OF AMERICA

10 9 8 7 6 5 4 3 2 1

This book is dedicated to
KIM CAMPBELL:
friend, suspense writer, critiquer.

Your ready opinion
always casts new light.
Thanks for helping me grow.

●

Prologue

*T*all spiky pines stood alert, seemingly resentful of Kenzy Dixon's intrusion along the wooded path. Sunlight sparkled like a thousand fireflies on the Sabine River which ran parallel to the trail. The river had a hum of its own, a song of belonging that coursed strongly in Kenzy's bloodstream. The twelve-year-old was sure her heart would slow its beating once she left the piney woods behind and headed North. East Texas never looked so much like home as it did now . . . knowing she was about to leave it and her best friend, Rose, forever.

Kenzy's green eyes misted over. How would she ever tell Rose she was moving? How could she say goodbye? Somehow her parents had found a way to borrow the money needed for traveling expenses. Now, they planned to take that offer to manage a boardinghouse in Cambridge. Massachusetts, of all places. The end of the earth!

"Are you deaf?"

A brown-haired, black-eyed girl raced toward Kenzy. Her calico bonnet shielded the afternoon sun from the girl's face, but Kenzy would recognize Anna LeGrand's petulant tone anywhere. Though separated in age by only a year, Kenzy thought her neighbor acted like a spoiled baby most of the time.

"I've been calling you for at least two miles. Open your ears, McKenzy Dixon."

"You haven't done *anything* for two miles in your entire life, Anna, and you know it." Kenzy quickly hid her tears, pretending she was swatting away the dust Anna's hooped skirt kicked up along the sandy path. Kenzy wrinkled her nose and sneezed for effect. Maybe then Anna wouldn't ask why her eyes looked puffy.

How did Anna expect to go swimming in that hoop, for goodness' sake? She probably didn't plan to swim with the rest of the girls, come to think of it. Bet Anna had prissed herself up for the boys again. Kenzy and Rose didn't play that silly game. They discovered earlier that summer that the boys showed off for those girls who never got into the water—girls too afraid to get their hair wet.

But that never lasted long. The real fun came later. The Miss Prisses had to go home because the metal that replaced difficult-to-purchase bone in their hoopskirts heated up from too much sun.

Instead of hoops, she and Rose always wore their fathers' long johns beneath their dresses. They stripped down to the red longhandles the moment they arrived at the cove, then dove in. She and Rose played leapfrog or swung from the tree limbs out over the river, just like the boys. But not today. Mama and Papa wanted her home to help with the packing. She couldn't go swimming with Rose . . . not today, maybe not ever again.

"Would you quit crying, Kenzy? I didn't kick up that much dust!" Anna crossed her arms and frowned.

"What's got . . . achoo! . . . you in a tangle this time?" Kenzy countered, giving one more sneeze for good measure.

"You mean you don't know? Rosella didn't tell you?"

Anna's hand splayed across her chest, forming a fleshy tent over the row of buttons that lined her shirtwaist.

Kenzy waited for Miss-Mind-Everybody's-Business to quit gasping like she'd sucked in a lungful of cayenne pepper. They both knew Anna was in no danger of expiring and couldn't wait to tattle.

Spinning halfway around, Kenzy glanced at the path she'd just traveled. Rose was nowhere in sight. They had agreed to meet halfway, but the talk with Mama and Papa had taken much longer than expected, forcing Kenzy to be at least fifteen minutes later. Maybe Rose had gone on ahead without her. Or maybe she thought Kenzy had changed her mind and went home.

Anna's exaggerated gasping grew louder. With a sigh, Kenzy quit ignoring Anna's tactics. "I don't have time for guessing games, so who's supposed to have told me what?"

"Rosella Whitaker, of course. Your dearest and closest . . . your supposed-to-be sister. Why do you think she's not here yet?" Anna's brows arched like bronzed wings. "She thought you would never find out. But I did."

"Find out what?" Kenzy stared hard at the eleven-year-old. What was she up to? Rose wouldn't tell anyone anything before she told Kenzy.

"I always warned you she wasn't your real friend. She only wanted you around so—"

"That's Rose you're talking about. My very *best* friend. You better watch real careful what you say, Anna LeGrand." Kenzy's hands knotted into fists, ready to defend Rose.

"Kenzy! Wait up!"

Filled with relief at the sound of the familiar voice behind her, Kenzy turned. Her fists unknotted to wave. A quick study of her friend's face made Kenzy's stomach hurt and her throat feel as if she'd swallowed a clump of prairie grass. The tears she'd fought so hard to hide from Anna now sprang into her eyes like water from a primed spout. How could she tell her that she couldn't go swimming with her this last time? That she couldn't spend the afternoon staring up at the clouds and talk about their futures? Would they become strangers once she moved away?

Kenzy blinked hard, forcing back the hot sting of tears. Instead she focused on Rose, storing every detail to be remembered later. Long legs made Rose taller than Kenzy and helped cut the distance that separated them. Strawberry-blonde hair, like a pony's tail in full run, whipped against the satchel strapped to her best friend's back. Always prepared, that Rose. No telling what she carried in the bag.

But it was Rose's eyes Kenzy would remember most. The color of a Texas sky just as night passed into dawn. The kind of eyes that made Kenzy feel better when she peered into them. Silver-gray. Always caring. Usually calm.

Not today. They were almost blue. Twinkling like they did when she had some great secret to share. A secret that seemed to have made her very happy. If only Anna wasn't here. Kenzy didn't mind sharing some things with Anna, but she'd always suspected her neighbor resented Rose for choosing Kenzy to be her best friend.

Normally, Kenzy ignored Anna's snippy remarks as long as they weren't targeted directly to Rose. But today was not the day for Anna to test Kenzy's patience. She would tolerate no criticism of her best friend.

"Where have you been?" Kenzy thought of a dozen things that might have detained Rose.

"Go ahead and tell her, Rosella." Reproach sharpened Anna's tone.

"Tell me what?" Tired of Anna's insinuations, Kenzy glared at the younger girl rocking on the heels of her kid boots. Kenzy moved closer. Anna stumbled, backing away. "If you've got something to say, just say it." Kenzy's fist knotted again, her legs bracing for a fight.

"It's not me you should be so nasty to, McKenzy Dixon." Anna pointed a finger at Rose. "Ask *her* who loaned your parents the money so you'd have to move.

Ask her how they got enough to travel and for that prissy academy you want to attend. But most of all, ask Miss Royal Rosella why she wants you out of town." Anna's finger tapped the side of her cheek. "Hmmmm. I wonder. Could it have anything to do with making you leave so Noble will pay more attention to *her*?"

"You take that back, Anna! You take that back right now or I'm gonna—"

"Stop it, Kenzy!" Rose grabbed Kenzy's fist as it raised. "You'll get in trouble for hitting her."

"She shouldn't tell such lies!" Kenzy glared at Anna, though her words were meant for Rose. "And she sure ain't gonna tell one about you as long as I'm around to hear it."

"I *did* ask my parents for the money," Rose said quietly, her hand pressing gently over Kenzy's fist. "I-I thought you'd be really pleased."

Kenzy's eyes widened in disbelief. She stared hard at Rose, trying to understand. Rose was a peacemaker who didn't like to see anyone fight. She would say just about anything to prevent Kenzy from getting in trouble for scrapping.

"You know the best thing we can do for Anna is to pull out a few plugs of hair," Kenzy insisted. "Maybe then she won't go around spouting such vicious lies."

"She's telling the truth, Kenz. I meant to tell you myself, but . . . well . . . she told you before I could." Rose's frosty glare at Anna could have melted the snow off the Rockies at their wintery best.

Confusion filled Kenzy as Rose shifted her satchel and linked their arms.

"Think about it, Kenz. You have to work so hard to help your parents earn a living, you hardly ever get to go to school. Now you can go to that academy in Cambridge." Rose's voice lowered, even trembled. "I-I thought about it a lot. A whole lot, Kenz. The only way you're ever gonna be what you want to be is if you go to that fancy school and take lessons from that architect fellow."

The enormity of what Rose offered hit Kenzy full force. Rose was always generous, always making certain Kenzy didn't do without. One of the wealthier class in San Augustine, her best friend didn't look down upon a sharecropper's daughter. Instead, she'd befriended her and always made Kenzy's harsh life a little easier.

Gratitude for her friend's kindness dimmed beneath the other emotions Anna had stirred within Kenzy. "You're too good to me, Whit." Kenzy's affectionate name for Rose came as naturally to her as the wind rippling reeds along the bank. "But I can't accept. When would we ever pay you back?" *What if I failed*, she added silently and immediately hoped that failure was not an inherited condition.

They both knew her parents dreamed big, but nothing ever happened. The Dixons were good people. Worked from dawn to dark. But as hard as they tried, they just couldn't seem to get ahead. Kenzy never considered they would leave the one place she'd felt more at home than any of the countless towns where they'd lived. In her four years in San Augustine, she'd found a best friend and the place where she *wanted* to belong. Most of all, she'd discovered Noble Stockton—the boy she just might marry someday.

Maybe her parents would dislike working at the boardinghouse. The first time one of them complained about anything in Massachusetts, she would beg them to return here. *Please let them listen*, Kenzy prayed.

"Everybody knows the Dixons have to borrow from Miss Euphemia all the time. They're as poor as that dark devil gypsy boy, Rem Parker, and his grandmother. They won't ever pa—"

Rose pushed Anna. "You stop that right now, Anna LeGrand, or I'm going to tell your mama about what you did at church last Sunday."

Surprised by her friend's show of anger, Kenzy wondered if Anna would dare push Rose back. But Anna was smarter than she looked and elected not to strike back. A good thing, 'cause Kenzy was ready to yank out *all* of that brown wad of hair now!

"See if I care, Rosella Whitaker. At least I'm telling the truth." Anna backed up the trail, her words growing bolder the farther away she got. Her gaze shot to Kenzy. "Instead of being so mad at me, why don't you ask Rose the real reason she wants you out of town?"

No matter how much Kenzy wished she could ignore Anna's insinuation, her neighbor had planted a seed of doubt in her mind. Enough to make her stare in question at her best friend.

Rose's arm relinked with Kenzy's, tightening in reassurance. "As if he even looks at me. Noble thinks you're the smartest girl he knows. He's told me so."

Kenzy's heart soared. "You and Noble talked about me? He thinks I'm smart?" A dozen questions raced to mind. "When did you two talk without me? Why didn't you tell me about it?"

"He tells me all the time . . . even when you're around."

"Oh." Kenzy decided she needed to pay better attention. But how many more times would she get the chance to do that? "He's fifteen," she announced realizing that, by the time she was old enough to return on her own to San Augustine, he would probably be engaged or married to someone else. Noble was fifteen years of blond-haired, blue-eyed, bronzed, make-her-breath-stop *man.* "The handsomest boy in the whole world. You think for one minute he's going to remember *me* after I'm gone?"

The boy she and Rose idolized was someone special. He always listened to all Kenzy had to say and never laughed at her for the wrong reason. But he also never failed to make *her* laugh. She'd even dreamed of Noble . . . ever since he made Eb Wheeler apologize for putting crawdad eyes in her lunch.

At ten years old, she'd promised herself she would marry Noble. But Rose decided a long time ago he was the boy she liked most, too. Since then, they'd both

made it their aim to find out as much as they could about
him. Each agreed that one could be the bride and the
other the bridesmaid, depending on which of them Noble
eventually chose as his wife.

An ugly possibility sprouted in Kenzy's mind, one that
spread like a fast growing weed. At first, their pursuit of
Noble had just been to compete. But as they headed toward the expected marrying age of fifteen for young ladies, she and Rose seemed to have a few spats with each
other. None that they couldn't get over. But . . . could
there be any truth to what Anna said?

Sickened by the turn of her thoughts, Kenzy searched
for reason. Never would she believe Anna over Rose.
That went without saying. But her relief was short-lived.
No matter what the reason, the Dixons were determined
to move to Massachusetts.

Wind whispered in the tree crowns. Leaves spiraled
and danced, then rushed along the path ahead of them.
Kenzy felt dizzy, too, as if she were spinning around
and being rushed to some place she didn't want to go.
She tightened the link with her friend's arm. Well, she
wouldn't be gone for long. She'd see to that!

The lump in her throat seemed to swell to the size of
Texas as Kenzy told Rose that she'd only been allowed
enough time to explain why she couldn't go swimming
today. Disappointment etched Rose's expression, urging
Kenzy to reassure her best friend. "I'll be back. I mean
it. I'm coming home as soon as I convince Mama and
Papa this is the best place in the whole world for us to
live."

Wind whipped Kenzy's thick, auburn mass of curls
making it feel as if a dust devil whirled through it. "You
can tell that to Noble when he walks us to church tomorrow. But make sure he doesn't think I'm listening. I'll sit
behind you and pretend I'm talking to Anna and . . . no,
I'll tell him. My parents never keep a job very long, you
know that. It won't be a lie."

"You know how he hates lies. I know you'll come
back. But shouldn't you tell him that you'll *try* to be

back soon? That everything depends on your parents?"
Rose reached into the satchel she had strapped around
her shoulder and pulled out a roll of parchment, a capped
inkwell and quill. The inkwell was made of the finest
Irish crystal, the top an ornately carved ring of gold.
"Here, take this."

Hesitantly, Kenzy reached out to accept the writing
material. "What for?"

"So that you can write me while you're gone. I've
even included money to mail the first few letters. When
that runs out, I'll send more."

Kenzy shook her head, thrusting the instruments back
at her. "I can't take them."

"Whyever not?" Rose insisted. "I'll write you about
all that goes on here. And I'll tell you about Noble, too.
Maybe he'll even send you a letter or two himself."

When he's not busy courting you. Jealousy tasted sour
in Kenzy's throat.

"Please, Kenz. It would mean a lot to me if you'd
take them. Then I'd *know* I could hear from you, and
you wouldn't have to depend on your . . . you wouldn't
have to wait on money for postage."

"Thanks." Kenzy finally accepted the gift, knowing
Rose was right. Postage and parchment would be low
on her family's list of necessities—especially enough to
write Rose as often as Kenzy intended. She couldn't let
pride keep her from being able to talk to Rose, even if
it would be only on paper. Kenzy would await every
letter with so much anticipation it would literally hurt.
If she couldn't be near them, at least she could keep
informed with what they did. "You will write? Truly?"

"Every day I can."

Kenzy blinked hard, fighting back the tears that
sprang from the deep well of friendship. "We really have
to say good-bye, don't we?"

Rosella nodded. "But remember what we promised?"

"We were only eight." Kenzy studied the braided hair
rings each wore on the forefinger of her left hand. After
knowing each other a few months, they had vowed to

become blood sisters since neither had a real sister. Kenzy decided they would be different than others who sealed such a pledge. They would pluck hair from their heads and braid it into rings to be swapped then worn on their fingers.

The girls touched hand to hand and repeated the vow they'd made in unison. "Now and forever, always together. Sisters."

1

July 1865
San Augustine, Texas

Twilight gripped the countryside with a cooling mist, causing long shadows to fall upon the land. The threat of a summer tempest flashed in the distance while low-hanging clouds seeped fine droplets of moisture into the red soil of East Texas. Loblolly pines edged the acres of ancient hardwoods and the new land Rose Whitaker had purchased. They loomed dark and towering, their trunks almost black from rain.

"Better put tarpaulins over everything. I'll go see where Euphemia and the boys wandered off to," Kenzy announced to the carpenter hammering away at his assigned task. "Danger's moving our direction."

Another glance at the sky sent her scurrying to the wagon for lanterns. They'd waited too long to leave. She knew better than to linger. Soon it would be raining *and* dark.

"It's just a sprinkle." Noble Stockton raised his six-foot frame from a bent-knee position and stretched his arms, yawning loudly as he relieved sore muscles. His tongue darted out to catch the freshness.

Kenzy swallowed with him when he shed his chambray shirt and picked up the hammer again, purpose lighting his periwinkle eyes. She could almost taste the rain's sweetness, increasingly aware of how it flooded the forest with a fragrant muskiness. The sight of Noble's bare back flooded her senses, drowning her best intention to treat him as anything but her hired hand.

Though she now believed her initial attraction to Noble those many years ago was merely a childhood infatuation, here she stood, gaping at him and warming like a lit coal.

"We won't melt," Noble insisted. "Besides, Strut and I can get this flooring finished if we'll work another half hour or so. By the time you find those three scatter-bugs, we'll be done."

A bald man ducked his head and peered out from the shaft of a rock chimney. *Now, how had he managed to get in that position?* Kenzy wondered. He was supposed to be mortaring the stone from the inside.

"Is everything all right in there, Strut?" She cocked her head. "Need some help?"

With a glance first at Kenzy, then at his fellow worker, Strut grinned from ear to ear. "Got me a grand idea! Think I'll shed me some garments like Noble did so it won't be so dang hot . . ." His head disappeared from view, but he kept talking. "Just need . . . a minute . . . to twist around 'yhear and I'll . . . well, spit in my face and call it rain! Dadgum skinned the hide plum offa . . ."

A string of colorful maledictions exited as the aging handyman changed positions. "There!" His short, wiry legs dropped to the hearth's stone flooring. "Peeled the hide right offa my nose. Probably stunted my growth a mite while I's at it." His hazel eyes glanced about, as if measuring the extent of his audience. Suddenly he grinned. "Wouldn't want to damage any of the pickings when the ladies come a'calling."

"Bad word choice, Strutter Ol' Man." Noble tried to keep a straight face but failed.

Everyone laughed. They all knew Strut Cuthbert was barely four-foot-eight, but he thought he walked taller than any man in the territory. The sad truth was that God in His mysterious wisdom had molded Strut into an extreme hank of homeliness to counter his giant-sized love of himself.

"Reckon it'll bother Euphemia?" Strut rubbed his nose, until it became one big crimson bulb. "Maybe she won't mind so much . . . if I take off my shirt like ol' Nobi there."

A wink at Kenzy spun her halfway around. She hoped Strut would be more worried about his best gal than the blush heating *her* cheeks.

Try as she might, it was more difficult than Kenzy ever imagined to view Noble's muscular frame and sunshine-colored hair without longing for what might never be. He had been the Adonis of her letters—the golden boy who lit the way through the darkness of her dreams.

She came home for many reasons: to build the orphanage Rose wanted, to construct a building of her own design and to keep her word that she would return. But the most important reason of all would be tested this afternoon. She faced Noble, studying him as if he held the answer to her future. Was her need for him merely an infatuation or did she sense that he somehow possessed the power to cast away the darkness?

"Best you keep your shirts on. We're not going to take any chances getting caught in a storm. And if we do, you'll need them to stave off the chill." Kenzy hurriedly lit two lanterns while the men did as told. She deliberately took her time about hooking one of the lanterns to the front and side of the tool wagon.

"Never seen such a fondness for burning wicks." Strut shook his head and pointed to the remaining lanterns setting in the corner of the tool wagon. His gaze leveled on Kenzy. "Gotta be at least five or six, I'm thinking. You and Euphemia got some kind of light show planned?"

"There are only four," Kenzy defended, willing her tone to remain calm. *One for each side of the wagon.* Now was no time to get into a discussion about lanterns. "The flooring can wait another day or two, depending on how long it takes to dry out." What she couldn't . . . wouldn't . . . say is that she must get back to Rosella's before nightfall.

Thank goodness the storm gave Kenzy an excuse to mask the real reason for her apprehension. With night came shadows and, with shadows, the unknowns over which she had no control.

The taste of dampening sawdust in the air made Kenzy's nose wrinkle. "I'll run down to the creek and see if Cordell is still washing that bell he wants hung up over the front door. Maybe Worthy and Euphemia will be with him." She watched the two men spread the first tarpaulin. "Now, make sure it covers—"

"Everything it can," Strut finished for her, instigating a smile from Noble. "Surely will. You can count on us. Now, you go on and fetch them. Us men'll see that everything's battened down."

"I'll be right back, and don't you try to do any last minute—"

"Fixing," said Noble as he nodded obediently at Kenzy.

Noble's gaze slanted toward the older man, his smile broadening into a handsome grin that dimpled one cheek.

Strut chuckled, immediately turning so she couldn't see his expression. The old man cleared his throat. "Sorry, guess I got too much of a whiff of that sawdust."

Worry festered within Kenzy. Strut had just turned sixty. He didn't need to be taking a chill or inhaling anything that would put him down with a cough. "Everything will just have to dry out on its own. Strut, you hitch the team. Noble, gather the tools. I'll—"

"Head on down to the creek," both men replied in unison.

At Kenzy's startled expression, the fellows roared

with laughter. Realization came slowly, burning her cheeks. She'd done it again—gone and told them to do what they would have obviously done anyway. "Sorry . . ." she smiled despite her embarrassment, "but I guess I *am* the ramrod of this outfit."

"Don't apologize, Freckle Face." Noble laid down his end of the tarp and grabbed the closest sawhorse and saw. "A list makes for good planning, and a good builder knows best what she wants done."

"A gentleman you are, my friend." Kenzy decided Noble was one of those rare individuals who was simply good through and through. Every ounce of that handsome hunk of muscle and goldenrod hair exuded an unparalleled kindness toward others. She doubted he had a mean bone in his body. "But I'm not sure Strut here will agree with you."

"I like 'em sassy, not bossy." Strut swaggered toward the horses. "Speaking of Euphemia, she's gonna shrink up that new bonnet if she don't get on up here. This is only a little spit compared to what's coming over that horizon."

The trio glanced to the southwest and saw flashes of lightning dancing over the countryside. Without another word, all three began their tasks in earnest. Kenzy raced toward the creek, aware that the buffalo grass seemed thicker with moisture, dampening her skirt hem.

Several minutes later, she broke through a barrier of live oak and white birch that paralleled the creek. Thank heavens, everyone was together. Kenzy took in great gulps of rain-kissed air, allowing her heart to slow so she could find enough stamina to speak again. Euphemia Jones was hard of hearing. Kenzy would have to yell if she expected the woman to notice her.

"Kenzy!" shouted the seven-year-old boy whose face lit up at the sight of her, setting the wanderers in motion toward Kenzy. Excitement danced in his brown eyes. "I found me the neatest place in this whole territory. It's right over here behind that big old tree. Looks like somebody wintered up in it." His voice hushed as he speculated, "Maybe even buried treasure there!"

"Now, Worthy, don't go filling her head full of doubloons and daggers." The Amazon-sized woman ruffled the ragmuffin's coffee-colored hair. "That's an old bear tracker's shack, and you know it." Euphemia Jones nudged her bonnet further down to shelter her eyes, unconsciously allowing the rain to dampen the long twist of gray braid that hung down her back. "Isn't mucha nothing there worth filling a trunk."

The tall, slim boy walking on the other side of the Amazon pushed up the spectacles that slid to the edge of his nose. He shifted the bell he carried in his hand, so she could see the burlap bag hanging from his waistband. "Oh, but you're wrong, Miss Jones. I found a *genus calypsos.*"

"What's that, Brainhead?" Worthy taunted as he took two steps for every one of Cordell's. "Some kinda gypsy germ?"

Kenzy didn't laugh. They all knew they were standing on Zephyr and Rembrandt Parker's former land. The Parkers had been gypsies. Though she didn't believe in their magic, particularly since both of them no longer walked this earth, she still felt a little uneasy about building an orphanage on land that others considered enchanted.

"It's a calypso, Knob Knees, a bog orchid bearing a single flower streaked with white, purple, pink and yel—"

"Cordell, Cordell, smart as a pup but slow as a snail." The chubby boy pointed a finger at the bag hanging from Cordell's waistband. "Who cares what you got in that old sack anyway? It's just some dumb old flower."

"Dumb old flower?" The nine-year-old's gray eyes narrowed, his hair spiked in carrot-red tufts. "This happens to be one of the rarest orchids in the whole country. It has about a million uses—"

"Yeah, like bruising your pants?"

Every eye focused on the multicolored stain spreading rapidly from the rain-soaked bag to the dampening pant leg. Cordell shifted the bell so it hid the stain.

"Boys, you can argue about this later when we're dry." Kenzy motioned to the blackening sky. "We need to hurry or we're going to be soaked to the skin." *And it will be difficult to light more lanterns to show the way.*

Euphemia wrapped her shawl around her. "Gotta go see Zephyr Parker before I head to town."

The insistence in Euphemia's tone made Kenzy's stomach knot with tension. The owner of the general store was known not only for her strong back, but for an equally strong mind and unbreakable will. "I'm sure Mrs. Parker will understand if you miss just one Saturday afternoon." Kenzy hoped the woman would listen to reason. "She wouldn't want you to take a chill—"

"She loved youngun's as much as anyone." Euphemia's violet gaze swept past Kenzy to the graveyard behind her.

"No, I meant . . ."

"I don't intend to let a few little raindrops keep me from visiting my best friend on her birthday," Euphemia persisted, clearly misunderstanding Kenzy's remark. "Besides, we both know that dear old soul would have been out here dancing in this barefoot and hooting it up with both those youngun's."

The thundershower was the least of Kenzy's worries. As the afternoon waned, night shadows threatened to blend with the ominous clouds. "But Miss Euphemia, we must head back. Rose already has enough to do preparing for the get-together. She'll fret about us if the rain starts in earnest, and she might take unnecessary chances."

The image of Rose rolling down muddied roads fueled Kenzy's insistence. "I'll tell you what, let's go on back to town. We'll all wash up and enjoy ourselves at the party, then tomorrow after church I'll take you there myself. I'm sure we'll need to clean off whatever the wind stirs up on the graves."

Thunder pealed overhead. "What's that you said,

child?" Euphemia shouted above the roaring heavens.
"Let's go do what?"

Kenzy tried to repeat what she'd said but another peal
of thunder warned that the danger was getting closer.
". . . I'll take you there myself."

"Thank you most kindly."

The older woman obviously misunderstood because
she turned and headed down the slope toward the scattering of tombstones and crosses that dotted a corner of
Parker land.

Whitaker land, Kenzy reminded herself as she
grabbed Worthy's hand and motioned Cordell to quickly
follow.

Worthy's eyes rounded as he realized where they were
headed. "They say there's a gypsy king buried straight
up in the ground." Hushed respect filled the boy's tone.
"And he don't like nobody tramping over his head. They
say you can hear him whispering to the blue jays, telling
'em to swoop down and pick the hair plumb out of your
skull so you'll get a pain in the head, too."

Cordell punched the boy on the arm, letting the bell
drop with a clank. "Who needs blue jays? We've already
got a pain in the head. You!"

Worthy swung back.

Wind whispered through the tree crowns, buffeting
Kenzy's skirts and caressing her cheeks with a surprising
warmth. As she struggled to pull the two boys apart, she
noted the air was damp. Sunlight waned. Night rapidly
encroached. Yet the wind held no chill. It seemed like
a human's breath—almost a pent-up sigh. A shudder
traveled through her. What nonsense to listen to a boy
who thrived on finding mysterious out-of-the-way places
and stretched any truth to its limit.

"Stop this right now." She willed her trembling voice
to find some level of authority. "You're entering sacred
ground. Let's show some respect, boys."

Worthy took one last swing before dodging the near-
est tombstone.

You can do this, Kenzy told herself. *You lit lanterns.*

It won't be completely dark when we go home. If we take too long, Noble and Strut will come looking for us.

"If it's so sacred, how come nobody but Miss Euphemia comes to visit it anymore?" Cordell's penchant for needing answers halted his fight with the smaller boy.

"This graveyard is for . . . others. People who don't practice the same faith as most of our neighbors do." Some of different religions, she added silently. Some who simply didn't live the Southern way of life and were punished for it. How was she supposed to tell a nine-year-old, much less a seven-year-old, boy about a prejudice they couldn't possibly understand? About a war that neither North or South understood.

Because the Parkers had practiced their gypsy beliefs, they were considered odd . . . dangerous . . . certainly not candidates to find eternal rest in the church's consecrated grounds.

Yet all Kenzy had ever known of Zephyr Parker was that the woman had cured ailments no one else could. Though Kenzy didn't believe half of what she heard about Rem Parker's grandmother, she grudgingly respected Mrs. Parker for using her "powers" to help people. How sad that her grandson stained what little honor the poor old healer had earned. Zephyr Parker went to her grave defending what she believed in. Rem should have done as much when his end came.

Lightning split the sky overhead, covering the countryside in a blinding flash. Worthy shot out like a cannonball toward an old oak tree that stood in the farthest corner of the cemetery. "Did you see that?" he yelled over his shoulder as he raced past Euphemia. "It's that gypsy king come to life!"

Realizing the seven-year-old's destination, Kenzy broke into a run. "Stop, Worthy!" Her eyes scanned the sky, willing the heavens into silence. "Don't go near the tree!"

"I'll catch him, Miss Dixon." Cordell vaulted over a tombstone.

Lightning streaked horizonally. In that blinding moment of sizzling light, someone shrieked. Cordell's spidery form hurdled over yet another tombstone. Kenzy's blood seemed to stop its flow, instantly chilling to the bone. Her nostrils flared, preparing to smell the burned sulfur of a storm-stricken tree . . . or worse.

Instead, the sweet smell of moist grass and pine needles mixed with the rain forced her eyes open. She focused on the small boy, breathing a sigh of relief when she realized the child had not run to the tree as she'd feared. Worthy now bent beside a dark form laying prone over a curious patch of flowers. A man? "Who would be out here in this?" Kenzy asked, hurrying for ward to help.

When Cordell tried to lean closer, Worthy pushed the nine-year-old away. Surprise etched Euphemia's face, her eyebrows looking as if they'd become fringe for her bonnet.

"Stay back! I found him, and he's mine. He just might be that gypsy king," Worthy whispered in awe. He pointed to the bandage wrapped around the man's forehead. "Look . . . somebody must been trampling over him real hard."

A silver earring in the stranger's left ear hinted at gypsy heritage, but his skin looked pale against his damp, midnight-colored hair. "Come away from there," Kenzy ordered. "He might wake up any minute. We don't know who he is or what he's doing on Rose's land."

"Yeah, if he ain't a gypsy king, then he might be one of those carbetbuggers." Worthy took two respectful steps backward, then added a third to get out of the man's reach.

"That's *carpetbaggers*," Cordell corrected. "The proper meaning for a carpetbagger is—"

"This man is no carpetbagger." Euphemia bent to put her hand on the stranger's forehead and glanced up at Kenzy. "This here is Rembrandt Parker, Zephyr's grandson."

"R-Rem Parker?" Kenzy's gaze swept over the tattered clothes and the sinewy outline of his body, trying to discern the physical changes years had dealt her childhood acquaintance. This was the boy who always beat her at leapfrog? The boy who knew the forest like he owned its map? The boy who had laughed at her flirtations with Noble?

Kenzy gauged the shallowness of his breathing. "But I thought he died years ago."

2

"*He* looks mighty sickly, but he's still got a breath or two in him." Euphemia took off her colorful shawl, draped it over the gypsy's chest, then glanced at the grass growing beneath the live oak tree. "Don't you worry none, Zeph ol' gal. We'll see his resurrection ain't short-lived."

Kenzy shivered as the store owner's emphatic words echoed with dark promise. If Rem Parker survived, the land on which Kenzy planned to build the orphanage would no longer belong to Rose.

Rose. The dinner party. What a dreadful situation. Returning with the man who could ruin all their plans would put a damper on the festive occasion, to say the least. The golden celebration Rose had planned to honor Kenzy's homecoming would now be tarnished with speculation.

Another look at Rembrandt inspired both shame and sympathy within Kenzy. His cheeks seemed flushed beneath sun-weathered skin, but his body shook as if a chill swept through him instead of the obvious fever. Rembrandt was ill, and their shared childhood far outweighed any resentment she felt for his intrusion into their lives.

The time he had rubbed the juice of a cattail on her

cut knee flashed to mind. In fact, he'd been the one to rescue her from going to school with lips the size of an ox tongue. Rem hadn't even laughed at her when she'd explained that she had rubbed beeswax on her mouth to make it shiny and forgot about the wax when she kissed her cat. How was she to know she was sensitive to the combination of cat fur and beeswax?

Come to think of it, how many times had she watched him pick a strange-looking weed or strip a flower of its petals to heal one of the swimmers' injuries? Devil magic? That's what Anna LeGrand claimed, and what Kenzy had wondered about on several occasions. She'd found it difficult to believe someone could know so much about such things and at such a young age. Yet, she'd also wondered how a simple act of kindness could beget anything evil.

Now was not the time to worry about the man's so-called powers. If there was any truth to the rumor, then he wouldn't be lying here out of his mind with fever. He would have found some herb to cure himself. Her Christian duty was to lend the poor soul a hand. That overrode any other consideration.

"Mr. Parker, can you hear me? Do you think you can stand?" Kenzy bent to touch him, gently shaking Rembrandt's shoulder. Despite his illness, the muscles beneath his clothing felt as if they were carved out of granite.

He shied from her touch, a low moan escaping from somewhere deep within him. Big expressive eyes— black as the ancient obsidian of Egypt—flashed open. Something reached down into the tips of Kenzy's toes, sparked, then branded goose bumps up her frame. His eyes closed as quickly as they had opened.

She'd forgotten the power of that midnight gaze. Forgotten how polished it became when he brooded. Forgotten how guarded his eyes looked when someone tried to talk to him about his reputation. Though Kenzy feared the night, Rembrandt's darkness of the soul frightened her more.

"We've got to get him out of this rain. One of you boys fetch Noble and Strut." Kenzy glanced at the older of the two orphans, but Worthy waved his hand and jumped up and down, demanding her attention.

"Me! I'll go get them." He turned halfway around to get a head start. "I found him."

"The boy has a point." Euphemia grabbed a leg and motioned for Cordell to grab the other. "Best send him before he splits those highwater britches I sewed him."

"All right." At least if she let Worthy go after the men, she wouldn't have to worry where the child might wander when she wasn't looking. Kenzy's gaze leveled on the seven-year-old. "We're counting on you, Worthy. Go straight there and tell them what we've found. Hurry and tell them exactly what I said. Nothing more."

"I will, Miz Dixon . . . ma'am." Worthy loped off toward the orphanage, calling back over his shoulder, "You can count on me."

"Count on him to stretch more yarn, if you ask me." Cordell bent to grab one of Rembrandt's legs. "Bet Knob Knees could out-talk Ol' Dan Webster himself."

"At least he's not afraid to speak up." Kenzy put her arms beneath Rembrandt's shoulders to link around his chest. "Everyone will always know exactly how he feels about things."

The semiconscious man twisted and turned, mumbling something indecipherable. His fingers dug into a clump of flowers at his side, clutching them as if they might moor him to the earth.

"Don't know much gypsy talk, but that sure sounded like he just asked you to hurry up." Euphemia hefted her end of their patient so his bottom wouldn't connect with the rock and the brambles along the way. "Best we stop worrying about what that child's gonna stir up and concern ourselves with getting this hunk of controversy hauled into town."

Rosella Whitaker breathed a sigh of relief as she spotted the wagon heading up the street. Its lanterns swayed like beacons in the wind. At last, Kenzy was home! What could have kept them at work so long that her friend would risk being out after dark?

"She's here, everyone," Rose announced to the handful of people gathered in the parlor to celebrate Kenzy's homecoming.

The upper crust of San Augustine society enjoyed the elegant furnishings of the Whitaker home. While a handful discussed the contentious politics of the day, others argued the inevitability of servitude under Northern Reconstruction. The main topic of the evening to this point was how Rose had managed to purchase real South American coffee, despite the exorbitant tax on anything coming from Mexico.

She had Noble to thank for that thoughtfulness. He had called in a favor owed by a friend. The man gladly made the special effort to get the coffee, knowing that Noble would repay the kindness ten times over. From the droplets of rain dotting the window and slight chill permeating the sill, Rose assumed Kenzy and the others would be ready for something hot to drink.

Glad she'd gone to so much trouble, Rose knew Kenzy would appreciate not having to come home to another cup of mesquite coffee. No matter how good it smelled, Kenzy hated the beans they'd been roasting lately as replacement for the hard-to-get staple. The fact that Rose managed this feat without Kenzy's help might just prove to her friend that she was still quite capable of taking care of herself.

"Dinner will be served as soon as they've all had time to freshen up." Rose spun her wheelchair around to face the window again and caught sight of her reflection. My, but her skin looked porcelain white against the silver-gray dress she'd chosen to match her eyes. She simply had to get out and get more sun.

Realizing her shoulders slumped slightly, Rose willed herself to sit taller in her chair. No one knew how much she longed to look people eye-to-eye once again.

Only you can do something about correcting that, she

told herself, staring past her image to watch the team coming up the street.

Heavy footsteps crossed the marble floor behind her, warning that one of her male guests approached. A beefy hand pressed none-too-gently on her shoulder as the guest leaned down and whispered in her ear.

"Isn't it a bit odd for those two to be working so late?"

"Orlan," Rosella maneuvered around, recognizing the voice belonging to the large man, "you of all people should know that circumstances have us all working late these days . . . if we want to keep our fortunes."

She offered the timber baron a patient smile and her hand. He bowed and pressed a kiss upon the soft kid leather glove. Though her words were offered in a teasing manner, Rose knew he understood her implication. She spoke of his late-night dealings with the carpetbaggers recently arrived in San Augustine. Confined to a wheelchair, her eyes and ears were always open to what affected their community.

"Touché, my dear."

A sable-haired beauty moved alongside Rose, tapping the baron with her ivory fan to capture his attention. "You really are too kind, Rosella." Though her words were aimed at Rose, Anna LeGrand's black gaze leveled on the man's face. "Why all the fuss, Orlan? Aren't my cousin and Mr. Cuthbert old enough to stay out as long as they prefer? Or," she batted her eyelashes elaborately, "were you trying to malign someone else's reputation?"

The timber baron nodded in deference to Anna's sarcasm, raising his palms and taking a step backward. "It was only my concern that the ladies might have caught a chill."

"Seems to me if the lady in question caught a chill, it would be to your advantage . . . wouldn't it?" Anna laughed and fanned herself elaborately. "Go join your little angry mob, Orlan. Or haven't you guessed already? Your gossip won't work tonight or any other night where McKenzy is concerned. Miss Dixon is Rose's best friend, and that simply supercedes anything you have to say! McKenzy got the contract. Plain and simple. How difficult is it to understand that the work has been given to a woman? Is that really so incomprehensible?"

"Perhaps I should take this opportunity to offer my adieus while we are still treating each other with tact. Rosella, thank you for inviting me to your lovely home. As always, you've been most gracious." Orlan half bowed to his hostess, then nodded briefly at Anna. "Good evening, Miss LeGrand. May I say that your company never fails to offend me."

Challenge sparked in Anna's eyes. "An equal pleasure, I assure you, sir."

"Don't go, Orlan." Rose rubbed the tension from the back of her neck, slightly raising the strawberry-blonde curl that dangled past her left shoulder. "Won't the two of you please put aside your grievances long enough to welcome Kenzy home properly?"

Understanding urged her to reassure him. "I know you feel wronged because I've given Kenzy the responsibility of building the orphanage. But it was meant as no slight to you, Orlan. I bought that piece of land for the sole purpose of giving her an opportunity to put her own designs to work. I fully intend to purchase any raw materials from you."

"A woman's place should be at home," Orlan and Anna recited simultaneously. Anna's laughter echoed across the parlor, abruptly halting as her attention shifted to the clamor resounding from outside the two-story home. "What's happening?"

Rosella swung around to discover a flurry of activity. Kenzy had just finished tying the team's reins to the hitching post and grabbed a lantern in each hand. The orphans she had taken into her care since her arrival a week ago were hurdling over each side of the wagon. Strut stood at the wagon gate, gripping a pair of legs threaded beneath his arm pits. Noble Stockton suddenly rose from a bent-over position in the wagon bed holding the other half of the man. "They're carrying someone inside."

Rose's announcement inspired a rush of curiosity seekers out the door ahead of her.

"You stay back, Rosella." Anna followed the townsmen's lead. "Looks like Kenzy's got things under control, as usual."

The door swung back, almost hitting Rose's knees. Not one to sit idle when help was needed, Rose swung around and rolled herself across the threshold. "How can I help?" she called out as her best friend issued orders with lightning speed.

"Prop the door open like you are," Kenzy replied, handing her the lanterns. "And keep these shining on the steps so we won't fall. We've got an injured man here. Where do you want us to take him?"

Before Rose could answer, Kenzy motioned to Worthy. "Fetch Jubal. See if he's still tending the Cartwright baby. Cordell, bring me those other lanterns, then unhitch the wagon and brush down the horses for me, will you? The rest of you quit standing there gawking and lend a hand."

"Third room on the left, gentlemen." Rose pointed behind her. "Downstairs."

The series of lifts and pulleys that allowed Rose to maneuver herself up to and down from the second floor landing would take too much time. "I'll be able to care for our visitor a little easier if he stays down here."

"Ain't no visitor, honey." Euphemia shook her head, her eyes narrowing to violet slits as she stared at each of the guests. "And, he might stir up a lot more trouble than you've got hospitality."

Puzzled by the store owner's strange criticism, Rose lifted the lantern higher to determine the unconscious man's identity. A wall of curiosity seekers stood in her way. She cleared her throat, hoping to capture Kenzy's attention. Kenzy glanced Rose's way, but immediately withdrew her gaze.

Something was wrong! Something so worrisome it had kept Kenzy out after dark. Something that involved this man? Just who was he?

"I promise, Brett . . . I-I promise. Will destroy him. Got to give him the . . . Stockton . . . trouble . . . nothing but trouble. I'm so tired . . . so very tired of it all." Incoherent words spilled from the patient's lips as he twisted and turned in fevered agony.

As if he'd seen a ghost, stunned surprise etched itself in Noble Stockton's handsome features. Rose felt his blue gaze searching for and finding her, locking on her as if it needed an anchor to reality. *Brett?* she mouthed silently, wondering if she'd heard the words correctly and sensing an unease stirring within the man she wanted to marry.

Noble shook his head.

But she could have sworn the sufferer had said Brett—the name of Noble's older brother. His dead brother. "But I was certain I heard—"

"He's talking out of his head." A frown creased Noble's brow. "You ladies get cleaned up and start the party."

It was as if Noble, like Kenzy, refused to look Rose in the eye. Rose intended not only to get to the bottom of their hesitation but to discover why Euphemia gave such a dire warning about their patient. "Would everyone move aside, please? Long enough for me to see whom I'll be tending?"

Obediently, the crowd parted and allowed Rose to move closer. She knew him. He was older, startlingly more handsome than his youthful features had promised, but the gangliness of youth had become the complexity of a powerful-looking man. "Rembrandt Parker," she whispered, suddenly aware of how this man's arrival could affect their plans for the orphanage . . . if he lived. Indeed an irony, since they all thought he had died in the war.

Rose felt as if she were offering a noose to the very man who might wish to hang her when he discovered she'd taken over his land. But moral duty required she come to the aid of an injured man if called upon to do so. No matter the man's name nor his intent. Rose glanced at Noble. "I'm sure my guests will understand that I can't join them until—"

"Strut can help me see to Parker's needs. No use all of us tending him. We'll have to strip these wet clothes off him anyway. Got any dry clothes we can put on him?"

Rose rolled her chair toward the closet under the stairwell, depositing one of the lanterns on the sideboy. "I kept some of Father's old things in a trunk. They might be slightly smaller, but they'll be warm at least."

"I'll get them." Kenzy moved ahead of Rose, grabbing the second lantern from Rose. "You stay where you are."

A flash of irritation blazed within Rose. She wasn't helpless. In fact she'd done just fine without Kenzy's help these past three years in the wheelchair. That's why she'd kept her injuries secret from Kenzy for so long. She knew Kenzy would have rushed home to take care of her instead of finishing her studies. "Thanks, but I know right where I put them."

Try as she might, Rose didn't quite keep the sharpness from her tone. Kenzy's expression looked immediately apologetic, consuming Rose with a wagonload of shame. How childish! Kenzy was only trying to help. If truth be known, her anger was targeted more toward Noble for denying what she knew she'd heard. But why? He wasn't a man given to lying.

She shouldn't have been so brusque with Kenzy. Rose smiled at her best friend. "You know, I could use some help, after all. I just remembered setting something heavy on top of the trunk the last time I went through it. Why don't we both work on getting it? I'll hold the light so you can look for them."

Perhaps she needed to quit worrying so much that Noble would think her too much of an invalid to court. Kenzy came home and had gone out of her way to see that Noble spent more time with Rose than he did with Kenzy. Her best friend's actions now were nothing more than overprotectiveness. To make things easier for Rose.

Why then couldn't she put their childhood rivalry over Noble where it belonged . . . in the past?

3

$\mathscr{S}$ound beckoned Rem from the deep exhaustion that had overtaken him at his grandmother's grave. He waited . . . listened . . . for movement that would alert his instincts toward self-preservation. But nothing more intimidating than an elusive hiss of flame seemed to threaten.

In the rain's aftermath, an odd silence filled the forest. He expected to be soaked when he awoke, but Rem's skin felt drier than when he'd first laid across Gran Zeph's grave. He allowed himself to close his eyes again for only the second time in a week. Sometime during his exhaustion, he must have stripped off his damp shirt—a common practice when he slept—especially on home ground.

Home ground. How long had it been since he'd been home to San Augustine? Four years? Hundreds of lost causes ago. A thousand lifetimes in the soul-searing hell of war between the States.

Rem's tongue darted out to trace the swell of his lower lip, finding it difficult to muster enough moisture from his parched throat to add a soothing balm. Light pressed warmly against his eyelids and cheeks, compelling Rem to open his eyes to the new day around him.

Light. He blinked several times to stave off the sting

of tears rushing to protect him from the glare. It was as
if the canopy of trees overhead had parted and a blazing
sun now shone down on him. If true, that meant he had
slept through the night in the open. Rem's body shivered
in response, his hands instinctively grabbing at the quilt
laying just below his shoulders.

Quilt? He flung off the cover and sat up, straining
through the wash of tears to search for any possible danger.

"He's awake."

The voice sounded slightly familiar, but Rem's memory couldn't quite place the deep baritone.

A blond man of admirable build rose from one of the
two occupied chairs stationed next to a reading table.
Dressed in blue chambray and nankeens stained with the
effect of an honest day's labor, the man moved toward
Rem with powerful strides. Rem recognized that walk—
that self-assuredness. Perhaps he hadn't awoken after all
and was still dreaming.

Fighting the dizzying remnants of exhaustion, he
wondered if he had finally reached his long-sought destination or if Noble Stockton's presence was simply a
fevered figment of his desire to deliver the burdensome
letter?

Rem's fingers raked through the hair at his right temple, testing the reality of the moment. Without a strand
of rawhide to bind its length, the shiny blue-black mass
inherited from his Romany ancestry fell past his shoulders. Another vexation to deal with when he reached
town. There would be questions as to how he'd received
the head wound. But first, he had to determine if the
man he'd sought truly stood a few feet away or if he
was an illusion. "Noble? Are you real?"

Uneasiness flared inside Rembrandt, but he shook off
the feeling as foolish. He had no reason to proceed with
caution with his childhood acquaintance. Still, he knew
the words within the letter and what discord they would
bring his friend.

Noble nodded, his blue gaze slanting to the smaller

man in Rem's company. "Better let Rose know her patient's awake."

"Kenzy's been up here every hour on the hour, keeping this place lit up like a candle factory. It's about time
for her to check the lamps and look in on this here fella
again."

The baldheaded man leaned over Rem and tugged on
his own aging earlobe. "Gosh amighty. Don't that hurt?"
Wrinkles farrowed his forehead as his hazel eyes peered
harder at Rem. "Never seen that earring up close. Always wanted to. Sure looks like the one Zeph wore. He's
definitely a Parker, all right."

"Stay back, old man," Rem warned in a clear voice
that belied his weakened state. Long practice tensed his
muscles like coiled springs ready to hurdle him into a
fighting stance. Though the older man's words hinted
that he knew Rem's grandmother, Rembrandt had been
tricked one time too many to ignore caution now. The
bias against his gypsy ancestry was a much longer-
waged battle than the one supposedly fought to free the
slaves.

"No need to get all riled up, son. Ain't nobody here
gonna hurt you." The balding man hitched up his belt
and squared his shoulders, his chest swelling to match
the expression of valor in his rumpled face. He glanced
at Noble. The rounded apple of the older man's neck
plunged the depths of his skinny throat like a sunken
lure. Just as quickly it rose and lodged midway. "That
is, if you remember your manners and who you're talking to."

Instinctively, Rem reached for the gun he had been
ordered to wear from the moment he'd left San Augustine with the first company of infantry volunteers under
the leadership of Captain Benton. Just as senselessly as
Benton and many of his townsmen fell during one of
the first battles of the war, so Rem reached now for the
nonexistent. He no longer carried the LeMat.

From the time of the dreaded massacre at Gaines Mill
throughout the years spent at war and, despite orders,

Rem refused to carry anything but a knife. A knife to plant and harvest the seeds of his labor. A knife to sow life, not take it away. A knife . . . to remind him that animosity, if allowed to flourish, stabbed deeply into a man's soul.

Rem realized that he was not only dressed in someone else's pants but was shoeless, as well. One of these men must have found the knife sheathed in the back of his boot. Now, Rem had only his wits to defend himself.

Not one to be intimidated and seeing the need to find an advantage, he thumbed the silver moon dangling from his left ear. "Take a closer look if you like, old man."

The short man blushed all the way from his neck to the top of his balding head. "Now, ain't no call getting testy. It's just me . . . Ol' Strut. Don't you recognize me anymore, Sowboy?"

"Mr. Cuthbert?" Rem recognized the nickname given to him by the one man in San Augustine who had found no shame in talking to a gypsy boy. Relief washed through him. Mr. Cuthbert took time to ask Rem questions about the seeds he and his grandmother collected, and why. After several such discussions, Strut told him that sowing the earth was probably one of the greatest responsibilities of mankind and boykind alike. The nickname the old gent had given him, Sowboy, stuck and gave Rem hope that somehow he belonged to this piece of land his grandmother had chosen to die for.

Even when one of the other boys in town found a letter Mr. Cuthbert had left for him and jeered at the spelling of his nickname, Rem hadn't let their oinks and piglet remarks destroy the pride he felt having earned the older man's respect and fondness.

Rem searched the revered face with new appreciation. The war had, indeed, aged everyone. "Last time I saw you, you had a full head of hair."

Strut laughed and rubbed the top of his head. "Done plucked it all out or them carpetbaggers would sure 'nough find a way to tax me for that, too."

"Go tell the ladies he'll take some of that soup now.

He's looking fit enough to lift a spoon." Noble's order put an end to the pleasantries between the long-ago friends. His blue eyes narrowed and focused on Rem. "Maybe even fit enough to tell me what you were trying to say when we carried you in."

Nodding toward the slouch hat someone had hung on the top of the bedpost, Rem inhaled deeply then let out a long sigh. "Got a letter in my hat that'll be of interest. Come a long way to give it to you."

Noble glared at the hat, reaching out to lift it from the post. "Why didn't you just mail it? It would have gotten to me eventually."

"Couldn't do that. Made a promise to your—" Rem's gaze slanted toward Strut, who held the door ajar and seemed to be listening to their every word. "—the man who entrusted me with seeing that you and you alone received it. Frankly, I wasn't sure you were still alive."

Rem shifted and planted his feet firmly on the ground. He needed to be prepared for the reading and the hostility that might follow. The message would be a hard pill to swallow . . . especially for a brother. One glance located his boots, a second estimated how much distance there was between Stockton and the knife that lay on the reading table.

"Something on your mind, Strut?" Though a question, Noble's tone echoed with demand.

"Yeah . . . all them pretty women in the parlor. I was just thinking how lucky they are that the handsomest of us three gents gets to go pay 'em a visit while you other two sit up here discussing a letter."

The older man shut the door behind him, but Rem shook his head at Noble and held up a finger to warn him that Strut had not truly walked away. A board in the hallway creaked as his weight shifted from one foot to the other. Rem smiled and deliberately spoke loud, "You know, the letter can wait, Stockton. If there are that many pretty women in San Augustine, perhaps I should get dressed and join the old man before he charms them all."

The narrow blue slits of Noble's eyes softly rounded as laugh lines fanned from their edges. His fingers retrieved the folded piece of paper hidden in the inner lining of the black slouch hat.

Just as Rem expected, Strut's footsteps rushed down the hall. He eyed the missive held in Stockton's hand. "Guess he wants more time with the women than he's wanting to find out what's in the letter."

"He's got a fervent belief that he's been put on this earth to court every woman in petticoats," Noble admitted before the smile on his lips sobered. He tossed the hat on the bed next to Rem and unfolded the letter. "The fact that many of our ladies have been widowed by the war makes this place a treasure trove for Strut Cuthbert. Now, what *is* in this letter?"

"A message from your brother." Rem waited as the other man scanned the words.

Noble's gaze focused on Rem, glaring. "This isn't his handwriting. What kind of foolery are you up to, Parker?"

Rem stood, needing to meet the man from an equal height the way he never had been able to do so socially. "No scheme, Noble. I wrote the letter but the words are Brett's. He couldn't write them himself. He was gutshot and dying. He asked me to write that to you, so you'd know the truth. I didn't add a single word, nor did I change a thing he said. It was his truth and not mine. I'm only sorry I had to wait so long to bring you the letter."

Color drained from Noble's face as he read more earnestly. Suddenly, anger flushed his skin a blistering red. "You're a liar! This is a lie! He would have never done that. Never allowed himself to . . ."

"Betray his men? His cause?" Disbelief emanated from Stockton like a tempest of Texas wind, battering Rem with its fury. "He wanted you to know . . . to understand why." Rem reached out to press a hand on Noble's shoulder and offer compassion, but Noble shirked away. Rem knew the hurt from both sides, betraying and being betrayed. "The thing he regretted most was that you would be disappointed in him. That you would not forgive him for dying without a hero's heart."

Recognition lit in Noble's face a moment before the man closed his eyes and buried his hands in his hair. The letter drifted to the floor like a leaf blown from its branch to die. Something Rem had said made him believe. And, with Stockton's belief, came the possibility of Rem's redemption.

"May I come in?" a feminine voice announced from the other side of the door. "Strut said you were awake, Mr. Parker, and I have some hot soup."

Noble rushed to the door to open it and allowed the woman in the wheelchair access to the room. He reached to take the tray braced on her lap. "Here, let me, Rose."

"Nonsense. It's one of the few things I do well in this confounded chair." The strawberry-blonde rolled up to where Rem stood and didn't blush at the sight of his bare chest.

Rem reached for his shirt someone had laid over the back of a chair. "I apologize for my appearance, Miss Whitaker."

"No need, Mr. Parker. You've been ill." Her silver-blue eyes welcomed him. "I'm glad to see you back on your feet. Look, Kenzy, he's much better now, don't you think?" Rose smiled at Noble. "You've done a wonderful job. Just as you always do."

Consumed with realizing that pretty little Rosella Whitaker now lived her life from a wheelchair, Rem hadn't noticed Strut Cuthbert and McKenzy Dixon join them.

Almond-shaped eyes the color of newly harvested sarsaparilla met his gaze directly. Long sooty lashes enhanced their emerald hue, complimenting the honeyed glow of McKenzy's skin and the thick mass of auburn hair that framed her face. Kenzy's mouth looked so sensual, he wanted nothing more than to test its lushness upon his lips. His breath stilled as a great craving consumed him.

But protocol demanded the distance between them, and he had to satisfy himself with merely tracing the full cleavage and soft curve of her hips with his gaze. Rem's blood ignited into a boil. Of all people he never expected to discover here in San Augustine . . . McKenzy Dixon. The troublemaker. The girl who meant to become "somebody." The girl he had never forgotten.

"Told you there was a letter." Strut tried to get around the wall of people blocking his way. "There it is on the floor . . ."

"I'll get it," a male and female voice announced in unison.

McKenzy bent to retrieve the missive near the hem of her skirt, but Rem bent at the same time to collect the wayward note. Their heads collided, causing his hands instinctively to reach out and prevent her fall.

Her full, generous mouth smiled easily. Tiny laugh lines hinted that she possessed a good nature. Though her cheekbones were now highly carved with the hand of maturity, the freckles patching her nose hinted she might still be impish enough to play leapfrog again. An idea full of interesting possibilities given the way she'd grown into womanhood.

"Th-Thank you, Mr. Parker," she said breathlessly. "I only meant to save you from having to bend over." She handed Rem the letter. "I thought you might not have a clear enough head. You've been feverish."

If I wasn't before, I am now, Rem decided, letting his hands linger a little too long for politeness.

"Ladies," Noble interrupted, averting McKenzy's gaze away from Rem. He took the soup from Rosella and placed it on the reading table. "Parker is obviously well enough to eat on his own. I suggest we all leave him to his supper and allow him time to gather his wits to meet the curiosity brewing among your guests."

He grabbed the handles at the back of the wheelchair and gently turned Rose toward the door, winging one elbow toward McKenzy. "May I have the pleasure of escorting you two lovely ladies to the parlor?"

Elation or something close to it, in Rem's opinion, lit McKenzy's eyes. So . . . the girls' rivalry over Stockton had survived the years. Was that why she had returned to San Augustine?

As if she felt Rem's attention focused on her, Kenzy's gaze averted to Rem. For a moment she stared, daring him to tease her as he'd done when she was younger. Rem wanted to laugh. Still as dauntless as ever. He'd admired that in her youth. The trait was even more fascinating combined with her beauty. Rem shrugged, yet arched one brow to let her know she hadn't totally escaped his taunting.

McKenzy's chin lifted in challenge before she shifted her attention back to Noble. "You and Rose go on and see to her guests. I'll be right down. I'm just going to add more oil to the lamps so Mr. Parker can have better light. Strut, will you see that Euphemia sends him some of that sweet potato pie?" She shooed the eavesdropper away. "Go on now, so he can have it while it's still hot."

"Durn!" Strut announced as Rem folded the letter and placed it securely back in the hat. The old man glanced at Rem, then at the hat, out the door at his departing friends, then back at McKenzy. "Durn amighty."

As soon as he left, Kenzy faced Rem. "Care to tell me what's so all-fired important about that letter, Mr. Parker?"

He wanted desperately to trust someone with the truth. Needed to rid himself of its burden. More than anything he longed to prove *his* reputation false. But the telling must come from Noble, for few would ever believe a gypsy.

Why then did he find it so difficult to deny the freckled face that once had given him reprieve from that unjust reputation? "You'll have to ask Noble. That's for your hero to say. And my name's Rem, McKenzy. Nothing more. And nothing less than when you and I were once almost friends."

4

$\mathscr{K}$enzy lay on her back, staring at the flickering shadows dancing upon the vaulted ceiling above the bed. Though past midnight, July heat still lingered in a room sweltering with the warmth of too many lit lamps. The last of the guests had left an hour ago and, by now, Rose and the orphans were probably asleep. The oil had all but burned out, leaving the acrid smell of long-used wicks to layer the room like a mist.

She needed to restore the light to stave off the growing shadows—a ritual performed without hesitation every night. But that would only add further heat to the room. Just this once, perhaps sheer exhaustion and the need for fresh air would eclipse her fear. Was it possible to close her eyes and truly forget?

They refused to comply.

Determined to conquer the chain of emotions that bound her to the light, Kenzy bolted to her feet and crossed the distance to the glass French doors that formed half the tower of Rose's home. She did not want to live with this dread the rest of her life. She *would* not.

Pulling back one curtain, Kenzy discovered the full moon offered a sweeping view of the stars. They gleamed like iced diamonds amid the ebony sky. Even

the wind-stirred canopy of leaves pressed against the tur-
ret's gingerbread moldings seemed less frightening here
where she could more easily distinguish their outline.
Her trepidation eased slightly until she forgot to stop
staring at the glass.

Look away, Kenzy warned. Instead, she focused on
the reflected image of herself in the glass—the image
she couldn't bear to stare at since that fateful night her
parents died.

Restlessness deeper than exhaustion compelled her to
reach out and cover the image with her palm, wishing
she could just as easily erase the wrong that kept her
from looking too closely in *any* mirror. If only there was
some way to change what had happened. To change *her*.

Tonight had certainly been full of change. Who would
have thought Rembrandt Parker would still be alive after
all this time? Where had he been since the battle of
Gaines Mill, and what would he do once he discovered
the construction of an orphanage on his land?

Kenzy stretched tired muscles, eyeing the second
story veranda. Fresh air was definitely in order, and the
moon lit the balcony well. Her hand shook as she
grabbed the doorknob with one hand and a lamp with
the other.

"This is nonsense." Before she could change her
mind, Kenzy opened the door and stepped onto the veranda. "What possible trouble could I find out here?"

At first, she saw the night as a single thing, a mass.
Now suddenly the details of it took shape and substance—the vast complexity of each branch, the deep-
ening hue of bark, the welcome coolness of air beneath
sheltering trees. Gooseflesh pebbled along Kenzy's skin
and raised the fine hair on her neck as if some night
creature crawled up her spine . . . or someone watched
her.

*Don't be absurd. Who would be out here at this time
of night?* She shivered, clutching her muslin wrapper
closely. With the other hand, Kenzy lifted the lamp
higher to shed light on the distance. Her toes curled

against the balcony's planked flooring, finding the cedar cool despite the lingering heat.

She took a deep breath and squared her shoulders, strolling to the edge of the ballastrade that formed the veranda's guardrail. A bird sliced the air above her, gliding without sound to land upon the steeple. The fragrance of earth and pine needles and the faint sweetness of white birch sharpened her senses. Kenzy retreated a step, distrusting the deceptive calm surrounding her.

Suddenly, the shadows filled with hundreds of sounds she could hear almost at once. The hoot of an owl. The raucous chatter of an invading racoon. Splintering wood, then footsteps.

Someone crying?

Did it come from inside the house or out in the yard? Discerning nothing in her line of vision, Kenzy swung the light on the recess of her room. Luck was against her. No one awaited her there. The crying echoed from the shadows below. "Who's out there?" She whirled again. "Where are you standing?"

No answer.

"I can't help you if I can't see where you are," she insisted, brushing back the auburn curls she'd loosened from their ribbon at bedtime. Perhaps the person would move closer into the light, then she could convince whoever it was to come inside instead of having to go out into the yard herself.

The crying intensified, becoming a childish wail.

"Worthy? Cordell?" Kenzy's feet seemed to take root in the planking. Her blood raced at the thought of one of the orphans out there possibly hurt and needing her help. Maybe Worthy was sleepwalking again. If so, she'd *have* to go get him. He seldom ever awoke when he dreamwalked, but his nightly excursions usually took him no farther than the parlor.

Perspiration dampened Kenzy's forehead as she attempted to calm the wave of anxiety rushing through her. *You're stronger than this, Kenzy. Whoever it is, he needs help and he needs it now!*

Taking courage in hand, Kenzy willed herself to move. She ran through her room and out into the hallway. Pausing at Rose's door, she stopped short. It was imprudent to wake her friend until absolutely necessary. Rose would have to deal with the chairlift to descend the stairs. Saving time and Rose's effort seemed more logical.

A quick check in the room across the hall confirmed the crier's identity. Cordell snored soundly, with a book spread over his chest and his glasses riding the tip of his nose. Worthy's smaller bed, however, was empty with the covers thrown back.

Kenzy raced downstairs and toward the front door, only to test her luck one more time. She approached where Rem Parker lodged for the night, then knocked firmly to announce her presence. "Mr. Parker . . . Rem . . . are you awake?"

No sound, no movement of any kind. After yet another knock and a slightly louder question, she opened the door just enough to peer in at the man to make certain he remained well. His bed was empty. Had he decided to return home? Surely, that wasn't him crying out there in the dark.

The wail had belonged to a child. She could imagine the curious boy following his "gypsy king" to learn what secrets Rem Parker might share. All she knew about Rem was that he'd won her respect as a youth, but that did not assuage her concern that he and Worthy were missing from their beds. She had wasted time in trying to get more help.

Kenzy berated herself, rushing outside and into the yard. Glancing furtively around, she saw nothing nearby. Surrounding shadows beckoned her closer, the wind whispering secrets through the trees. Terror sharpened her senses to a fine pitch, testing Kenzy's willingness to encounter the unknown. Why hadn't she stopped long enough to grab a gun?

The crying had been human, not a wounded animal's. And Rose kept her father's weapons locked away, as did

all Southerners who hoped to ride out this new storm
called Reconstruction.

If only to hear her own voice and be reassured, Kenzy
needed to speak. She fought the lump of trepidation attempting to lodge in her throat. "W-Worthy? Is that you?
If so, let me know where you are."

In the event, Parker was out there as well, Kenzy
added, "Is your gypsy king with you?"

"Miz Dixon?"

Though she could barely hear him, Kenzy exhaled a
gale of relief. "Yes, Worthy." She walked closer to the
copse of trees bordering Rose's property. "Where are
you?"

"I'm stuck. Way up here. I ain't seen my gypsy man
or I'da asked him to make his magic get me down from
here."

Glad to shed the horrible distrust that tainted her
thoughts, Kenzy offered a silent apology to Rem Parker.
Forgive me. She held the lamp high, craning her head
to see if she could spot him.

"Over here. Gotta come closer or maybe climb a little
ways."

She stepped between the trees and shone the light
among the next set of branches. Still couldn't see him.
Her pulse began to race. Kenzy glanced over one shoulder then the other, realizing that the tree trunks she
passed now looked like hidden adversaries blocking her
escape. *Breathe*, she reminded herself. *You're not alone
this time. It doesn't matter that you can't see him. Worthy can see you.*

If only the boy could come down on his own. At least
he was awake and aware of his danger. She peered harder into the foliage. "This one?"

"Yes. I'm here. Way up here." The fear in his tone
eased slightly.

"I'm coming up," she announced, setting the lamp
down at the base of the tree, then moving it farther away
to shed more light on the lower branches. Not wanting
her hair to fall in her eyes, Kenzy gathered its length

and tied it into a knot at the base of her neck. The thick curls would not stay bound very long. "Just stay put until I can reach you, Worthy. Don't try anything brave."

"You either, Miz Dixon."

Believe me, this is braver than I thought I'd ever be after Mother and Father's deaths. The need to alleviate his fear gave her hands a will of their own. Kenzy tested the heaviest of one of the lower branches, then swung her leg over the bough.

"Bet you're a real good rider." Worthy's hiccup signaled an end to his sobs.

Distract him. "I played leapfrog and one pony a lot when I was your age." She recalled the game she and Rose played, pretending that Noble was the sole rescuer in a mock battle that had left them afoot. Each girl loved being taught to grab his offered hand and catapult themselves into the saddle behind him. Locking her hands around Noble's work-hardened torso had been worth every saddle sore Kenzy suffered as a result. He had been her dashing knight, and she his damsel in distress. And when Kenzy particularly enjoyed the rescue, Rose remained the lady in waiting. Kenzy grinned, grateful for the amusement that eased some of her tension. "But that was a long time ago."

Her bottom rested on the branch now, as she strained first one way, then another to seek his location. "How high are you?"

"See that branch cracked in the middle? You prob'ly can't see it, can you? Well, anyway, don't step on that one. The monster broke it."

"Monster?" Kenzy climbed to a branch adjacent the broken one. "What monster?"

His voice sounded closer now, easing the racing of Kenzy's heart. The sight of him might come any moment, quelling all her apprehension.

"The monster peeped into me and Cord's window, then chased me up here when I came outside to look real close. It had mean-looking eyes, I tell ya. Dark as sin."

What did this child know of sin? She prayed Worthy's description resulted from his tendency to eavesdrop instead of experience. The child had seen more injustice than his years on earth. They must build the orphanage, for no other reason than to give this boy a decent home and a chance at life. Parker land or not.

The wind must have cast shadows or caused branches to scrape the boy's window, scaring him. But he obviously thought the monster real. She would wait until the seven-year-old was safe on the ground before explaining what really happened. Still, the question of whose weight had broken the branch remained. "Am I on the branch that wouldn't hold you up?"

"I told ya, I didn't break it. It's the last biggest one over your head."

That meant she couldn't go any higher to reach him. "Can you come down a different way than you got up there?"

"I ain't coming down, Miz Dixon. Not until the sun comes up or there ain't no more monsters."

"You stay right there. I'll find a way up." She hoped her tone held equal measures of assurance and authority. Scanning a different path to climb, she decided to test those further on her right.

Her toe fought to establish the next foothold. Make him talk, she decided, to keep them both calm. There . . . right leg up. "You must have been sleepwalking again." *Pull yourself up,* she encouraged, obeying her own command. A loup rippppp! rent the air.

"Did the monster grab ya?" the child called out. "Is it eating you alive?"

Her hem had caught on the jutting point of a snapped branch, badly ripping her wrapper. The coolness of the bark pressing against her thighs made her aware of where the garment had ripped, and she was grateful for the shadows that hid her indelicate situation. "Nothing so dramatic as that. My nightdress is hung up. I have to get it unhooked." The ripping worsened with every shift of her body.

"For goodness sake!" She fought the frustration that held her captive. If she forced the cloth, the gown would tear in half. When a rescuer came along, she would be found half-naked!

"Looks like we're going to have to sit out the rest of the night," the boy announced prophetically.

"Much as I hate to admit it, I'm stuck, too. Hold on awhile longer. I'm sure somebody will come along soon." *Maybe in three or four hours,* she didn't say, not wanting him to realize how long they might have to wait for dawn.

Her own muscles trembled as she fought shifting and damaging the material further. Minutes passed. She strained to hear anything human other than the sound of her own breathing and Worthy's shifting upon his perch. Finally, when the child kept yawning and she feared he might doze off, she decided the only thing she could do was sacrifice her modesty to secure his safety.

Suddenly, two hands encircled Kenzy's waist, lifted her slightly, then set her down on the branch just below.

"My hem is hung up on something." She quickly gathered the division of muslin, grateful for the man's strength.

"Not anymore. Now let's help you down, so I can get the boy."

"Th-thank you," she managed to say as she recognized Rem Parker's voice. Fortunately for them, he had come along when he did. Or . . . had he been there all this time?

She felt herself being pulled down once again and backward into a muscular span of bare shoulders. With one powerful motion, he regained his footing and cradled Kenzy in his strong embrace.

Her trembling increased.

He lowered her feet to the ground, sliding her exposed thighs against his length. "You're out of danger now," he whispered.

Every fiber of Kenzy's body stiffened. Muslin molded to his bare chest, the peaks of her breasts straining the delicate material. Embarrassment swept through her, sending added heat to the thigh still pressed wantonly against him. She immediately stepped away, more afraid of the invitation in his voice than she was of the velvety sinews beneath her touch.

"I'm fine." Kenzy's hair elected that moment to break free, cascading over her shoulders like a russet shawl. She mustered more calm than she felt, but this time her nervousness had little to do with wanting to get out of the dark.

"Good, then I won't be but a minute. Wait here. We need to talk."

About what, she wondered, worrying that someone might have already told him about the orphanage being built on his land. "Watch out. There's a broken branch a few feet higher to your left and several a little higher to the right of the big one."

Kenzy stared at his agile climb, her gaze examining him from boot heel to bandaged head. Powerful thighs. Slim hips. A splendid span of shoulders that would make any woman feel safe and men wary. Strange new sensations stirred within her, threatening to weaken her knees. Blood raced through her veins as if someone had opened a floodgate.

The rescue of the boy proved easier than she expected. No sooner had she gathered her wits and the lamp than the two nightwalkers joined her.

Rem bent down to look at Worthy, eye to eye. "Would you like for me to see you home?"

Worthy pulled up his waistband. "Naughhh, Mr. Gypsy Man. I ain't really afraid of no monster. I was just trying to catch him for you. Figured he was one of yours that done popped out of that cut on your head while you was lying sick."

"Rem . . . call me Rem, if you like." Rem patted his heart. "Unfortunately, all my devils still dwell here."

Worthy's eyes widened into saucers. "You're just joshing me, aintcha?"

Kenzy pointed. "Go home before he puts more ideas

into that curious little head of yours. Stop at the out-house before you go in. Be sure to put on some warm socks. You know how you—"

"I'm sure he knows the formalities." Rem halted a short distance away and watched the child's progress along the trail.

Worthy swung around one last time. "There really was a monster, Rem. It chased me up that tree, but I was lucky and climbed to the top . . . almost. Then I heard a branch break. Didn't get much of a look at the monster when it fell, but I sure heard it good enough. I didn't know monsters knew cuss words, Miz Dixon." The boy shrugged. "Guess I'd let out a few 'nosy snots,' too, if I hurt my foot like the monster did. I know it hurt 'cause the thing was limping after it fell. This ain't no whopper I'm telling, Gypsy Man. There really was a monster. I promise."

"I believe you, son, but you're safe now. Looks like you chased it away and saved us all from great harm."

"I did?"

"Seems to me it was gone before I ever got here, so I wasn't the one who ran it off. Now you go along and be proud that you've scared the fiend clear into the next territory."

When the gypsy clasped his hands together behind his back, the muscles of his arms and shoulders flexed. A fresh bandage tied back the midnight-colored hair that dipped well past his shoulders. A single silver earring hung from his left earlobe. A talisman? He looked as if he truly could harness the forces of the night.

Kenzy blinked and, suddenly, he stood in front of her. The shock of not seeing him move nor hearing his approach foretold the danger this man might impose if he were, indeed, as dishonorable as the townspeople thought him. Yet, he'd never given her reason to doubt him. She suspected her concern now stemmed more from her attraction to this enigma of a man than from any fear of him.

Though his eyes were in shadow, she sensed his gaze

upon her. The sight of him was equally compelling. His broad chest slimmed to an admirable abdomen and muscular thighs. Black trousers ended abruptly at knee-high boots, giving him the appearance of a highwayman. Devil or saint, he looked no less seductive. A sigh escaped her.

He gently took her hand and threaded it through his own. "Like what you see?"

The audacity! He'd read her mind, but she refused to let him know how his nearness affected her. "I'm tired. We should get back." She stared up at him, trying to discern the exact color of his eyes while she resisted the impulse to see how he tasted. Finding her throat suddenly parched, Kenzy's tongue darted out to wet her lips. *We definitely should*, she told herself, *before I do something I might regret.*

If she allowed herself, she could be lost easily in the spell he wove—a spell that gathered the forest around him as if he were a part of it and made him so compelling his presence diminished the night's hold over her.

She no longer met his gaze, grateful that her knees felt more stable now. Kenzy headed toward Rose's. Rem fell in step beside her.

"Why are you out here, McKenzy? Is this some sort of revenge for my beating you at leapfrog those many years ago?"

Indignation flared within her, halting her escape. "Unless that hit on your head has affected your memory, you should recall that I was trying to rescue a little boy who'd climbed too far up a tree. But I got stuck, too."

"We both know I meant why you elected to wait for me instead of seeing him home."

Betrayed by her own actions, Kenzy glared at Rem and hoped he could see every ounce of her anger in the moonlight. "Have you been so long at war, that an act of common courtesy is unknown to you? The house is not that far away, and he needed to feel proud that he'd been brave enough to beat the monster. He had to face the walk back alone."

"That sounds adamant, and as if we're talking about someone other than that child."

"I have no idea what you're talking about." But he was right on both accounts, wasn't he? She knew that one day she must face the fear that consumed her with such terror. She knew that she would have to do it alone. But the worst of his claim was that she'd wanted Rem to notice her as thoroughly as she'd examined him. Yet, he acted as if she'd deliberately set out to seduce him. "Do you still fancy yourself the man of my dreams?"

Laughter followed, resonating in his touch at her elbow. "I'm pleased you remember. Though it may have only been a game to you . . ." His features defined themselves more intensely. "I seldom make idle promises, McKenzy. And I may not be so easily resisted . . . if I decide to haunt your days *and* your nights." His teeth flashed white in the moonlight.

Of all the arrogance! Just because she'd played one too many games with him and lost. A loser's kiss when they were eleven did not give him the right to pay court now. She marched ahead, slinging the taunt back over her shoulder. "You've forgotten there's someone who will likely disagree with you."

"Stockton? Still the object of your and Rose's infatuation, I see. Certainly, he's a worthy opponent." Rem's calloused hand reached out to grab hers, gently stopping her progress. He imprisoned her fingers between his own and swung her around to face him. "But it's not respect that challenges you, McKenzy. If it was, then you would have never seen fit to let me near you and your friends. You wanted something more than the expected. Something grander than the easily obtained. You flirt with danger to make people notice. Well, I've noticed, Tadpole, and I'm up for the challenge."

She looked into his dark gaze and saw a hunger so raw it devoured any words meant to contradict him. The night hushed. The wind whisked his scent around her, and the moon shifted, allowing her to see the invitation in his eyes.

She should have been insulted. Instead, excitement summoned her, inviting Kenzy to test her bravado on the man and his comfort with the shadows. "I happened to like worthiness in a man. Respect is a fine reason to marry him. Do your best, Rembrandt Parker. I'm not your beloved forest you can read like a well-used map. As you just said . . . I'm a challenge. I'm that trail with dangers you can't even comprehend."

"And what if that trail leads me to your bed, Tadpole? Will you yield to my quest?"

The seduction in his tone caressed her as if he whispered heated promises against her neck, along her jawline, pausing inches from her lips. Kenzy's tongue darted out again to cool the hunger searing them.

His breath suddenly fanned her face. "If you continue to look at me that way, McKenzy, I'll skip all the gallantry and go straight to kissing you."

Powerless to fight his charm and unwilling to quell the excitement he'd aroused within her, she dared, "Kiss me then. Show me why you're the man for me. Let me feel—"

"Must everything be a list with you?" A deep chuckle filled the night. "I intend to do each of those things . . ."

His lips touched hers, imprinting their shape and texture into Kenzy's soul. The world careened in a dizzying dance of desire, then sent her cascading to some deeper yearning she could not comprehend.

At some point, she set down the lamp and buried her hands in the soft mat of hair covering his chest. Finding it silky to the touch, she wanted to feel more and wove her fingers through the thick mass that framed his face. When the white-hot tip of his tongue traced the sensitive edge of her lips, she opened her mouth to give him greater access. She pulled Rem closer to taste him more fully.

Suddenly, she lost control. It was as if she were trapped in a whirlwind, careening wildly over the prairie, down steep canyon walls, lifting to join the tempest that had given it birth. Excitement robbed her of breath, while longing forged a forbidden path from her reeling mind to the nether regions of her desire. His rough hand splayed, a thumb caressing one nipple straining beneath the muslin. Her body molded itself into his, wanting to be closer. Not knowing how. "Teach me," she sighed.

His palm slid down the curve of her hip, parted the ripped material to caress the bare skin of her leg. Suddenly, his hands cupped her bottom, pulling her closer until she could feel the pounding of his heart against her breasts.

Kenzy's eyes opened to find him looking at her. Black as the night that surrounded it, his gaze held the promise that only he could satisfy the indefinable need consuming her now.

"I'll do that and more," he groaned, pushing her away from him. "But after I'm sure it's me you desire and not just a release for the excitement Stockton left wanting in you."

5

When Kenzy came down to the kitchen the next morning, she was brought up short by the sight of her best friend's face. Rose looked like a rolling thundercloud.

"Rose, what's the matter?"

"Matter? Should something be the matter? Only that Noble has taken it upon himself to tell me how to run my business. It would have been different if I'd asked him."

Kenzy had never seen Rose quite so angry at the carpenter, but she couldn't imagine their childhood hero trying to dominate Rose. "What did he do?"

"He said that he would check with Orlan about a prime piece of property where the orphanage can be built."

"That's wonderful!"

"Wonderful is the last thing it is. Don't you understand? If Orlan Marsdale gets involved any more than he already is, you can bet he'll find a way to see that *you* are no longer the builder."

Though pleased by Rose's defense, Kenzy still felt the need to reassure her. "It's your money. You decide who to pay. Now, calm down, Rose. It sounds to me that all

Noble means to do is help you through this mess with Parker."

"I know of no mess with Rem Parker. At least not yet. Since we've already got the foundation laid and chimney set, perhaps he can be persuaded to let us continue. Shouldn't we give him a chance to help our cause? Surely a man with his background understands the need for war orphans to have a permanent place to live."

Kenzy pulled out one of the chairs at the dining table and sat. "Frankly, I'm surprised he returned to his land. He once told me the only reason he'd stayed in San Augustine as long as he did was because his grandmother claimed it would become her eternal resting place. Otherwise, he would sell the land and be on his way. Now that his grandmother is gone, what is there to bring him back but to pick up the money you paid for the property?"

Rose put the coffeepot and two cups on a tray, balancing the tray on her lap. When she felt it was secure, she rolled her chair to join Kenzy at the table. "The sale is no longer valid; he's alive. Maybe he's decided to settle down after all. Who knows, perhaps he *wants* to stay. The war has made us all care a little more about what we had before it began."

The midnight kiss Kenzy and Rem had shared came racing to mind. His words echoed with a promise that he had, indeed, returned for reasons other than to demand the return of his land. "Perhaps."

"Speaking of Rembrandt, did you hear what he said when they carried him to the guest room last evening?" Rose bent and rubbed her leg, grimacing.

"Something about a letter." Concern filled Kenzy as her friend straightened and poured the coffee. Rose's hands trembled. "Here, let me."

She refused to let go of the handle. "I can manage."

"Look at me."

Rose met Kenzy's gaze. "You're hurting." Kenzy gently placed her hand over Rose's and realized they both now wore their childhood "rings" on their smallest fingers. "I can see it in your eyes."

Her friend smiled. "My legs ache, not my hands. Won't you let me do this small thing for you?"

Withdrawing, Kenzy nodded and waited until her friend had poured both cups of coffee. "Thank you, hardhead."

"You're welcome, softheart."

Both women smiled because each knew that the nick-name they'd given each other had been swapped as surely as they had their rings. Rose was the softhearted one, Kenzy the more stubborn of the two.

"Now about Rem's ramblings. Did anything else make sense to you except for 'the letter'?" Rose took a sip from her coffee cup, glancing over its rim.

Rose seemed to be choosing her words carefully. Kenzy wondered what was so important about what Rembrandt had said. She tried to recall the moment but had difficulty shedding the cramped images and noise of people in the parlor to focus in on Rem's words. Then she remembered. When Rem had said Brett's name, she'd felt Noble almost drop the man. "He said Brett. Do you think he meant Brett Stockton?"

The cup Rose held banged sharply against its saucer, setting the cup on end and spilling coffee across the table. "Oh my, I'll get a towel and clean this right up."

Kenzy bolted to her feet and got the dishrag before Rose could even turn her chair around. "Sit still. I've got it." She wiped up the mess and put the soggy cloth into the dishpan. "I'll take care of that in a few minutes. Now, mind telling me why this has got you so upset?"

"I-I did something I'm not sure I should have."

"And that something has to do with Brett?"

Silver-gray eyes searched Kenzy's face. "Yes."

The pause was maddening. Kenzy felt her friend's scrutiny. Was she looking for a reaction? God in heaven, what had Rose done? A terrible possibility mounted in her mind. Even as she gave it voice, she refused to believe Rose would do such a thing. "You didn't . . . I mean, you and Brett weren't . . ."

Embarrassment stained Rose's cheeks. She shook her blonde head adamantly. "Nothing like that. It's just that before he left, I had a long talk with him. I don't think Noble would appreciate some of what I said to his brother. If he ever finds out . . . if that letter is truly from Brett, Brett may have written things I never meant for Noble to know. Things I'm not sure I could easily explain."

Kenzy waited, thinking her friend would tell her the dreaded words she'd spoken. But Rose closed herself off now, leaving Kenzy to approach the subject another way. "So you think that what you told him will make Noble angry enough to stay away?"

Rose wheeled her chair around and carried her cup to the dishpan. "He might never forgive me." She rolled to the table and gathered the tray and coffeepot, placing it on her lap. "Finished?"

"Not quite yet." Kenzy stood and took a final sip, following Rose to the wash station. "Why don't you tell Noble what you heard and ask him who sent the letter? No use worrying about this if we both misunderstood what we heard. The man was feverish, and Noble's brother wasn't the only person in this world with that name. This all might be pointless."

Rose squared her shoulders and blew out a long breath. "You're right, Kenz. And I'll do just that on our way to the orphanage this morning."

Pleased that her friend would be on location if Rembrandt decided to return home, Kenzy smiled. She didn't know all the exact details of Rose's purchase. It would be best for Rose and Rem to discuss the transaction. All she knew was that Rose had paid for the property and the money was held in trust for Rembrandt or any Parker relative who could prove a rightful claim. "I'm glad you've decided to join us for the morning. I can't wait until you've seen the fine job the men have done on the chimney. It's fireproof enough to last through Armeggedon."

"That's just what will happen around here, if we're right about what we heard."

"Armeggedon?" Kenzy handed Rose a towel, dipped the saucer into the suds, then dunked it in the clear basin of water. "I'll wash, you dry. Surely, it can't be as serious as that. Just what *did* you say to Brett Stockton?"

Rose grabbed the saucer and dried the china until it squeaked. She stared at it as if it were a mirror and she could see her reflection. "Something that will make Noble hate me for the rest of my life."

By the time they neared Parker land, Rose's stomach had twisted into a cold, hard knot. Kenzy, bless her heart, had tried to ease Rose's misgivings by fostering Noble's good humor. Unfortunately, he was in no mood for teasing.

"Why did Parker have to come along? I thought he was sick." Storm clouds brewed in Noble's blue eyes, though his words were a deadly whisper. "We don't have time to play nursemaid if we're going to get this built before the first frost."

Rose squirmed on the driver's bench, wishing now she'd elected to sit in the back of the wagon with the rest instead of next to Noble. "He asked for a ride home. Since he didn't have his horse with him, I thought it only neighborly to offer to take him there." Frustration filled her tone. "We were going there anyway."

"Does he know about the land yet?"

"I told him. I wanted him to understand why I did what I did."

He signaled the team to veer to the left of a pothole. The roadway was still damp from the rain, but not so muddy as to bog them down. "And what did he say?"

Still puzzled by the gypsy's reaction, her palms flew up in question. "He said, 'A godly goal, Miss Whitaker. Certainly, there is the need.' "

Noble's gaze met hers. "That's it? No recriminations? No demands?"

She shook her head. "Nothing but a compliment. He acted as if I'd done little but pluck a flower from his field."

"His culture doesn't believe in owning land. They like to move around a lot. Nomads, they call them." Noble swung around to glimpse his passengers. "But I wouldn't trust the man. I'm not sure gypsies even believe in the same god we do. Are you sure he meant it as a compliment?"

She shrugged. "Near as I can tell." Then Rose decided he had left her the perfect opening to lead into the real reason she'd sat near him and asked the others to sit in back. "About that letter he gave you . . ." Rose felt Noble's body stiffen.

"How do you know he gave me a letter?" Noble flicked the reins, ordering the horses into a swifter gait.

"At least you don't deny it. There was a letter, wasn't there?"

His gaze swept over her. "You know there was."

"And it was from your brother, wasn't it?"

He blinked and sucked in a deep breath that exited as a hiss. "Yes. Parker tell you that?"

The knot in her stomach tightened. "He didn't have to. Well, was it from Brett or wasn't it?"

Noble turned away, his lips taking a downward turn. "It's possible. It said something only Brett and I knew about."

Sensing his stormy mood, yet wanting to soothe his ire, Rose reached out a hand to touch his forearm. She gulped back the fear that threatened to surge from the pit of her stomach to stifle her words. "Whatever he said, you can tell me, Noble. There's nothing we can't discuss."

"You're right." He shirked away. "There is nothing. Nothing that matters now anyway. He's dead and gone. The letter won't bring him back."

"I've never known you to lie to me before."

He glared at her. "I haven't lied to you, Rose. Not now, nor will I. I just can't tell you right now. There are things I need to think about."

"Don't you see? You lied when I looked at you while you carried him to the guest room. You knew I'd heard what he'd said, but you shook your head as if to tell me I was wrong."

"I-I thought you were asking me if he was out of his head with fever." He couldn't meet her gaze any longer. "He was sick but still conscious enough to deliver the message."

"Another lie, Noble? We both know you did so because of other reasons."

"Be my friend enough to leave it alone, Rose. At least until I'm sure if I want others to know about the contents and why Parker brought it to me."

She told herself she would keep quiet out of friendship; but, truth be known, Rose wanted to stall the inevitable she knew she would one day face. Despite the reprieve, curiosity enveloped her. Was Noble's hesitancy because he must now fight the suspicion that she had somehow caused Brett's death?

"I'll leave it alone for now, as you've requested. But someone else heard the same thing. I can't guarantee the town won't know about it come evening. They'll be just as interested in what might be the last letter from the hero of Gaines Mill."

She wouldn't let him know it was Kenzy who had overheard. Their friendship demanded her silence for the moment. Yet, jealousy rose at the thought of Noble discovering Kenzy's knowledge and possibly asking her advice in the matter. He often relied on her best friend's ready opinion.

He needed to know that someone else had confirmed the letter's origin. Someone who rarely kept secrets to himself. "Little Worthy tends to have big ears and can fit under beds and other places well. You might want to be more watchful of what you say and to whom, if this is to remain a secret," Rose said.

"No telling who he's told. I'll put him to work beside me all day. That way, I can keep an eye on him."

"He and Cordell are supposed to hang the bell this morning. That will keep him in sight and out of the way for a while."

The rest of the miles passed in silence between the two. Even the boys had hushed, everyone marveling at the rain-washed beauty of the countryside. Blueberries and the lush green raspberry leaves formed a kaleidoscope of color along the base of the young pines that lined each side of the roadway. The greenery was deep and looked slick now like new paint, the trees planted in such straight lines the empty avenues between them seemed to race away to paths unknown. The air filled with tiny, silver umbrellas of dandelion seeds blowing in on the morning breeze.

"Why so quiet, you two?"

Kenzy's voice echoed from nearby. She must have scooted up to be heard.

"Have you been friends for so long, you don't have anything more to say to one another?" the architect teased.

Rose elbowed her for being so blunt.

"Ouch!" She glared at Rose, then took the hint. She sucked on her finger. "Must have gotten a splinter. I just thought I'd let you know that Mr. Parker says we can continue to build on the land. You can stop worrying that your carpentry has been wasted, Noble."

"That's good to know." He commanded the team past two ducks swimming in a rain puddle. "Which leaves the question of where he plans on staying while he's here."

Rose had never heard such a lack of welcome in Noble's tone.

"I'm staying on my land," Rembrandt Parker answered, his tone brooking no argument. "Until I've settled a few matters."

Rose half turned. "But you just told Kenzy we could still build. I assume that meant you're willing to accept the money I gave for your land originally."

"Providing shelter for these homeless children is a larger need than my own. But I must insist upon dividing the property. I won't sell the ground where my grandmother rests, nor the alcove where she planted her herbs."

No one needed him to say he wouldn't sell where her blood had been spilled. Everyone knew that Zephyr Parker had defended her right to live her life and conduct her business in the ways of old. The fact that an angry husband believed her "witch's potions" had killed his wife and son in childbirth did not deter the healer from offering her medicines to others. Only when the husband's anger caused a fire that burned off her garden and claimed Zephyr's life, did she stop fighting for her right.

"I'd be pleased to buy all but that portion, Mr. Parker." Rose admired his demand. "And if you decide to leave when things are settled, I'll buy that from you, too, and see that it's always properly cared for."

"The kindest offer I've ever received, Miss Whitaker." Gratitude shone in his eyes. "Thank you."

"You're welcome. Call me Rose. If we are to be partners in this, we should call each other by our given names."

The team bounded into a jarring trot that forced Rose back around and the others to grab hold. "The team smells the sawdust." Noble's tone rumbled over the jingle of harness and the groan of osage wheels against damp earth. "They know water waits ahead to slake their thirst."

But Rose knew better. Noble had flicked the reins ever so slightly when she'd given Rem the privilege of using her first name.

Could Noble be jealous?

6

$\mathcal{L}$ong past noon, Kenzy walked down the path that led to the Parker cemetery. While the men and boys ate the picnic lunch she had prepared for them, she decided to go see what was keeping Rose and Rembrandt. Rem had suggested he take Rose to the cemetery in the wagon to save her from having to use the wheelchair in the mud. But the pair should have been back long ago.

Before Noble cripples himself, she decided. He must have walloped his thumb out of sheer distraction. She kept watching him glance at the road instead of paying attention to what he hammered.

No wagon at the cemetery. No grooves in the damp ground that revealed the wheelchair had been put in use. That was odd. Kenzy shielded the sun from her eyes and peered into the tamarack and pine just southeast of the graveyard. The stream where she'd found Euphemia and the boys yesterday ran all the way through the property. Somewhere along the winding bank should be the alcove Rem had talked about.

Within a few seconds, she spotted the wagon. The wheelchair no longer stood tied against the back of the driver's box. Rose must have decided to take to her chair and get a closer look. A possibility that didn't sit well with Kenzy. Wouldn't the ground near the creek be muddier and more difficult for Rose to maneuver across?

The trees grew so thick there, images and distance faded into the emerald understory of bush and leaves. Noble would not be pleased that her friend and the gypsy were alone and out of sight, no matter that they were supposed to be conducting business. Kenzy decided to join them, in case the carpenter abandoned his meal and came searching. "Rose . . . Rembrandt? It's lunchtime."

The team cropped grass as she approached. One of the horses looked up and sniffed the air.

"It's just me," she announced.

"A distinctive scent."

Breath fanned her neck. Kenzy shivered and swung around, startled by Rem's nearness and the fact that he'd obviously changed clothes. If possible, he looked even more exotic, standing there dressed all in black. Her hand splayed against her throat, forming a barrier to the wall of shoulders standing in front of her. It was then she noted the spirals of dark hair adorning his chest where the buttons of his shirt had been loosened. A red bandanna had been knotted around his neck—a colorful banner against his beautiful dark matte skin. She attempted to swallow the lump of attraction that had risen to dry her throat. A glance upward showed her how well her height fit his. "Y-you should let someone know when you're that close."

"When I'm sneaking up on you, you mean?" His lips lifted slightly to one side, defining a well-carved jawline.

"You're laughing at me." Her hand returned to her side as she allowed irritation to quell the temptation he posed.

"At your offer of lunch, my dear Miss-Must-Know-Everything." One brow winged upward. "You came to see if I had taken Rosella into my notorious clutches, didn't you?"

"I did no such thing." She scanned the area behind him for sight of his horse or a place where he might have stored his belongings. The Parkers had never built on their land. They'd only harvested his grandmother's herbs and whatever they needed to feed themselves. Kenzy had always wondered where they went to get out of the cold and rain. "I simply meant to warn the two of you that lunch was ready and that, as hungry as those boys are, you best get back to camp if you plan on eating before supper." She eyed him from hat to boot tip, lifting her chin to defy the grin that broadened after her inspection. "You've changed."

His teeth flashed white against his tanned skin. "Have I, or is it just the clothes?"

"Don't laugh at me." Kenzy's fists shot to her hips. "And just when did you manage to do that?"

Another glance awarded her with the sight of a covered wagon perched on high wheels. Windows graced the side of the wagon visible to her. Double doors at the front opened onto a wide, porchlike board. The wood's deep toned, natural-colored oak looked heavily varnished. Once brightly colored eiderdowns hung across thick branches, airing in the sun. "Is Rose there?"

He removed his hat and combed his long fingers through his thick hair, causing the earring to flash and his muscles to flex. The dark gingham shirt defined the powerful vee of the gypsy's torso. A chuckle escaped him. "Care for a closer look?" He smiled. "Though I doubt she's there."

Kenzy concentrated on the pinestrewn pathway so he wouldn't see the tumult of sensations his innuendo stirred within her. "Why isn't she with you? She could be stuck in the mud."

"Now, isn't that a twist? You came running down here because you feared she *was* alone with me. Now you're asking why she isn't. Why are you blowing hot and cold, Tadpole? Afraid the Gypsy Man might find someone else and kiss her like there's no tomorrow?"

"Yes," she admitted through clenched teeth. "Because I don't know what you want from me . . . from Rose. Why did you really give her permission to buy the land? This was your chance to pay back everyone who ever treated you wrong in this town. You and you alone could cause the orphanage not to be built. What hidden reasons do you have to be so accommodating?"

Rem grabbed her elbow. In defiance, she jerked it away, expecting him to grab her again. Instead his hands lowered to his side.

"I don't have to defend my actions or explain my reasoning to anyone, McKenzy. Least of all to a tadpole who is so jealous that she can't bear the thought of any man paying interest in her rival."

The slap struck swift and hard. Her fingerprints shone sharply against his swarthy cheek. "Don't ever talk to me like that again, do you understand? Rose and I are best friends. There's not an envious bone in either one of our bodies for the other. You're just a stranger here, Rem Parker. A stranger who needs to mind his own business."

He rubbed the blistered cheek. "Then mind yours, Miss Dixon. As your holy book says, 'Do unto others as you would have them do unto you.' You do that, and we just might be able to work things out between us."

"What happened yesterday? Did that fever swell your ego? Since when do we have anything to 'work out' between us?"

"Since I decided to make you mine."

Kenzy marched toward the alcove, throwing her challenge over her shoulder. "You should be so fortunate, Mr. Parker. Now, help me get Rose and her wheelchair into the wagon. She doesn't need to be out here all day."

Rem fell in step beside her. "I imagine she knows what she needs and what she doesn't better than you or anyone else for that matter. She seems to be a capable woman."

Feeling the necessity to defend herself, Kenzy disputed his insinuation that she interfered where she was not wanted. "Rose knows whatever I suggest has one purpose, and that is to make her life easier."

"It has nothing to do with making her look less competent in Stockton's eyes, then?"

Fury unlike any she'd ever known consumed Kenzy,

halting her steps. She glared at him. "I've done nothing since I've been here but made sure she's in his company, and he has plenty of opportunity to see all her fine qualities. Don't you dare accuse me of trying to make her look weak in my favor. And don't try saying that Rose said such either."

Rem half bowed. "You're right, and she wouldn't. I've overstepped the boundaries of good taste. Excuse me, Tadpole, I must have been mistaken that you still have interest in Stockton. Unfortunately, my heretic raising gets the better of me and forces me to speak my insight." He reached out to lift her chin. "Your eyes look like frosted emeralds when you're provoked. A vision worthy of a slap or two."

"Rose!" she called out, needing to put an end to this exchange. The man was seduction at its best and she too ripe for the plucking. She hurried down the path, past the shelter of trees. "Where are you, Rose?"

"Be mindful where you step," Rem instructed behind her. "There are seedlings everywhere. You'll damage the tender roots."

"Over here, Kenzy. Isn't it simply lovely?"

Rose's voice drew her to a path that swerved right. She followed only a few short steps until she understood why her friend's voice was filled with such awe. Before them rose a natural arbor. Flowers and vines formed a half moon of greenery around an inlet pool fed by a tributary that ran from the creek. A riot of color dotted the ground, forming a dozen patterns but looking somehow whole.

"How beautiful." Kenzy glanced at Rem despite her earlier anger. "Your grandmother must have been a remarkable woman to have grown something so lovely and to make it last. I thought it had all burned."

"She knew only how to put good in the world. That was her true genius. That and not caring what others thought of how she went about it. And it did burn." His voice grew deep and somber. "But as the blessed soul once told me . . . out of ashes comes a new beginning."

His hand swept to encompass the alcove. "Out of the
burned soil came new, stronger herbs. Waiting here for
my return."

"I heard she was quite a healer. It's a shame she was
caused so much grief." Rose's face reflected her genuine
sympathy more than did her words.

"You would have liked her, and she, you. In fact, she
would have already twisted my ear for not offering you
some of that lavender and mugwort for your joints. Pardon me for asking such a personal question, but your
legs are aching today, aren't they?"

Rose lifted her hand from where she'd been rubbing
her thigh. "Wh-why, yes, they are." She stared at where
he pointed to the ground. "Lavender will soothe my
pain?"

"Mixed with mugwort, it will. It's not a cure, mind
you, but it helps ease muscles that bunch too tightly.
When GranZeph's bones started aching just before a
good rain or snow, she always took a healthy dose of
the tonic she made with the two herbs."

"Tonic? Not a lotion?" Alarm blazed through Kenzy.

"I'd like to try it." Rose scanned the rows of colorful
herbs. "How much would a batch cost me?"

"You said you wouldn't allow me to return any of the
fee paid for my property once I collect it from the
banker. The concoctions I make for you shall bear no
cost."

"No." Kenzy bent on her knees to stare squarely at
Rose. "Don't give up now. There may be a specialist
who can help you. Some doctor from back east whom
you haven't had an opportunity to see yet. One who's
returned home from the war and knows more how to
help you. *I'll* help you, Rose. I'll find the best physician
in the whole country, the whole world, for that matter.
Please don't take an unnecessary risk."

Rose smiled gently. "I appreciate your concern, but
Rem's grandmother was known for the wonders that
happened when she was called in to heal. Right now, all
the hope I have left is that her grandson might have

inherited that same gift. I need a miracle, Kenzy, and I need it now."

"You can't take something that hasn't been tested by real doctors. I've heard of people trying such elixirs and going out of their minds." Kenzy's eyes pleaded with Rembrandt, challenging him to deny her words. But he refused to speak. "He's been gone since the beginning of the war. Four years, Rosella. Who knows what's happened to these plants since he left. How do we know that he remembers his grandmother's formula? A little too much of this or that could prove disasterous."

A weariness settled over Rose's features, one that Kenzy had never seen before. Rose sighed deeply, the look in her eyes more imploring than her tone.

"Don't you understand, Kenz? I have tried everything I know to make my legs stronger." Tears bubbled in her eyes. "For three years and despite the insufferable war, I sought out every doctor who supposedly specialized in my condition. True, the war kept most of them busy and it was difficult for me to arrange a visit with them. But I came away from those examinations certain of one thing. They can't help me. They've done all they can. They all agreed on one thing . . . because my legs hurt, there's a chance I can one day walk again. If it takes believing in some magic gypsy potion to regain the proper use of my legs, then that's what I intend to do."

"Bravo." Rem clapped his hands like an enthusiastic audience member at an opera house play.

Kenzy rose and faced him. "Can't you see she's desperate? Don't take advantage of her discouragement."

"I happen to think Rose is making a wise choice, McKenzy, and that *is* the point here. To let Rose make her own choice."

"But it's only hearsay. Wive's tales. Sorcery to comfort the sick and afraid."

"My grandmother was no *drabarni*. I'll not defend her so-called 'sorcery' to anyone." Anger exuded from Rem like a perfume. "Just as I would never belittle her memory by giving Rose something I had not tested thoroughly." He moved to take hold of Rose's chair and rolled her to the wagon. "So, Miss Whitaker, it's up to you. Do you allow me to help or do you join with everyone else who's never taken the time to learn my people's ways?"

Noon sun reflected through the windows of the Whitaker home, radiating in motes that made the house seem to glow from within. The door stood ajar and the distinct aroma of baking bread filled the air, reminding Rem of days spent over his grandmother's pots and earthen kiln. Others had called GranZeph's cooking instruments cauldrons, as if to insinuate she was a witch conjuring medicine and mayhem. The only magic she had been guilty of creating was delectable morsels that satisfied even the most finicky eater.

He reined the dappled gray to a halt and dismounted. If the food tasted as good as it smelled, he hoped the baker was a kind soul eager to show hospitality.

After hitching the horse to the post, Rem retrieved two carefully wrapped jars from his saddlebags and headed up the stone walk to the porch. A scan of the woman's property familiarized Rem with its well-kept grounds, fresh paint and ornately carved columns. Designing an escape route had been a habit of his since before the war and one he relied on now. Trust never came easy to a man whose people had battled with scorn their whole lives.

If a house could mirror its owner's personality, this one surely did. *Genteel. No false facades. Sturdy enough to withstand a storm.* From what little he remembered of her, Rosella Whitaker had seemed all those things in her youth. As far as he could tell now, time and circumstances had only strengthened her. But he'd also known her as a follower—someone who did whatever McKenzy Dixon suggested. The Rose he glimpsed yesterday at the alcove definitely had split paths with her friend somewhere along the way. Which was good, if she meant to oppose Kenzy's mistrust of his medicine.

The war and life had taught him that to prolong anything only made a wound fester and weaken the body. The sooner Rose began taking the dosages, the quicker her legs could regain their full ability.

Shifting the jars to one hand, Rem knocked. Hopefully, Rose would answer the door. He did not feel like sparring with Kenzy today, wanting only to restore the wagon he and GranZeph had called home and await Stockton's decision about the letter. Though Lee's surrender freed Rem of military obligations, he was bound by a higher duty to honor the promise made to his grandmother. Bringing medicine to Rosella Whitaker was the first step in keeping his promise that the garden would not lie fallow. Her land would be used to heal.

A minute passed. Two. After a second knock, finally heavy footsteps heralded someone's approach. Rem braced himself for a less than enthusiastic welcome.

"Why, Rem Parker! Whatever are you doing here this fine Sunday afternoon?" Euphemia Jones wiped her hands on her apron. Wisps of gray hair had pulled away from the long braid she wore, but her violet eyes shined with a healthy vitality that defied any age. "I thought you might attend church, being as how it's your first Sunday back. Come on in, boy."

Rem took off his hat and waited until the woman allowed him inside. "Good afternoon, Miss Euphemia. You're looking particularly lovely today, and no one but you would have saved me a pew."

"Ain't nothing a good wash up won't do." Euphemia dusted a speck of flour from one cheek and waved away his comment. "And you're wrong. I expect Strut would've sidled over for ya."

Remembering Miss Euphemia had always been hard of hearing, he wondered if she'd thought he said *dusty* instead of *lovely*. Rather than correct her, he offered the store owner a quick peck on the cheek in question. She giggled like a schoolgirl and gave him a hug.

"Landsakes but you've grown a sight since I seen you last. Zeph would be proud that you've grown into such a long drink of water."

He eyed her with affection. The woman had been his grandmother's dearest friend. Miss Euphemia would always have a special place in his heart no matter if she never extended to him the same accord she'd shared with his grandparent. He sniffed the air. "And you've become a pretty good cook if whatever that is tastes as good as it smells."

"I offered to watch Rose while the others went to church. She's two lips shy of her best smile this morning, and I thought a One-Two-Three-Four cake would be just the thing to make her feel better. They serve it at the Caledonia Hotel, and it's her favorite. I'm this close," she left a slim gap between two fingers to show the measurement, "to figuring out exactly how much sassafras should go in it."

"Sounds delicious." Rem glanced at the empty chair-lift that rested against the wall opposite the stair railing. "Is she upstairs? Will I be able to see her?"

Euphemia nodded. "Rose is in the sitting room, enjoying the sun. Wanted some tea earlier. She hates lying in that bed and letting those legs get the best of her. Doc Jubal ought to be here pretty quick to give her a look-see. He had to go into Nacogdoches, and I expect him back today. If he heads home, he'll get the note I left on his door. If he makes church, Kenzy will bring him back with her."

She held a finger up against her mouth. "But don't say a word about his coming to Rose, mind you." Euphemia signaled him to follow her upstairs. "She ain't

one to complain and worry folks, even when she has
every reason."

When he found her, Rose didn't seem in any great
pain. She sat in her wheelchair behind a table. The curtains in the window had been pulled back to allow in
the light. Her laughter, as she stared at something outside, was soft and reminded him of the tinkling bells his
grandmother used to hang in the trees that shaded their
vurdon when they camped. GranZeph said the chimes
invited the wind to cool the wagon, refresh their steeds
and soothe their sleeping quarters from the summer heat.

A blanket spread over Rose's lap hid her legs, but
Rem had learned from years of handling the wounded
that the severity of an injury did not always compare to
how much the patient complained.

Euphemia announced his presence.

"What a pleasure to see you again, Rembrandt."
Silver-blue eyes turned to focus on Rem. "I trust you've
settled in and are having a pleasant first Sunday home.
Did you find your *vurdon* in order?"

He nodded, pleased that she remembered the name of
his people's mode of transport—their home on wheels.
"Yes, everything was exactly as I had left it."

"Extraordinary good fortune," Rose remarked, "considering all that has occurred in the area in the past few
years. Carpetbaggers, raiders, even deserters. Thieves of
every social persuasion. I'm surprised there was anything at all left when you returned."

It was difficult to agree with her, for Rem knew why
his possessions had remained untouched. They were
considered gypsy—tainted. Not even good enough for
the dregs of mankind to steal. As a guest in Rosella
Whitaker's home, he would bow to her optimism. She
was a kind woman who did not see with his eyes. "Good
fortune, it is then. Regrettably, I believe it more the
power of superstition waging war against a would-be
robber."

He strode across the room and set down the two jars
of tonic on the table next to her. "Now, in answer to

your first question, my day would be much more pleasant if you'd accept this small token of appreciation for your kindness in nursing me back to health."

"The mugwort and lavender?" Rose lifted one jar, her thumb rubbing the pottery as if by doing so she could make the medicine's potency rise to the top like cream. Gratitude lit her gaze. "You remembered."

He half bowed. "An easy task at the moment, although I'm not sure that won't change once McKenzy returns."

"She'll come around. Kenzy's just wary of anything she has no experience with. She means well." Rose motioned him to take the chair opposite her own, while she poured tea into a cup. She handed him both cup and saucer. "Cream or sugar?"

"Neither, thank you."

"Euphemia, dear, would you mind going downstairs for another cup, then join us?"

"Sure thing, Rosie." Euphemia waddled over and took the teapot. "And while I'm at it, I'll refill the pot. Got a little surprise for you, too. Ought to be just about done. Wanted it ready when Kenzy and the boys returned."

A smile lingered on Rose's lips as she waited for the woman to leave. "She's such a kindhearted soul, don't you think? And her surprise smells absolutely delicious."

"It looks like you've got lots of good friends to watch over you." Rem took that moment to survey Rose Whitaker from the marionette curls that covered her delicate forehead to the dainty slippers at her feet. She was a fine measure of a woman. If she ever regained the use of her legs, Rose would be taller than Kenzy and with a slightly less provocative figure. Her hair shone like sundappled strawberries, haloed by the light coming through the window. The fetching curls could never compare to the thick, rich auburn hue of Kenzy's hair, but then he supposed another man might be of a different opinion.

"I'm more fortunate than most." She sipped her tea, then suddenly began to cough, sputtering as she fought another blush. "Forgive me. I didn't mean to im—"

"Don't apologize. It's no secret that I can count my allies on one hand." He eyed her over the rim of his cup, testing how well she took teasing. "Perhaps *we'll* become great friends, and the association will absolve my reputation?"

"Being my companion hasn't made Kenzy any more popular since her return." Rose set her cup down and stirred the tea with her spoon. "I just wish everyone would see that she isn't trying to be domineering; she simply wants to prove herself to them . . . to me."

Rem admired Rosella for her loyalty to her friend. Loyalty was one trait he'd coveted above all. But the few companions of his youth, his comrades in arms during the war, even his own grandmother had, in the end, deserted him. She preferred to die for her land rather than choose life with him. Odd, that Kenzy now reminded him of GranZeph—a woman whose will could not be easily swayed. Admirable, yet frustrating. "Seems to me someone who's bent on proving herself to everyone else just might have something to prove to herself," he offered brusquely, angry at himself for finding fault with his grandmother. It was unkind to think ill of the dead.

"And what is it that I have to prove?" Kenzy asked from behind him. She entered the sitting room and untied the ribbon from beneath her chin to loosen her bonnet. Plopping down on the settee that graced one wall, she pulled the bonnet from her head and put it next to her. "Pray tell me, ol' soothsayer," she leveled a skeptical gaze at Rem, "what do you foresee?"

Kenzy looked beautiful, despite her gentle scoffing. Though he normally left the practice of fortune-telling to others of his tribe, he could not resist the challenge in Kenzy's eyes. Rem poured a portion of his tea into the saucer, stirred the remainder of the liquid in his cup, then narrowed his gaze to examine the tea closer. "Interesting."

"I'll say it is." Euphemia bustled into the room, carrying the fresh tea service. "The three of you look like a dust devil just whisked through here. What's got you so ruffled?"

Rose leaned closer, motioning to Rem's cup. "What do you see?"

Kenzy stripped off her gloves. "Tea grounds. Nothing more. We're being played for fools."

She was half right. Rem frowned, wishing he had not chosen to seek the wisdom of the leaves. "Only if you make a gypsy speak a language foreign to himself, will he lie."

Because Kenzy had once opened herself to his friendship, honor demanded that he not treat her as his people might a total stranger who mocked him. He would embellish the truth only slightly. "Fool you will be if you do not accept who you are, McKenzy Dixon. Live not for what others expect of you." His voice deepened to a dramatic whisper, aware of the effect it would have on the doubters. It took all his effort to squelch a chuckle. "Perhaps the answer you seek lies within the question you wish to ask us all."

"And what question is that?" Curiosity filled Miss Euphemia's tone.

He'd wanted only to tease, but a second glance at the tea surprised Rem. A question truly burned within Kenzy. "Whether those around her are merely scavengers feeding off her life or true comrades."

Rose gasped and dropped her cup.

"Now look what you've done!" Kenzy blurted, bolting to her feet to help Rose. "If she as much as burned her—"

Euphemia rushed over, set down the tray and began dabbing at the tea that had splattered Rose.

Fury danced in Kenzy's emerald eyes as she grabbed the tonic from the table. She thrust the jar in front of Rem, covering the sight of his cup. "I suggest you keep your predictions and your potions to yourself. They will do nothing but bring her harm."

Seeing that Rose was not burned and the mess easily cleaned, Kenzy's anger cooled to a slow simmer.

"Seems to me if anyone has spent his life seeking everyone's acceptance, it's been you."

She dropped the jar into his cup, spun on her heel and stormed out of the room.

"She didn't mean—"

"No need." Rem waved away his hostess's defense of her friend and rose. "I suppose I deserved that. Ladies, I shall see you again. I regret not being able to stay long enough to sample your cake, Miss Euphemia. Perhaps another time. I think an apology is in order."

The slamming of the front door told him that Kenzy had taken her tantrum outside. He hurried downstairs and out the door after her, almost running into the children coming up the walk—Cordell and Worthy, the two orphans who rode in the wagon with them out to the building location.

He managed to sidestep the smallest, ruffling the boy's brown hair to reassure him he meant no harm. "Pardon me, Worthy. I'm in a hurry. Didn't mean to startle you."

"What's going on?" Puzzlement etched the seven-year-old's forehead. "Miz Dixon looks mad enough to spit cactus. Y'all have a fight?"

"It's called a spat, snailbrain." Cordell looked over the rim of his glasses at the smaller boy, then at Rem for confirmation. "A lovers' spat."

"Let's just call it a difference of opinion." Rem wanted to set the record straight for the time being. They weren't lovers . . . but the possibility definitely had its appeal. "I don't fight with women."

"Better watch out anyway, Gypsy Man," Worthy called after him. "Miz Dixon's full of spit and stubborn as a woodpecker."

"I'll keep that in mind. Did you see which direction she took?"

"Headed toward Doc Jubal's like her bustle was on fire. He ain't back, though. I coulda told her that, but she was hell-bent for high country and wasn't listening."

"Better not let Miss Euphemia hear you say that, Worthy," the older boy warned. "She'll make you swallow a tub full of castor oil to clean out your mouth."

"What'd I say?" Worthy's eyes widened, appealing for support. "You heard me. All I said was hell-bent for . . ."

"I'd love to stay and referee, but I want to catch Miss Dixon." Long strides carried Rem up the street. He caught sight of several people—Union soldiers ogling two women with parasols, Noble Stockton and Strut dressed up in their Sunday best.

When he finally spotted Kenzy, purpose fueled her stride. Protection of her friend spurred her quick steps. Part of what she'd said was right, no matter how much he denied it. He had been fighting for acceptance all his life.

The apathy he presented to others who directed their prejudice toward him had become a private hell. Isolating himself evolved into a defense against the pain of being an outcast. Outwardly, he shrugged off the criticism by pretending he didn't care. Inwardly, he felt as if he alone battled the bias toward his ancestry. He'd even joined the rebel forces to prove that he could not only live alongside the people of San Augustine but was willing die beside them.

A stupid mistake, Rem learned almost immediately. A childish mistake he managed to live through. Yet there were no cheers for a returning soldier who had survived when everyone else in the unit died. The brand of coward hung over his head. Coward, or worse . . . traitor. When would he stop being labeled and simply be considered a man?

He wondered if Kenzy would ever see him as such. Not in the shadows of the night, when he'd been unable to resist the fire in those green eyes and kissed her with all the desire of a man who'd seen too much death—a man who needed to taste life once again. Instead, he wanted her to view him as a man in the broad light of day. With all his faults and his strengths. To kiss him in front of everyone who mattered to her.

"Quit following me."

The nearness of Kenzy's voice startled him. She stood several feet away now, her hands on her hips, the same fire blazing in her eyes. Her spine was straight, her countenance unyielding, her voice cold as a north wind. She had never looked more beautiful. The desire to indulge his fantasy twisted like a dull pain in his gut.

Kenzy seemed unaware of his struggle as she moved a step nearer. "If you have something more to say . . . then get it said. Otherwise, take your tea leaves and leave me alone."

Resentment chilled his blood, every muscle turning to stone in its wake. He disliked her bossiness as much as he admired her spunk. "All right, I will. I said some things to you at Miss Whitaker's house that I shouldn't have."

Her feet rocked backward and forward, revealing her impatience. "You certainly shouldn't have. It's a good thing the boys were not back yet. If they'd heard such nonsense, no telling what kind of ideas you would put in their heads. Cord would have been up all day and night trying to determine if there was any scientific reasoning in your reading. And, Worthy . . . well . . . I shudder to think what wild tale that child would have spread by sundown."

The woman's attitude could get on his nerves, if he let it. That, and the fact that she did deserve an apology. "I should have waited until we were alone before I told you what I saw," he said begrudgingly. "I didn't mean to make you feel so uncomfortable that you would choose to run away."

Her gaze met his squarely. Her breath took on the chug of a steam engine. The material of her shirtwaist rose and fell with each breath, defining the swell of her bosom.

"Don't flatter yourself. I've never run away from anything in my life."

Temptation shattered Rem's resentment as if it were a stone thrown against glass. She was too adamant; he, too willing to provoke any response from her. "Even from this?" he asked as his lips branded her with a searing kiss.

In the broad light of day.

In front of everyone on the street.

Despite all his imperfections.

8

*S*omething indefinable changed between them as Rem kissed her. With her insides trembling, Kenzy unthreaded her arms from around his neck, hating the way her fingers ached for one last touch of the silken hair that framed his handsome face. Black eyes, that moments ago had been filled with a dare, now stared at her with intensity. She felt the heat of their desire melting away any sense of propriety she still possessed.

"I didn't mean to make you feel so uncomfortable that you would choose to run away." His words echoed in her mind as she squeezed her eyes shut, trying against hope to silence the sensations that coursed through her bloodstream. But every nerve ending pulsed with the erratic beat of her heart. Every breath mingled with his. Every fiber of her being cried out to move closer and be cocooned in his warmth. Kenzy couldn't resist the memory of his kiss as it seeped in deeply, somehow soothing the numbness that had iced her heart since her parents' deaths.

Never before had she believed any man, even Noble, could make her lose her bearings again, forget her obligation to someone important to her. But here she stood in the middle of the street, kissing him like he was the one man who could rescue her from the nightmares. She allowed herself to be lost in his kiss rather than completing her search for Jubal. She'd placed her own desire over Rose's needs. What kind of friend was she? For that matter, what kind of daughter had she been?

Run away? Perhaps Rem was right. She had run, because she was afraid of looking too closely at the truth and discovering that she'd been right all along. Her parents died because she'd lost her way, and Rose became bound to a wheelchair because Kenzy had led her astray.

Though she'd not been there physically to warn Rose about the stagnant pool, Kenzy knew, under normal circumstances, Rosella would never have dared to swing from the tree limb, and drop into the water. Rose had always accompanied Kenzy's escapades, relishing the adventure they found together. Her friend didn't have to say that she'd taken such a chance just so she could write and share the details with Kenzy.

The moment she'd seen Rose in the wheelchair, Kenzy had known that she was to blame for Rose's affliction. She'd encouraged her to live life more daringly. And now Rose was doing it again. Taking chances on potions that might harm her. All because Kenzy had once told her to grab hold of life.

Well, she would heed her own advice. She'd find Jubal and make sure Rose didn't suffer because she wanted to prove she was just as daring as Kenzy. She'd not give Rem Parker another chance to make her lose control. A small part of Kenzy mourned that decision, sensing the loss of something she couldn't quite name. Something that challenged her fear of the unknown.

Noble can make me forget, she reminded herself silently, taking assurance from the fact that she knew him and his ways like the orphanage's floor plan. That's what she wanted now . . . certainty, convention, comfort. A life within her control. "Don't ever kiss me like that again."

"No slap?" Rem turned his face, offering his jaw. When she didn't comply, a twitch revealed he had braced for her retaliation. "Then, your response must have been as I imagined. *Mutual*."

"A gentleman wouldn't take such liberties in front of everyone." Kenzy became aware of the gathering townspeople. Gossip would spread like sand blowing in the wind. She stepped backward and nearly tripped on the hem of her dress. "A gentleman wouldn't boast."

"I'm no gentleman. Ask any one of them. And believe me, Tadpole, if you had offered one speck of resistance, we wouldn't be having this conversation."

His gaze seemed to bury itself deeply within her.

"What the good people of San Augustine don't know is that my magic won't work unless you want it to." He reached out and toyed with the auburn curl dangling over her shoulder. "And you do want it to work, McKenzy. I see it in your eyes. I tasted it on your lips."

Kenzy prayed for a gust of wind to fan her cheeks and cool the rush of longing that heated her skin. How easily he read her. Like the tea leaves?

No, she wouldn't listen to such nonsense. Her own body had betrayed her! All because his eyes tempted her with secrets hidden in their depths and his lips dared her to profess the mysterious feelings he conjured within her. Feelings that made her aware she was searching for something different than designing structures to fulfill her life. Kenzy wanted more than to prove her worth. She needed something beyond what she could provide for herself.

Was this unusual hold Rem had over her magic? She could not deny his claim nor explain the sense of loss that overwhelmed her now. Her chin lifted to defy him, unwilling to humble herself completely. Yes, the kiss was mutual. *There, are you satisfied?* "You've made whatever point you intended. If you're quite finished in using me to anger the others, then I have to be on my way. Jubal will head off somewhere else if I don't get to him soon."

"We both know why you're in a hurry to leave, and it has nothing to do with finding the doctor. Go, Tadpole, before I remember how beautiful your eyes are when passion burns brightly within you. Go, or I'll be sorely tempted to show you why you should stay."

Frustrated, Kenzy returned home without Doc Jubal. She'd posted a note beside the one Euphemia had left on his door, giving explicit instructions to find her before he examined Rose. By accompanying the doctor, Kenzy hoped that Rose would be less likely to send him away and more willing to allow an examination, if only to pacify her.

To Kenzy's surprise, Orlan Marsdale's horse and several buggies were hitched in the foreyard. Anna Le-Grand's sleek new roan raised his head as Kenzy walked past. She paused long enough to stroke its flank, admiring the beast's rich, red coat. "That's all we need today . . ."

Kenzy slid her palm along the magnificient horseflesh until she reached the animal's nose and stroked it. "A dose of those two quarrelers would make anyone sick if they weren't already."

The roan bobbed his head. Kenzy giggled. "Guess you above all others would know—huh?"

His nostrils widened a second before blowing out a hot stream of air.

"Sounds like horse sense to me." Kenzy laughed and headed into the house.

"Rose, I'm back," she announced, wondering if her friend could hear her for all the ruckus. The sound of Orlan's booming voice echoed from the parlor, accompanied by someone's skill with the piano. The protectiveness Rembrandt had kindled earlier within Kenzy now burned with a brighter flame. If the timber baron was in the parlor that meant Rose had left her sitting room and, out of courtesy to her guests, come downstairs. She wasn't well enough to go up and down the lift. Whatever her visitors discussed could wait until another time when she felt better.

Just before Kenzy reached the doorway to the parlor,

a tiny hand snaked out from inside a duster on a nearby coatrack. Startled, she started to throw back the floor-length coat and demand to know Worthy's intentions.

"They're fighting mad," his childish voice whispered from inside the coat. "Better not go in there."

Small boots, barely noticeable under the hem of the black riding slicker, shifted. Kenzy pulled the material back and found his brown eyes looking up at her innocently and a forefinger pressed against his lips. A laugh bubbled up from inside her, but she didn't dare encourage him. Instead, she stifled her amusement and frowned, hoping she showed a shred of disapproval. "Come out from there this minute, Worthy. I told you it's impolite to listen in on other folks' conversations. I'll see to it they take their vexations somewhere else. Rose doesn't need to be—"

"But they're mad at *you*, Miz Dixon." Worthy's eyes narrowed, his chin lifting defiantly. "I *gotta* listen so I could tell you what mean things they're saying."

About me? She ruffled the boy's head affectionately, aware of how she'd grown to care for the child in just a short time. Pleased by his equal concern for her, she wondered what had been discussed that would compel him to worry. "Well, your loyalty is on target, but your method misses the mark."

"Huh?"

"Never mind. I'll explain it later." Kenzy wondered why anyone would be angry enough with her to call a meeting; and, from the looks of those buggies out in the yard, with some of San Augustine's elite.

She began to speculate. "Rose wouldn't have sent for anyone just because we disagreed on whose medicine to use. Come to think of it, I'll bet Orlan found a way to convince her to replace me. That has to be it. At least, that makes the most sense at the moment. Lord knows Marsdale is envious. Whatever his intentions, there's nothing I can't handle." Kenzy realized that she talked more to herself than her small listener. He was probably confused by her prattling. "So you quit worrying about me."

Worthy shook his head. "Ain't nothing like that, Miz Dixon. Mr. Marsdale is mad 'cause you up and kissed the gypsy man. Said you're kissing a coward who ran off and joined the other side. Left men in the field to die so he could save his own hide."

She'd heard the rumors circulating since Rem Parker's return, but she hadn't wanted to believe them. The boy of her youth would never deliberately disappoint anyone; he wanted too much to belong. It didn't make sense that he would join up with rivals who hated him worse than they did his fellow Rebs. But the man who came back seemed a loner who no longer cared what others thought of him. "What else did they say?"

"I didn't hear it all 'cause that lady playing the piano was playing that fancy stuff real loud. But I did hear them saying something about you laying down lots more than bricks out at the orphanage." Puzzlement furrowed his brow. "What does that mean, Miz Dixon? We got boards and bricks and some stones. Ain't we supposed to lay all that down?"

A firestorm of fury flashed through Kenzy. She glared at the parlor entrance and back at the boy. "Yes, we are, and what it means is that I will have a few things to say to Mr. Marsdale before he leaves. Now be a good scout and round us up a piece of cake and some milk. Rose and I will be there shortly . . . after I've gotten rid of her guests."

"What if somebody starts shooting?" His question held the sincerity of a soul who'd lived through the horrors of the country's recent conflict.

"Nobody gets shot for kissing someone. If they did, they'd have to shoot every woman whose husband, son, father or brother came back."

"So you did kiss him?"

Worthy stared at her mouth as if he could see the imprint of Rem's kiss. Although it wasn't visible from the outside, Rembrandt branded himself deeply into her senses. Kenzy fidgeted under such youthful scrutiny. If she couldn't explain her action to a child then how did she expect to contend with Marsdale? "It was more like *he* kissed me. But that isn't the issue, now is it? What I do is nobody's business but mine, and no one but *I*," she stressed, "has the right to decide whether I allow the kiss or don't."

"Did you get any of his magic?" Worthy reached up and touched her bottom lip. "Did it rub off?"

Magic? There was that word again. Rem's kiss had captivated her, warmed her with such a spellbinding intensity that she'd been enthralled beyond words or action. Once she regained her senses from the mesmerizing effect of his embrace, she had found her response to him exasperating. And his amusement at her response incorrigible.

"Nothing rubbed off." She disliked disappointing the boy. "It was just an everyday kind of kiss. Certainly not one the town should be up in arms about. Now, I know a little boy who's going to have lots of new spelling words to keep him occupied for the rest of the day if he doesn't haul himself out of that duster and hightail it to the kitchen. Ask Miss Euphemia to cut us a slice of the cake she made. Which will it be . . . cake or spelling words?"

The seven-year-old disappeared down the hall and into the kitchen. Kenzy's smile faded. She took a deep breath, squared her shoulders and entered the den of denouncers.

Anna LeGrand sat at the piano, providing background music to the conversation being carried on between Orlan, Rose and several townspeople whose names Kenzy couldn't remember. Orlan's cohorts, no doubt.

Everyone hushed and faced her.

"Please don't stop on my account. Gossip's an old bonnet that's fit me a long time. I'm sure I've been the subject of conversation before now." She strolled over to the sideboy and wondered what they would all say if she decided to pour herself some sherry. Liquor might

dull some of the senses that still hummed with the tune
of Rembrandt's kiss, but drinking it would certainly
color their conversation further.

"How did you know we were discussing you?" Orlan
frowned at her.

Thunderous music escalated then fell at Anna's fingertips, giving dramatic effect to his question. She half-
turned, tossing back her sable-colored hair while laughing. "Perhaps it's because you were shouting so loud
you could have heard it clear to Nacogdoches. Or . . ."
One eye winked at Kenzy. "Because there's a gypsy in
town. Is it possible that phantoms he's employed are
listening in on our discussions?"

Kenzy wasn't sure if Anna was mocking the man's
superstitions or if she meant to imply Worthy's eaves-
dropping.

"I have no time for that gypsy nonsense and neither
does San Augustine." Orlan hooked his thumbs underneath the lapels of his brocade vest and rocked on his
boots. "I say the faster the orphanage goes up, the
quicker the Northerners will offer us amnesty."

Rose rubbed the back of her neck. "Orlan, please sit.
We all want it built as soon as possible. That's never
been an argument, but amnesty will be based on more
than improvements made on the land they're taxing."

Orlan sat on the edge of the davenport, filling it with
his large frame. He leaned forward, knotting one fist on
the table that divided his hostess's wheelchair from her
guests. "Once the orphanage is in use, they'll look more
favorably on our township. Why, Captain Mullins himself sent a message to his superiors about our plans.
Apparently, there are several children up north who have
lost their parents and homes to the war. He seems to
think a way to win back trust is to show what we can
do to help repair what was undone. We simply can't
allow any more time to be wasted."

Kenzy moved behind Rose and kneaded the tension
knotting in her shoulders. "We haven't lost any time,
Marsdale, even with that last storm. Noble and Strut

were able to cover everything before it got too wet. You're worrying about delays that just aren't happening."

The pianist let her fingers race down the keys until they fell off the end, as if plummeting from the top of a hill. "Take the plunge, Orlan dear," Anna challenged, laughing when the baron's cheeks puffed up like a squirrel's after a successful scavenge. "Or perhaps I can find more delicate words to relay what he's implying." Her black eyes leveled on Kenzy. "In other words, he's complaining about time he thinks should be spent wooing the enemy instead of each other."

"Does this have to do with me and Rembrandt Parker?" Kenzy felt Rose stiffen beneath her touch. "If so, that's none of your affair. It happened only this afternoon, and we were nowhere near the orphanage. Sundays are my day away from work. What I do on my own time should not concern you. And, if you'll remember, Parker was brought in two nights ago nearly unconscious. Hardly time for me to get to know him much less set my sights on him."

"Yet you know him well enough to kiss him." Orlan twisted one edge of the thickly waxed mustache that bracketed his frown.

Surprised by the impulse to defend Rem, Kenzy's temper flared. "We have been acquainted with one another a lot longer than I've known you. I would think you have better people to spy on than me, Marsdale."

"Got you there, big guy." Anna's finger pretended to slice her neck in half.

Kenzy never knew for sure if Anna was on her side or whether she simply liked to watch someone best Orlan. Her childhood neighbor had been nothing but congenial since Kenzy's latest arrival in San Augustine. It was hard to believe she once was the girl who had caused her and Rose so much trouble. Remaining behind had brought Anna closer to Rose in friendship, apparently eliminating any envy Anna had previously harbored.

Rose's hands gripped each armrest of her chair as if she intended to rise. Instead, her neck straightened and her head lifted. "I'm going to say this once, Orlan, and I hope you're truly listening this time. I consider you a friend, and I've been patient with you because of my respect for your family."

She motioned to the oval picture hanging on the wall next to the sideboy. The tintype revealed a woman holding a child in her lap, with a handsome man standing behind them.

When Rose began to talk, Kenzy quit rubbing, aware of how the enunciation of each word warned the others that no more insinuations would be tolerated.

"My father always revered your father and thought highly of you . . ." The pause in Rose's compliment made Orlan shift to his weight to the other foot. "I, better than most, know that financing the orphanage would gain us favor with our overseers."

Murmurs rippled across the room.

Kenzy scanned the faces of the townspeople in attendance. To have Rose speak in anything but a benevolent tone immediately captured everyone's attention. Pride filled her at Rose's resolve to be heard.

"I gladly pay the cost, first to help my friend, second to provide a home for children who need one, and third to ease the strife between us and the Federalists. But I also know that *you* are aware that whomever constructs the building will most likely win several contracts from the new government."

Surprise darted across Orlan's face, and Kenzy realized her friend had leveled the man's true motivation right to its foundation. She could almost feel Rose staring at him and wondered how long he could endure the intensity of her reproach. Rose might sit smaller in a chair, but few stood taller in determination.

Just as Kenzy expected, the man blinked and sat back in a less threatening manner.

"I decided Kenzy would be my architect long before I ever discussed the possibility with you." Rose rolled closer. "I won't sit here and allow you to impune her dedication to the project just because *you* think she's taking longer than *you* think is necessary. As far as I'm concerned, Kenzy can involve herself with whomever she pleases outside of her project."

"With Noble?" The timber baron looked as if he were backed in a corner.

"There's nothing new going on between her and my cousin that I know of." Anna swung around, rustling the flounces of her white muslin dress. When she stood, she grimaced, slightly favoring one foot by shifting her weight to the other.

"You're hurt." Sympathy softened Rose's tone.

Anna sat and reassured her, "Twisted my ankle. It'll be fine in a few days, I'm sure." She glared at the baron. "Noble and Kenzy are just good friends and have been as long as she and I have known each other. Perhaps someday they'll even marry. I think they'd make a fine couple who'll raise healthy sons. Don't you think so, Rosie?"

Rose's hand rubbed one leg in response. Her silent nod did more damage than if she had spoken. The breath went out of Kenzy as surely as if someone had punched her in the stomach. Anna's defense did nothing but clarify the true problem left unresolved by Kenzy's return. It wasn't whether or not she could do the job. It wasn't if she allowed her private life to interfere with her professional one. All of these accusations centered on the one obstacle she and Rose were unwilling to face—giving up the dream of becoming Noble's bride.

"Cake, anybody?" Euphemia carried refreshments into the room, followed by Worthy, Cordell, Noble and Rem. "Looks like the whole town's turned out." She lifted the cake and smelled it. "Gotta admit, I put my toe in it."

Worthy's eyes ovaled into chocolate saucers. "Put your toe in it? Euuuwww!"

"That's just an expression." Anna's criticism bit sharply as she gathered her reticule, preparing to leave. "*If* you get a little older, we'll tell you what it means."

"I ain't listening to nobody with mean eyes."

Mean eyes? Kenzy watched Worthy bristle as Anna walked past him and wondered why animosity radiated from boy to woman.

Rem Parker moved alongside Kenzy. "Without wood the fire will die. The child fuels Miss LeGrand's temper."

Despite wanting to ignore Rem's presence, curiosity got the best of Kenzy. "Do you have any idea why she dislikes him?"

"Didn't she say she twisted her ankle? I wonder if it could have happened from a fall."

Something stirred inside Kenzy's memory, causing her to stare at her former neighbor's strides. Though Anna tried to disguise the severity, she walked with a definite limp. "What reason on earth would Anna have for peeping inside the boys' window?"

"*Rose's* window," Rem's whisper reminded ominously.

9

After cultivating GranZeph's garden and making the wagon livable once again, Rem spent the next week getting to know the two waifs who visited him whenever they got in the way elsewhere. Not that he minded. Cordell's countless questions about the herbs forced Rem to remember all GranZeph had taught him. Playing hide-and-seek with Worthy had its value, too. Spending time with the boy reminded him of the carefree days of his own youth, swimming and chasing daydreams. Laughter and the joy of simply existing had started to heal that part of Rem sorely bruised by the war's injustices. But reality was never more than a stone's throw away.

July had passed into the sweltering heat of early August during the ten days he'd been gone. The rumor mill that fueled the blistering lies about his activities in the war had apparently added another speculation to its stream. Upon his return today, he'd been greeted with a jeer by one of the townsmen. It seemed everyone in San Augustine thought he'd left town and moved on.

Rem elected not to explain his hunt for the difficult-to-find herbs that needed replenishing in the garden. Instead, he reminded the man that privacy was a courtesy extended. The man looked at him as if he spoke with a forked tongue.

The herbs Rem searched for grew in the deepest part
of the Big Thicket, and few knew their exact location.
Admiration for his grandmother's tenacity remained
with him since the first day she'd shown him the path
to the treasure trove.

"Feel your way, Nikolo," she had told him years ago,
using Rem's middle name rather than the first given him
by his American grandfather. She pressed his hand
against her heart. "Feel its pounding? That is the special
sense of knowing within us. If we trust its beat, we will
be rewarded with our prize."

"How do you know, GranZeph?" he remembered asking, staring through the verdant wall of pines. The forest
had been darker there, a hodgepodge of green blending
into black and deeper greens. Sunlight filtered through
the canopy, shining like beams from tiny lighthouses.
But neither grandmother or grandson would have cared
whether they worked by sunlight or shadow. Both were
nomads of the night, knowing it only as an extension of
day.

"What you see can be deceiving, dearheart, but what
you feel here never bears false witness."

How many times had he heard her say such? How
many times had he marveled at how soon they'd found
the clusters of pennyroyal, woodruff and more. Time and
again this trip, he found no truer trail than the one where
he stopped to remember what she'd taught him and listened.

Others called her talent magic, but her true gift had
been knowing herself, listening to her inner heart. Her
miracles of healing were often the result of compelling
others to hearken their own heart wishes rather than ap-
plying a poultice.

Perhaps that's why her death left him so empty, so
unwilling to fight anymore to belong. Not another soul
on this earth understood him. Not another soul cared to
listen to the truth he wished to live. Not another soul
dared see through his darkness.

Memory drifted away like a forest mist. He wiped the

grief that spilled from his eyes, dampening his sleeve. The movement wafted the spicy, agreeable odor from the red-brown roots he held. Angelica was his grand-mother's favorite herb, and she had discovered its many uses. He intended for her grave to be bordered with the greenish-white umbrella-shaped bunches that would later blossom.

As he dismounted, he carefully placed the angelica on the saddle blanket, hobbled the gray's front legs and removed the horses' bridle. From his pocket, Rem pulled out a large carrot he'd dug up at sunrise to preserve its sweetness. "Here, Kumpania, something for you while I visit Rosella. Thank you for allowing me to ride upon your back, my friend."

The horse accepted his gift and nodded its head, as if answering him. The Rom, Rem's people, valued horses above all other animals and never failed to give thanks for the comfort offered to their people.

A shout behind him urged Rembrandt to turn. A hive of activity met his gaze. A crowd worked at the orphan-age today, but from this distance he could not decide how many had joined Kenzy and her crew. Long, limber strides ate up the distance that separated Rem from Cor-dell.

"Hey everybody, Rem's back!" the boy called over his shoulder.

Cordell's enthusiasm pleased Rem. He couldn't re-member the last time he'd gotten such a welcome. Checking to make sure the angelica would be safe with-out having to wrap it, he searched through his saddlebag for the piece of linen he'd stored. The boy halted in a rain of pebbles and dust a few feet away. Rembrandt offered him the linen. "Brought you something."

"For me?" Cordell pushed back his glasses, pleasure lighting his face. "Gosh, you don't hardly even know me." He swung around to show the smaller boy, who ran as fast as his tiny legs could carry him. "Look, Mr. Parker got me something."

"Can I see?" Worthy stood on his tiptoes to get a better look.

Curiosity sculpted Cordell's expression. He unfolded the linen to reveal a handful of leaves. "These aren't familiar to me. Bet they're something special."

"Wood sorrell." Rem offered to hold the others while Cordell examined a leaf. "The juice from those will remove stains on just about anything. I thought you'd appreciate having some of it around the next time you stain your pant legs or rub your knees in the grass. Add water and steam them over a low heat, then soak the stain in the juice a couple of hours and you'll never know they were damaged."

"Ahh, it's just a bunch of dumb old plants." Worthy frowned, hooking his thumbs in his pockets and kicking the dirt with one boot. "Glad you didn't bring me nothing."

"Guess I'll just have to take this back and give it to some other boy then." Rem reached into the saddlebag once more and pulled out the gift he'd bought in Nacogdoches on the way back. "Don't suppose you're a bit interested in having one of these?"

"Let me see it." Worthy grabbed at it before remembering his manners. "Please."

Rem complied. The seven-year-old frowned. He put the thing in his mouth and blew hard. Nothing came out. "You ought to get your money back. They left out the music." He handed it back.

"It's not a flute, Brainrot. It's one of those refracting magnifying tubes I heard about." Respect echoed in Cordell's tone. "It's got mirrors and something they call a lens to make faraway objects look closer. They say that's how Grant could outmove Lee. He could see our men for miles and knew just where to strike."

"Ain't no such thing," Worthy argued, reaching for the tube despite his disbelief. "Who come up with such a notion?"

"Take a look if you don't believe me. And by the

way, it was an Italian explorer, Galileo, made the first one way back in the 1600s."

"What's an Italian?"

"Just hold it up to your eye instead of your mouth."

Worthy did as Cordell instructed.

"Twist that round piece in the middle and the tube will extend itself," Rembrandt encouraged, impressed with the older boy's knowledge.

"Holy Moses, will you look at that! I can see clear to town."

"Let me try." Cordell tried to touch the tube, but Worthy jerked away.

"Huh-uh. It's mine and I'm gonna look at everything before anybody else does." Worthy gripped his present tightly and flashed Rem a grin that stretched from ear to ear. "This is just about the best present I ever got in my whole life, Gypsy Man. Now, I can see as good as I hear things."

There won't be only one monster running around here. Rem chuckled, knowing he'd probably get a piece of Kenzy's mind on the subject. Thinking of her drew his attention to the hilltop where he noticed a wave of workers heading toward him and the boys. "Suppose you take a look with that glass and tell me who's coming."

Worthy swung the tube around and started rattling off names. "Kenzy, Strut and Miz Euphemia, big ol' Mr. Marsdale and that piano lady with the mean eyes. Don't guess you've met her yet. Rose is behind them with Noble rolling her chair."

"Looks like they're coming to welcome you home," Cordell proposed.

"A nice prospect, but I'm sure they have some other purpose."

"Oh, yeah." Worthy lowered the glass. "We forgot to tell you something real important. I kind of heard the grownups talking about it a while ago and just told Cord before you rode up. Hadn't had a chance to go check on it, but you sure ain't gonna like it none."

Accustomed to hearing bad news, Rem watched the

others' progress. "I'd rather hear it from a friend, Worthy, than someone who won't necessarily care how much it affects me."

"Tell him." Cord punched Worthy in the arm. "You're the one who heard them talking."

The boy pointed to the trees that sheltered the stream. "Kenzy said someone tore up your garden, that everything is a mess. She started to straighten it up but was afraid she wouldn't remember the order of things. I think she was 'fraid you'd come home and see her digging around in it and think she done it. Kenzy would never do that, Gypsy Man. She ain't that kind of lady."

The garden? His grandmother's legacy? Rage boiled inside Rem like none he'd ever felt during the war. It was the final straw. He'd given everything and gladly. Now, the one thing he wanted to keep only for himself lay in ruins. Maybe it was time to cut his losses and retreat into the forest, never to return to the world of the *Gaje*.

Kenzy ran to him, but Rem stepped backward, silently warning her to keep her distance. No one in San Augustine had more reason to destroy his garden than did she.

"We all thought you'd left." She brushed back a wisp of auburn hair that had dislodged from her braid, sharing a glance with the others who joined her.

"So I've heard."

"We have some unfortunate news for you." Her green gaze slanted toward the location of the alcove, then back at Rem. "There's no easy way to tell you this but just to say it."

"There's no need." Rem scanned the throng to see if one would unveil a twitch, a gleam of victory in the eye, a shuffle of feet that might imply penitence and, therefore, participation in the sabotage. Either none were guilty or someone was very good at acting. "The boys have already informed me. I stopped to see the children, and now it seems I have much to do. Good day to you all. I hope the construction is going well."

"Wait." Noble pushed Rosella's chair closer. "Rose just suggested that we all go with you. We've finished early for the day because the mortar for the second chimney has to set. Might as well help you while we can."

"With this many hands, it wouldn't take much time for all of us to set things right." Rose patted the blanket on her lap. "I have the perfect place to carry things back and forth." She enlisted the others' opinions. "What do you say, everybody?"

"That's a great idea." Euphemia elbowed the large man in the duster. "How 'bout you, Marsdale? Sit behind that fancy desk so long you got any backbone to bend?"

"Not for the likes of that scoundrel. I refuse to help a man who'd run out on his own unit in the thick of things."

Tension filled the air. Marsdale was spoiling for a fight, but Rem didn't take the bait. If that's what Marsdale wanted to believe, nothing he could do or say would change it. Still . . . Rem's gaze met Noble's. *You could end this*, he silently challenged Brett's brother.

"Speak up, man," Noble countered. "Defend yourself."

"Yeah, speak up," Kenzy echoed.

Rem recognized the carpenter's intention for what it was. He'd been waiting for the chance to irritate Rem into reading the letter. Rem wouldn't let him off that easy. He'd promised Brett that Noble would do the telling, and all Rem had left in this world was his word. "I've got nothing to say."

"No coward ever does." Marsdale's mustache twisted with each word.

Fighting off the need to ram his fist down Marsdale's beefy throat, Rem's fingers opened and closed. Instead, with slow deliberation, his gaze examined the man from hat to boot. The baron swallowed hard enough that it jiggled his collar, assuring Rem that Marsdale realized he'd been found lacking.

"You have no proof he turned traitor." Surprisingly,

it was Noble who defended Rem. "No telling what a man might do given the situation." When Rose reached up and patted Noble's hand, her encouragement fueled the fierceness of his words. "We've all got to get on with our lives and put the war behind us. Start pulling together instead of working against one another. None of us here are, and never have been, the enemy."

"I'm all for everyone helping." Strut rubbed his balding head. "Means less time burning my scalp and finding better things to do."

"Like sparking Miz Euphemia?" Worthy snickered. "I seen you two akissing back yonder."

"Who's he been kissing?" the Amazon-sized store owner yelled, obviously not having heard the boy's words. She pinched Strut's earlobe, eliciting a yelp from her beau. "I told you to quit chasing the whole herd or the milk's gonna clabber on ya."

"How can we help, Rembrandt?" A lady with sable-colored hair stepped forward. "You don't remember me, do you? As many times as you dunked me in the Sabine, I'm insulted you've forgotten how much you detested me."

"Anna? I thought you'd sailed to Europe."

"I did, but managed to come home at the best possible time." She patted Rose's shoulder. "Our Rose had just learned of her affliction, and I felt privileged to help her during those trying days."

An awkwardness layered the gathering. Kenzy looked uncomfortable, and Rose became busy arranging the blanket around her legs. Apparently, the two friends had more to overcome than their mutual interest in Noble. Kenzy didn't want Rose to form an attachment that could compare to the one they'd shared for so many years. How long would the wound be allowed to fester before one of them brought it to a head and endangered their friendship?

"I've always found Miss Whitaker to know her own mind." Rem unhobbled his horse and gently clutched the angelica. "No matter who among us thinks we know what's best for her."

He winked at Kenzy, hoping she would take the teasing amicably. For the briefest moment, he noticed a silent dare pass between her and Anna LeGrand before both quickly masked their expressions.

Kenzy folded her arms across her breasts, amusement dancing in her eyes. "If you think that little announcement will stop me from giving her my opinion, you don't know me as well as you should."

Though she directed the words to him, Rem was certain they were equally targeted to her rival. Anna had better watch out. She was treading dangerous ground if she intended to push Kenzy out of Rose's life. Kenzy was a fighter, had always been, and Rose was the driving force behind Kenzy's ambition.

In their youth, Rem had watched Kenzy's attempt to impress Rose, seeking her respect by doing things everyone found too difficult or frightening. In his opinion, she had measured her life against Rose's and gauged her success, or lack of it, by how it compared to her friend's. He could see the motivation behind her actions easily because he saw that part of himself within her. "Looks like I won't get a better offer anytime soon, so let's delay no longer."

The irony of Rem's words were not lost on the crowd and they laughed.

Neither was the miracle that had just occurred lost on Rem. For the first time in his life, people outside his family had extended him a willing and intentional hand in friendship.

10

To watch Rem separate the dying root from the good was both fascinating and agonizing. Like a mother tending her infant, his long sculpted fingers picked the soil free of any refuse. Kenzy couldn't hear the soft words he muttered because Noble and Rose were trading quips that ended in giggles. As she strained to listen to Rem, Kenzy decided he was cooing words of apology.

She'd forgotten that about him—his insistence upon thanking the earth, the animals, even the wind for the privilege they extended him. The first time Rem had ever expressed his gratitude in her company, she thought it only a young boy's effort to impress her. After all, back then, Rem had been little more than a scrawny collection of legs and a black hank of hair.

But he was no scrawny boy anymore, and it was torment to work beside him and watch him gently swaddle each root with the newly gleaned soil. His body emanated an agile strength as he moved from one pile to the next, examining the damage and testing each root to determine its fate.

Those that could not be replanted, he handed to Euphemia or Cordell who immediately took them to Rose for safekeeping on her lap.

"What's this for?" Cord reached out to take the handful Rem offered. "Catnip, isn't it?"

"Yes, and if you add horsetail branches and stems, along with some southernwood, then boil it for about fifteen minutes, it will make your hair grow."

"You could use some of that, Strut, Ol' Man." Euphemia elbowed the man beside her.

"Better boil him up a whole new crop." Anna opened the gunnysack she carried, allowing Noble to empty some of his and Rose's horde of herbs inside.

"Don't need none. Got plenty up there." Strut patted the long strand of hair he combed from back to front to hide a portion of his balding head. When he touched the strand, its unnatural position shifted, leaving muddy fingerprints in its wake. "Well . . . somewhere up there."

Euphemia glared at Anna, then dusted Strut's head with her hand and finger-combed the strand back into place. "That you do, darlin', but it doesn't hurt to plant new seed now and again."

Kenzy bit back a smile, knowing the old dear still saw himself with the wealth of hair he'd enjoyed in his youth. A perpetual misconception since the man loved to preen at anything that reflected his own image.

Rose's laughter mixed with Noble's, drawing Kenzy's attention. Noble bent over the wheelchair, whispering something in Rose's ear. Rose looked tired, yet her cheeks stained a becoming shade of pink as his hand cupped hers and gave it a gentle squeeze. Kenzy glanced away, feeling as if she were infringing upon a private moment between the two. What had he said that would make him squeeze her hand with such clear affection? Envy, green and prickly as cactus, pierced Kenzy's good humor.

A chuckle beside her forced Kenzy to turn from the disturbing sight. Rem had rolled up his sleeves, exposing his powerful forearms. She watched as a slow smile stretched his lips and his dark eyes sparkled with amusement. She knew he knew.

Unwilling to let him think she harbored a speck of

jealousy toward her best friend, Kenzy decided to prove just how *not* jealous she was. "Noble, you and Rose take some of those plants back to the wagon and make a place for them to ride without being scattered. While you're there, go ahead and light some lanterns so that'll be one less thing to do when we head in. Check the chimney and see if we've used enough mortar or need to add another layer tomorrow. Anna, the boys and I can help Rem finish up here."

"Better make that *boy*." Strut wiped the dust from his knees and helped Euphemia stand. "Me and 'Phemia will start chasing Worthy, if you plan to leave anytime soon. That little look-yonder ain't nowhere in sight. He took off with the magnifier thingamawatchy about a half hour ago."

"We've done just about all we can do for now." Rem stood and bowed his body backward as his palms reached high over his head. He stretched, his thighs tightening and flexing, setting off a powerful ripple through his muscular frame. Beads of moisture covered his forehead and streaks of exertion stained his shirt.

When his palms came to rest on the small of his back, something pulled taut within Kenzy. She felt like an arrow, held tight by invisible strings she couldn't comprehend, aimed toward a mark she felt compelled to make, sensing she could easily soar. Heat skittered along her skin. Even with the shade of trees and a slight breeze blowing from the creek bank, the afternoon was still hot and would linger long past sundown.

Sundown. They had to round things up and leave. Make sure plenty of lanterns were lit. Kenzy fanned the rush of anxiety that erupted within her.

"Wishing we were closer to our old swimming hole?" Rem unfastened one button. Two.

The possibility that he might remove his shirt distracted Kenzy's thoughts from the fact that the afternoon waned. She had worked in the sweltering warmth beside Rem all afternoon and, indeed, daydreamed more than once about their days spent swimming and lying on the

---

112 *DeWanna Pace*

bank to dry. Back then, she'd never paid much attention to his appearance, she'd been so fascinated with his way of perceiving life. Now, she would not be so distracted by his mind and wished he would strip off the gingham so she could admire the controlled power of his body.

Try though she did, Kenzy couldn't stop the thoughts and had even included herself in the daydream wearing little more than her chemise. A dangerous combination, considering how the years had honed Rem Parker from that gangly stretch of legs to such a fine form of muscle and bone. And lips. She couldn't forget the well-seasoned skill of his lips. The fact that Rem's skin had regained a healthier tone only added to the sensuality that exuded from him.

"I can't remember the last time I've been swimming. Been too busy and . . ." Kenzy glanced at Anna to make sure she wasn't close enough to hear. "I don't want to offend Rose."

"Swimming would probably be good for her." Rem planted another root. "It would be wonderful exercise and would work the soreness out of her legs."

"You don't know how her injuries happened, do you?" Kenzy was surprised no one had mentioned it to him, particularly Rose herself.

"They resulted from swimming, I take it."

Kenzy's head bowed as remorse washed over her. She stroked the hair ring on her finger. "It was the anniversary of a pledge we'd made to always be a sister to one another. I lived with my parents in Massachusetts, and she wanted to do something wild and exciting in our honor. Something I would have had us do if I were here. Unfortunately . . ." Kenzy looked away, unable to stare any longer at their bond of friendship. "That dive from an outcropping I had always been too afraid to make landed her in a pool of tainted water. Seemed harmless at first. But ever since, her legs have grown worse. Now, there doesn't seem to be a doctor in the country who can help her."

His hand reached out to touch her. "It was a choice *she* made."

His compassion spread like a balm over her tortured soul, offering a moment of reprieve from the pain of responsibility. Kenzy blinked back the sting of tears welling in her eyes. She stifled a sniffle, making her nose twitch as she tried to hide her guilt over Rose's condition. But he was supposed to have special powers of insight, wasn't he? Maybe she would never be able to keep anything concealed from him.

Surprisingly, the fact that he sensed her turmoil, coupled with his ability to discern the truth on his own, became a relief from the pressure building inside Kenzy since her return to San Augustine. She hadn't been able to speak of her remorse. Not to Noble. Not to Rose. Not to anyone. She could never find the right words to say. Never find enough words to speak how sorry she felt or what she would do to change things.

"She would never have made that choice if it hadn't been for me. Rose is not a risk-taker." The sting of tears blinded Kenzy now. "She's practical and thinks everything out to the last detail. That day, she decided to be me. To please me. She wanted to write and impress me with what she'd done. Well, I'm impressed all right . . . impressed with the fact that I've ruined her life. She would be well now if I hadn't always urged her to take chances."

"That does it for today." Rem dusted his knees.

Kenzy grappled with the guilt seeping from her like holes in a sieve. She had to get a grip on her emotions before Rose noticed or she'd be questioned all the way home. Rose needed to relax and enjoy the drive, not be concerned about the fact that Kenzy had been crying.

Noticing that Rem unknotted the bandanna from around his neck, she expected him to wipe his hands but, instead, he gently dabbed the corner of her eye where a wayward tear now trickled.

"You're wrong about Rose, Kenzy, and you're definitely wrong about her taking risks. Look at her."

Rose rolled up the path toward the construction site. Instead of pushing her chair, Noble darted back and forth in front of her, encouraging her to beat him to the top. Playfully, Rose maneuvered her chair to the left and right, countering each of his moves. Kenzy'd never seen her look more tired . . . or happy.

"She's taking a huge chance that Stockton is man enough to love a woman bound to a chair." Respect echoed in Rem's voice. "She never hides the love in her eyes for him. Everyone can see that. Yet she's not afraid to show him and leave herself open for disappointment, perhaps even for rejection. She has to trust that he is a man who has no secrets of his own." His tone demanded Kenzy's gaze to meet his. "I think that's the bravest deed any man or woman on this earth could ever do. She's a risk-taker, Kenzy, because she listens to her heart's wishes. Someone very wise told me that when I was younger. I'm only beginning to understand that now." He handed her the bandanna. "Now, I offer it, and this kerchief, to you."

A wealth of emotions enveloped Kenzy—gratitude that he'd wanted to ease the guilt she felt, anger that he'd made a point of showing her how much Rose and Noble cared for one another, awe that he could readily admit his respect for such a display of affection when his own life had been so riddled with scorn.

This brooding man had a gentler depth that needed to be brought into the open. Perhaps if she, and others, tried a little harder to be his friends, Rem could shed the stigma of being born among a people most refused to trust. Perhaps, if they all took the time to know the real Rembrandt Parker, they would come to respect the man within him.

"Thank you." She accepted the kerchief, though she was thanking him for so much more. For caring enough to ease her remorse and for giving her insight into her heart. He didn't seem so daunting at the moment, so dark with emotion.

The thought made her glance at the sky. The red-orange flames of sunset streaked the broad expanse, setting the countryside afire with its hue. To the east, a smoky-gray line formed a rainbow over the canopy of trees, warning that night would come sooner than they could gather everything and be on their way.

Kenzy shivered, despite the lingering summer heat. Rose would have all the lanterns lit in time, she reassured herself. Rose understood. Hopefully, Strut and Euphemia would track down Worthy and they all could be on their way home as quickly as possible. "We're going to have to head back now, Rem. Rose said you could use her kitchen to salvage any of the herbs for your potions. She noticed the size of your cooking hearth near the wagon and said you needed a larger place to cook this much."

"I knew I was going on a hunt and would be away for a while. The elixir I made Rose just needed a few minutes boiling so I only set up a tripod and one pot." Rem nodded. "It would save time if I could use her stove . . . after her evening meal has been prepared and the stove is still hot. I think I'll take that offer, if she'll let me cook dinner for you all. As a thank you for your help today."

"She's stayed out here much longer than she intended, so she needs to rest this evening. Euphemia's already promised one of her neighbors she would dine with them, so your offer is tempting." Kenzy shrugged. "Everything I cook tastes like shoe leather."

Anna LeGrand approached, her gunnysack looking half full. "It's time I headed back, too." Her nose wrinkled up as if she were holding a skunk. "What do I do with these?"

Kenzy grabbed the sack. "I'll see they're taken care of. Thanks, Anna, for pitching in to help."

"Yes, thank you, Miss LeGrand." Rem half bowed. "I'm indebted."

"Believe me, it was my pleasure." A smile darted across her face and ended as a sparkle in her black eyes. Just as quickly, a frown creased her forehead. "Whoever tore up your garden should be chased out of town. It's a real shame."

Kenzy watched as the woman turned and limped her way up the hill to return to the wagon. Maybe she was wrong, but she thought Anna too helpful today, particularly to a man she had despised as a boy. The woman didn't have *that* much compassion for anyone. But what would she gain by destroying Rem's garden? Did she think it would make him leave San Augustine?

He would have never come back to the people who had ridiculed him and cost his grandmother's life unless he meant to settle here. Which made sense to Kenzy. Why start out somewhere else where he would be new bait for the gossipmongers? At least here, he was old news. From what he said about making a promise to his grandmother, Kenzy suspected nothing would drive Rem away. Not Anna's lifelong prejudice against him. Not whatever secret he shared with Noble. Not even her defiance of his remedies.

Was it possible to gain that much control over himself? Over his fears?

11

By the time they gathered their implements and found Worthy, twilight had settled in around them. Kenzy became impatient with Anna, who insisted that Rose sit in the back of the wagon with the others. It made more sense if she rode next to Noble on the driver's box. Though it would take a few more minutes to make the change, Kenzy countermanded Anna's suggestion. "Why don't you sit next to Noble, Rose? At least when you rock and sway with the ruts, you'll have a stable seat beneath you instead of those wheels."

Part of the lantern light disappeared for a second, sending Kenzy's heart racing until she realized Worthy had lifted the lantern from the nail on the outer panel and set it down on the wagon bed. "What are you doing with that, Worthy? Put it back so we can see the way."

"I'm trying to see if this is a lightning bug. Can't tell."

"You won't tell in the light, genius," Cordell chided from the other side of the wagon. He reached out and swiped at the lantern, shoving it several inches away. "Can't see the bug's caboose lit up unless it's dark."

"Be careful! You'll catch something on fire or put the light out." Kenzy grabbed the lantern, her voice breaking and revealing which of the two possibilities she considered the worst.

"Would you like to ride up here with us, Worthy?"
Rose patted the empty space alongside her.

"He'll be fine back here." *Calm down.* Kenzy knew
she overreacted and had drawn attention to herself, worrying Rose needlessly. "Think of all the trouble Rose
went through to light them. Now, let's all take a seat so
we can get her home and out of the night air." Perhaps
the others would believe her anxiety sprang from concern for Rose's health rather than from fear.

"It's still quite warm." Rose settled in beside Noble
and thanked him as he spread a blanket over her legs.
"And I can make it home just fine. I'm tired, but it's a
good tired." She eyed the man sitting next to her. "I
can't remember the last time I've done so much work
and had even more fun doing it. Thank you for the wonderful day."

"My pleasure."

"Tie your horse to the back of the wagon, Rem."
Kenzy rattled off several orders in an effort to speed up
the process and get her mind on other things. Watching
Noble and Rose eyeing each other with such affection
ignited the envy Kenzy had tried so hard to hide.

"Now you got all that, Sowboy?" Strut chuckled. "She
ain't one for running things, mind you, but if you got
any questions or need any help, feel free to ask her."

More than one in the crowd snickered.

Realizing her nervousness made her sound terribly
bossy, Kenzy adjusted her command to a question.
"Rem, will you please ride next to the herbs so you can
make sure they don't shift?"

"That's better. A little sweet talk'll get things going
quicker than any amount of insisting." Strut's teeth out-
shined the glow of his hairless head as he looked to
Euphemia for approval. "Ain't that right, ol' gal?"

"Shuck that skunk-eating grin off your face, Crop
Top." Euphemia folded her arms beneath her ample
breasts, defining their fullness. "Calling me old ain't my
idea of sweet talking."

"Like I said before . . . I'll take sassy over bossy any day. Come here, you sweet young thang."

Laughter rippled across the wagon while Strut tried to cuddle up next to Euphemia.

Worthy lost interest in the grownup banter and his lightning bug. "Hey, there ain't no room left! Can I ride your horse, Gypsy Man? Can I please?"

Rem nodded. "With Miss Dixon's approval."

Worthy out there on the horse? In the semi-darkness, away from the light? She would worry about him all the way home. "It's best you sit here in the back. Maybe next time when you can see more what you're doing."

"I ain't afraid of no dark."

His bravado stung Kenzy. She breathed in the night air, then exhaled it slowly. *He's just a little boy trying to prove he's brave.* "I'm sure you aren't. But the horse needs to meet you, and you should become better friends before you ask him for a ride. Isn't that right, Rem?"

She realized she was prattling, making up an excuse as she went. But once said, the reasoning seemed sound.

The look on Rem's face told her she hadn't fooled him. "Yes, you should always ask for Kampania's permission. But . . ." Rem stared intently at Kenzy. "He cares not whether you ask by day or night. He merely listens to the whispers and responds."

"Everyone ready?" Noble waited until all but Worthy answered. When he turned to check on the boy, Worthy gave a reluctant nod.

"I couldn't be more ready." Kenzy listed a whole inventory of tasks that would be waiting for her when they got home.

The children groaned.

"I just remembered I've got to bake that pie for Bernie May." Euphemia patted Strut's knobby knee. "Told her I'd have it for Sara Janell's birthday tomorrow."

Anna yawned and stretched her arms. "Well, I'm not going to do another solitary thing the rest of this evening except lift my fork. This helping-your-neighbor work is too exhausting."

Strut tried to wrap his arm around Euphemia, but couldn't encompass her complete width. "Guess I'll help 'Phemia bake that pie."

"You mean you'll help me eat that pie." Euphemia scooted slightly, lowering her shoulders to fit underneath Strut's arm.

Kenzy smiled at the older pair, aware of how much the two cared for each other. Strut might openly flirt with the widows in town, and Euphemia might let him, but everyone knew the old codger would sit in Euphemia's pew come Sabbath.

"That means me and four-eyes'll have to help Miz Dixon." Worthy propped his elbows on his knees. "Grownups sure can think up things they forgot when there's chores to do."

"A worthy insight, son."

Everyone moaned at Rem's obvious pun.

"We stand properly chastised." Rem patted the space he'd left open between him and the herbs. "Or rather, we sit properly chastised. Miss Dixon, care to join me?"

The empty place next to Rem and the wheelchair roped to the driver's box were the only options left. Though riding next to Rem had its own risk, it seemed the lesser of two perils. Kenzy could never dare sit in the wheelchair that shackled Rose's life. If she did, the determination that dammed her guilt would surely burst, and she would never be able to stop the tears.

Kenzy gathered her courage around her like an invisible cloak. A shiver traveled from the top of her head to the heel of her slipper. Though she blamed her uneasiness on the encroaching shadows, she knew it also stemmed from the prospect of riding so close to Rem. She sat beside him, stretching her legs to form a barrier in front of the gunnysacks. His thigh touched hers, heat igniting where their bodies made contact. Streamers of desire rushed through her.

"Snug," Rem remarked, lifting one hand to rest along the side of the wagon and, by happenstance, around her shoulders.

Taking lessons from Strut, was he? Kenzy scooted over a few inches, elbowing Rem in the side. "Smug is more like it."

He threw back his head and laughed deeply, a full-throated guffaw that drew everyone's attention.

"What's so funny?" Worthy crawled over Anna's legs to get closer.

"Watch out, I've got a sore ankle." She fussed with her skirt and frowned at the boy.

"He didn't mean to, Miss LeGrand." Cordell reached into his pocket and grabbed a kerchief. He began to dust Worthy's bootprints from Anna's hem. "He's just nosy sometimes."

The seven-year-old swung around and glared at Cord. "Who told you I didn't mean to? I know she's got a sore foot, and I know how—"

"Apologize to Miss LeGrand." Cordell snapped the kerchief like a sling shot across the smaller boy's pantleg.

"I ain't gonna. You ain't my boss, and she ain't my mama, so I don't gotta like her. Ain't that so, Miz Dixon?"

Kenzy found it less distracting to referee the children's argument than to tolerate Rem's body inching toward her. The moment she leaned forward to counter his move, his arm slid between the side of the wagon and rested against her hip. Her other elbow shot backward.

"Pardon me." Rem's breath fanned her right cheek. "One of the sacks shifted. I thought you hadn't noticed, and I was trying to scoot it back."

"I noticed, and it wasn't the only thing that slid." The others were waiting for Kenzy to answer, but the man obviously enjoyed pestering her. Fingers traced a trail over her hip, splaying to test its width in his hand.

"Perfect. That ought to do it."

Half hooded, Rem's eyes looked even darker in the growing twilight. "We should try our best to like everyone," Kenzy insisted, hoping to encourage Worthy. Instead, her words seem to sanction the gypsy's explo-

ration of her waist. He nodded and grinned, further exasperating her. His wandering hand slid upward,
touching the underside of her breast. It was a good thing
the shadows prevented anyone from seeing his impertinence!

Or had they? Kenzy found herself leaning away from
the lantern light only to allow him further access to the
swell of her bosom. She twisted slightly. "You do, however, have control of how often you tolerate the company of some." Kenzy grabbed Rem's hand and shoved
it away, shooting him a look that warned she had insight
into the future of his fingers if he didn't keep them
where they belonged.

But Rem was insistent. His palm slid from her breast
to caress her hip once again.

The man's audacity had no limit! She ought to demand his apology, perhaps even slap him for good measure. Yet a part of her thrilled at his daring and his
tenacity. He was a man not easily swayed. That made
him enormously appealing to someone who was tired of
fighting for control so she did not seem weak. How
would it feel to give in to such a man and lose control?

Worthy wiggled a seat between Rem and Kenzy, re-
leasing her from Rem's maddening touch and her speculation. Kenzy's hand automatically reached out to
smooth her dress but stopped when she felt the heat of
flesh that had transferred from his clothing to hers. Suddenly, she felt cloaked in intimacy with a man who
might prove to be nothing but trouble. Intimacy that
promised to rouse more from her than the docile devotion she gave to Noble. An intimacy that beckoned her
to lose herself to passion in his arms.

Thoughts of disloyalty sprang to mind, slowing the
beat of Kenzy's heart and cooling her ardor. She cleared
her throat and willed the desire that coursed through her
to bank. Never before had she considered any man other
than Noble to share her bed. Never before had she felt
such wondrous new sensations. Yet tonight, Rem Parker

aroused such a wanting within her she'd forgotten the danger of night and its shadows.

But she mustn't forget. Ever. Loneliness and grief rose like smoke from the pit of her heart to vent themselves. "Let's be on our way, Noble. We wouldn't want to get lost."

Worthy yawned, leaning back against her and draping his legs over the gypsy. "Yeah, I'm kinda tired."

The team jerked into motion, causing Kenzy to wrap an arm around the child to make sure he rode comfortable and safe. He yawned again, nuzzling his cheek against her. Her fingers gently delved through his hair, smoothing the silken strands. Worthy sighed, and soon his breathing slowed.

Kenzy marveled that he could so easily fall asleep, despite his disappointment about not riding the horse and his dislike of Anna LeGrand. How Kenzy wished for the trust and innocence of youth once again.

The jingle of harness, the low conversation between Noble and Rose and the *clop-snuff-clop-snuff* of hooves against dirt became a rhythm, lulling Kenzy into a false sense of security. Her head bobbed with the wagon's motion, but the solace of sleep eluded her. There was too much to do when she got home. Rose needed tending to. Household chores had been left undone. She didn't know how long Rem would stay to use the stove, and someone would have to clean up after him.

She glanced up and realized that pine trees lined both sides of the pathway. Their trunks had dissolved to coal-black silhouettes. The leafy canopy overhead rustled and shifted in the imperceptible wind, setting shadows into motion and making a chill race up her spine. She could almost feel someone's breath blowing against her neck. Could almost hear the night whispering.

Stop this, she scolded herself and sat up straighter to square her shoulders. *You're not alone. You're not afoot. Everyone is together. Noble will see you safely home.*

Worthy shifted his weight, pressing on an already cramped leg. She must have moaned aloud because

Rembrandt suddenly lifted the child and cradled him in his own lap.

"Heavier than he looks, isn't he?"

She reached out and grabbed one of the unused gunnysacks, draping it over Worthy as a blanket. "I hadn't really noticed."

"Not one to complain, are you?" Rem kept his tone to a whisper, for the others seemed to be dozing.

Respect filled his voice, pleasing her. "I suppose not."

"Mind if I ask you a few questions?"

"Only if I can answer the ones I like."

"You don't talk much after sundown, do you?"

She felt his gaze probing her. Did he suspect? Kenzy tried to laugh off his observation. "Not according to Strut. He's right, you know. I do tend to tell everybody what to do."

"But you mean well. Your heart's in the right place."

Gratitude warmed her. "Sometimes I get so caught up in telling everyone how something should be done that I forget they might want to do it their own way. I'm just trying to keep them from making a mistake like I ha . . . I mean from making a mistake that a little forethought might prevent."

"What have you done that's so unforgivable, Tadpole?"

The gratitude chilled to caution. "I don't know what you mean."

"I think you do. Otherwise, you wouldn't try so hard to protect everyone else. You failed someone . . . maybe even yourself. And I suspect whatever took place happened at night."

The cry of a loon pierced the silence. The air thickened with tension. Startled by the sound and Rem's perceptiveness, Kenzy found it difficult to breathe. She hunted for an explanation that would convince him, detour him from the course their conversation had taken. She wasn't ready to share that part of her life with anyone. Especially not with a man she wasn't sure she could trust. She had told no one the truth of the night her

parents died. Not even Rose knew the entire story. *An-*
swer his question with one of your own. "Did you read
this in your tea leaves and forget to tell me?"

"I didn't have to." Rem pointed at the lanterns. "You
insisted on every one of those being lit. When I woke
at Rosella's that first evening back, you came in and
checked to make sure there was enough oil to burn
through the night. You tense every time your eyes stare
out into the passing countryside. It doesn't take tea
leaves to know you're uncomfortable with being out
here now."

Change the subject. But to what? Her mind raced to
latch onto something that would distract him. Finally it
latched on the letter Rem had given Noble. She could
only hope the question would be effective enough to
ward off further inquiry about her troubles. "I'm no
fortune-teller myself, but I'd say you and Noble are the
ones hiding something. I know about the letter you gave
him. At least I know he read it and handed it back to
you. Strut told me. What I don't know, however, is the
content of that letter. Nor do we understand why Noble
would feel compelled to lie about its existence."

Rem's shoulders suddenly looked like they were made
of medieval armor bracing for battle. "Oh, there's a letter. As to what it says, that's up to Stockton to discuss
with you . . . or with anyone else, for that matter."

The wagon halted. The outskirts of San Augustine lay
like an amber haze in the distance. Lights from neighbors' houses invited the laborers home.

"Why are we stopping?" Kenzy took the opportunity
to stand and stretch her legs. Everyone roused from their
dozing, echoing her question.

Rose lifted her head from Noble's shoulder and
wrapped her shawl more tightly around her. "I-I'm
afraid I asked him to. I'm not feeling well and thought
if I could stretch my legs, I might begin to feel better."

Kenzy was over the side and on the ground before
she realized lifting Rose from her perch would be difficult.

"I'll get her." Rem handed the boy to Euphemia, stepped over the pile of herb sacks, then swept Rose up into his arms. "Miss LeGrand, Cord, get those extra sacks and cover the place where I sat. Yes, like that." Rem waited until the two completed his instructions. "May I prop her legs on your lap, Miss Euphemia? She needs to elevate them above her waist so the circulation will improve. Reviving the blood flow will ease some of the pain."

"That's what Jubal told me." Rose's arms locked around his neck. "You must have studied regular medicine as well."

"Some. Now, if you don't mind, I want you to try to rest the remainder of the journey. That's it. Close your eyes and think of the most pleasant place you've ever been. See it?"

"Yes."

"Shouldn't Kenzy get back in the wagon?" Anna's gaze slanted to the place next to Noble, encouraging Kenzy to take Rose's former seating arrangements. "So we can—"

Rem shook his head, silencing Anna. He began talking in a monotone to Rose. "Your eyes are beginning to grow tired. No one and nothing needs your attention. You have accomplished everything you could possibly do and are now completely at rest . . ."

He slowly slid his arm from under Rosella, letting her lay back on the gunnysacks. Euphemia tucked in the hem of Rose's dress to provide a cushion of material that would be a comfortable buffer between them. All the while, Rem continued his monotone.

Anger flashed through Kenzy. What kind of wizardry was that? Certainly not something any real doctor practiced. Yet, whatever he said worked. The lines of pain in Rose's face didn't look near as defined. Her breathing slowed to a steady rhythm.

"Climb up and ride beside Noble," Anna suggested. "Might as well take advantage while you can."

Anna's words irritated Kenzy. She'd never take advantage of being with Noble, especially when Rose was ill. "*You* ride with him. I want to be back here with Rose in case she needs me."

Instead of climbing out of the wagon, Anna stepped over legs to get to the front. Her foot slipped at one point. "Pardon me."

Kenzy flinched, certain that her neighbor had stepped on Rem's herbs in the process.

Anna turned around backward and sat on the driver's box. She frowned at Kenzy. "I was only trying to help, and you know why."

Rem raised a brow, making Kenzy feel two inches tall. Did he think she and Anna were united in a conspiracy against Rose? If so, he judged her unfairly. Just as she misjudging him? What wrong was there in using no other power than a calming tone and soothing words to mesmerize Rose into relaxing?

"Thanks, Anna," Kenzy said through gritted teeth as the woman swung around to face the team, "but the only help I need now is to get Rose home as soon as possible."

Give the devil his due. The old saying reverberated through Kenzy's thoughts, mixing her opinion of what she'd just witnessed. Once they got Rose home, Kenzy intended to find out where he had learned such a skill.

12

The lamplight in Rose's room did little to ease Kenzy's panic. Tonight, she wished she could endure the shadows so she didn't have to witness the pain dulling Rose's eyes. Kenzy wiped the sheen of perspiration beading her friend's hairline, willing her hand not to tremble and reveal how upset she was by Rose's condition. "Rest awhile, Whit. I'll see that everything gets done."

When Kenzy grabbed the covers to tuck them in more tightly around Rose, Rose reached out to stop her.

"No need to fuss over me. I'll be fine come morning. I just overexerted myself today. But I'm not sorry for one moment of it. I'd take this pain for the rest of my life if I could always be assured such a lovely day. I felt more alive than I have in a very long time." Her eyes flashed a hint of the excitement she recalled. "Did you ever see Noble so playful?"

"Never." Shame that she'd felt even a moment of envy earlier soured in Kenzy's stomach. She had to admit that Noble seemed totally at ease in Rose's company. But who wouldn't be? Rose never expected anything from anybody but to be themselves. Not that Noble was uncomfortable in *her* company. They just talked business and, more often than not, discussed Rose's plans.

Kenzy stared at her dear friend and wondered for the thousandth time how the two of them had ever become so close.

The auburn braided ring Rose wore had never looked so stark against her porcelain-white skin. Concern beat a rapid drum against Kenzy's breastbone as she realized how delicate Rose looked. Her bone structure might keep her from ever being considered small, but sometimes Rose looked as if she might crumble if Kenzy reached out and touched her. When had that transpired? And how could it be reversed?

Rose had always seemed the stronger of the two friends, no matter that Kenzy tended to tell her how to live her life. But that had always been an unspoken agreement between them. Kenzy ruled, yet bowed to Rose's greater wisdom when necessary. The give-and-take of their relationship suited them both. Now, Rose's well-being was entrusted to Kenzy, setting into motion her worst fear. What if she failed Rose like she had her parents? Kenzy would never forgive herself.

"Is Rem still downstairs?" Rose sat up, lifting her hair off the nape of her neck. "It's really hot in here. Think we could do without some of the lamps?"

"One or two perhaps," Kenzy conceded, willing to test the bounds of her fear in favor of comforting her friend. "Lean forward so I can fluff your pillows. There, is that better?"

"You're avoiding me. Are those Rem's herbs I'm smelling?"

"Yes—the ones he couldn't dry and store for later. Why? Are you hungry?" Kenzy shifted her hip from the bed and stood. "Rem kept a pot of soup heating, hoping your appetite might return. Everyone but he and Noble went home. Noble's down in the parlor trying to pretend he's dozing, but he's too concerned about you to rest."

"I'm not hungry." Rose shook her head slightly, her hands rubbing her thighs. "I just wondered if Rem could stir up another batch of his lavender potion. I used the last of it last night. If Noble is still there, ask him to come up. I won't have him waiting all night. I'll be fine, and he needs to get some sleep . . . in his own bed."

"I'll send someone after Jubal. He's supposed to be—"

"I don't want Jubal." A deep sigh escaped Rose. "I asked for Rem and his herbal medicine."

Rose's tone was more insistent than Kenzy ever remembered. "But what if that's the reason you're hurting tonight? You don't know how your body will react to something that hasn't been tested and tried by professionals. I think you should just lie back, and I'll send someone after—"

"Kenzy, please, I don't need to be fussed over. I don't want Jubal to come here and tell me everything he's already told me a dozen times." Rose's eyes fluttered closed, and her words exited in a soft whisper like she was trying to gain a child's attention. "Please, can't you understand? There's no use in us arguing about this. I know you think I'm wrong for trusting Rem. Just do as I ask and let me decide what's best for me."

"All right." Kenzy felt properly chastised, realizing she had taxed her friend's strength and amiability. She tried not to be offended, but the helplessness she felt in dealing with Rose's pain overwhelmed Kenzy. The only way to fight the feeling of inadequacy was to make certain she kept busy. "I'll get Noble and talk to Rem."

When the door closed quietly behind Kenzy, she took a deep breath and exhaled it slowly. Tears stung her eyes but she blinked them away, fighting off the impulse to give in to her fears and frustrations about Rose. What good would crying do but show her uncertainty?

Yet frightening possibilities shaded Kenzy's thoughts as she plodded downstairs to the kitchen. Rose's affliction seemed to be worsening rather than getting better. Could it be that Rem's medicine was somehow responsible and Rose was experiencing a reaction? Or was it possible *she* was the cause of Rose's declining health?

Blame became an unwelcome cloak, weighing heavily
upon her shoulders.

"Why so serious looking, Freckle Face? Rosie's all
right, isn't she?"

Noble's voice startled Kenzy out of the mire of her
thoughts. She stared down into the carpenter's face and
noticed that he looked as if he could use the sleep Rose
instinctively knew he needed. Halting at the second step
from the bottom, her eyes leveled with Noble's blue
gaze. "She seems to think she will be if she takes more
of Rembrandt's concoction. I wish we could talk some
sense into her, but Rose truly believes it works."

"You look tired." Noble reached up and caressed her
cheek. "Why don't you go eat some soup, and I'll look
in on her for a while."

A wan smile lifted Kenzy's lips. Anytime he'd ever
touched her in the past, she'd felt like a firecracker being
lit for the Fourth of July. Her affection for him sparked,
but not enough to ward off the weariness that enveloped
her or the voice of jealousy that wanted to deny him
access to Rose's bedroom. It *had* been a long day. She
was being petty. "Rose'll love that. I won't be long."

"Take your time. It's no problem whatsoever."

The sound of Noble's bootsteps hurrying upstairs echoed his eagerness. "No problem," she repeated his words
in a sad whisper. There would always be one as long as
both she and Rose intended to become Mrs. Noble
Stockton.

Kenzy turned the corner into the hallway that divided
the kitchen from the greeting room and stairway. Instantly, thoughts fled, leaving trepidation in their wake.
Someone had forgotten to light the lamps. The only il-
lumination available shined through the window at the
end of the hall. The quarter moon offered little if any
solace.

She blinked, willing her eyes to adjust to the shadows.
It was then she sensed him. Silent. Looming. Exuding a
scent more intoxicating than any potion he could conjure—the mystery of the man himself. Rembrandt.

"Why are you standing there in the dark?" Kenzy's hands reached up to straighten a nonexistent wisp of hair. Goose bumps raced along the surface of her skin. Just so he didn't think he'd frightened her, she challenged, "Shouldn't you be watching your herbs?"

White teeth flashed like lightning across a midnight sky. "Not when there's something more interesting to watch in the hallway."

Irritation rose to quell Kenzy's uneasiness. "It's impolite to lurk. And, I have no idea what you're talking about."

Rem stepped closer, his features defining themselves more fully. "Don't you? Stockton missed a prime opportunity, in my opinion. A caress on the cheek is nice, but *I* would have kissed you."

His earring flashed in the moonlight, reminding her of just how unorthodox the man had become. His daring and the danger his presence exuded secretly seduced her, enticed her to test his claim. A thousand tingles ignited within Kenzy, threatening to blaze into full-blown passion at any moment. She was grateful for the lack of light, glad he could not see how shaken she was by his powerful presence. "Are all gypsies as egotistical as you?"

An ironlike band gripped Kenzy's arm. "Egotistical, Tadpole? No. Full of unbridled passion? Yes. Certain of what we wish to claim as our own?" His voice deepened to a husky whisper. "That's the reward for listening to one's own heart."

The iron band gentled. Rem pulled her back into his arms, even as she half-heartedly struggled to break free.

"Kiss me, Kenzy," he whispered against the top of her head, his breath fanning her hair. A knuckle gently tilted her chin upward until their eyes met. "You know you want to."

"Damn you," she hissed, unable and unwilling to say *Stop!* She wanted him to kiss her again. Completely and with wild abandon.

Rem's mouth claimed hers, melting Kenzy into the

muscular plane of his chest. Her arms threaded themselves around his neck, pressing her so close she felt the moment his heart began a faster rhythm.

The touch of his hands subtly altered. His fingers drifted over Kenzy's face, traced a tender trail down her throat, massaged the tension from her shoulders. Large and warm, they applied a gentle pressure that left waves of sensations in their wake. Kenzy arched against him, revelling in his exploration.

Desire infused her, blazing from the trembling core of her being to master sense and sensibility alike. The only thing that mattered at the moment was the bliss felt in his arms and the silent, sensuous tune to which their bodies hummed. She felt like dancing, knowing the movements would be hers and his alone to perfect.

His touch was heated magic, his kiss a beacon to the shadows of her heart. Though she didn't understand why he held such control over her, Kenzy acknowledged her willingness to surrender herself to his power and the possibility it promised.

"I smell something burning," she whispered through the haze of passion that clouded her senses, wanting the kiss to last longer.

"It's me." A husky chuckle rumbled from Rem's throat. "And you started the fire."

His ardor thrilled Kenzy, easing the uncertainty of submission into an ego-strengthening confidence. Still, he didn't have to look so smug. "Don't gloat."

His nose wrinkled. Immediately, Rem released her. "The herbs! They're burning!"

They raced to the kitchen to find several pots boiling over.

"Grab a couple of towels and set that small one off the heat. I'll get the big one." Rem became a blur of activity, finding pot holders and a tin sheet to keep the pots from searing the tabletop. When he removed a lid from his pot to let steam rise into the air, a spicy fragrance layered the kitchen. "Good. It doesn't look like it's entirely lost, but we probably won't be able to salvage the herbs at the bottom of each pot."

Kenzy grabbed a spoon and lifted the lid on the smaller vessel. Vapor escaped into the air as thick as the passion that slowly drained from her senses. The heavy odor of camphor forced her backward. "Whoa! This one could turn a herd of buffalo."

She tested the bottom of the broth and lifted the spoon to see if it was crusted with blackened ingredients. Grimacing at the sight, Kenzy warned herself not to scrape any more or she'd ruin the rest. "I'm not sure this batch faired so well."

Taking a close look then smelling a spoonful, Rem nodded. "It's still usable. Thank the moontide, it's only to be used as ointment and not ingested."

Not to be eaten? Was he making something other than his lavender and mugwort potion? "Is all of this . . ." Her arm waved to encompass all the cookery. "To become ointment?"

"You sound angry. I thought making the excess into liniment would please you. After all, even Jubal uses lotions to ease pain."

Opposition renewed itself within Kenzy. Once again she had allowed her attraction to Rem to eclipse her duty to Rose. She immediately told him about Rose's request. "I should have said something sooner," Kenzy admitted, "but Noble will keep her occupied until you can go up."

"I have some of the ingredients, and it won't take long to boil a batch. The stove's still good and hot. I just need to clean up this mess I made."

"I'll help." Kenzy grabbed a rag and wet it from the basin containing soapy dishwater. Her thoughts went to the pair upstairs. "I have nothing better to do at the moment."

"Feeling sorry for yourself, are you? He has every reason to be infatuated with her. Rose is a lovely woman." Rem cleaned off a spot on the stove, lightly tapping his fingertip to test the intensity of its heat. "This one will work. How about handing me that sack lying next to the flour bin? No . . . yes, that one."

"It's no concern of mine if he likes spending time with her. Or she, him." Kenzy refused to let Rem believe she felt defensive. She took a look inside the gunnysack, spotted several plants and shrugged. What she knew about herbs could be written on a child's slate. "Seems odd that such strange looking things could contain such power."

"Sometimes the stranger something seems," Rem delved into the bag and lifted out the lavender, "the more it needs someone to value its potency."

This was talk of more than herbs. Was this his way of asking her to accept his method of healing? Or did he mean to imply his need for acceptance? Kenzy had seen him deny that need ever since she met him, but she knew it continuously returned to taunt him like a perennial weed in the garden of his ambition. "Perhaps it should simply be glad for its resiliency and forget what others think. Strange is simply a point of view. Opinions shouldn't matter."

"No, they shouldn't. But they do and can sometimes hurt . . . unknowingly or on purpose."

Kenzy stared at Rem's profile while he poured water into the fresh pan and placed the lavender and mugwort inside. Had her lack of belief in his ways hurt him?

Uncomfortable with the blame he insinuated, she defended herself. "If you're talking about me defying your efforts to heal Rose, I couldn't possibly hurt you. She won't even listen to me about it anymore. You've done your job well and convinced her yours is the magical ingredient she has to have in order to recover."

"Is that what angers you so, Kenzy? Is that why you kiss me with a fire so ardent it singes my soul, yet you can't accept me permanently in your life?" His eyes darkened to midnight black. "You can't endure the thought of someone other than yourself having power over sweet Rose. You don't want me anywhere near you, because that means I'll be near her. And, as long as I'm near, she just might listen to me and help herself. But there is another reason you don't want me too close, isn't there? You know that if we kiss, you might possibly lose control of yourself. And that, Kenzy, requires a price you think too costly to pay. I'm right, aren't I? I see it in your eyes."

Kenzy turned her head away, but he grabbed her shoulders roughly and made her face him. "I have no power over Rose, Kenzy. Just as I have none over you . . . unless you want me to. Rose believes I can help her. That's the battle we all must face sometime—finding the courage to believe. Her affliction happens to be physical. Others of us . . . well, we have different kinds of wounds. But no matter what we suffer, there will always be a reckoning with how much we allow ourselves to believe. I don't think it's Rose's faith that bothers you, but rather your own fear that she might actually find a way to cure herself and not need you quite so much."

Her fingertips pulsed with the need to slap him, but Kenzy resisted the urge by curling them into fists. No need to cause a possible spill of the precious potion meant for Rose. Or so she told herself, so she could ignore the grain of truth his accusation planted in her mind. "Rose and my relationship is none of your concern. And you've never been more wrong. I will celebrate the day she finds a true cure."

"Even if letting her decide for herself is part of the remedy?"

"I do not interfere!" Kenzy remembered the others in the household who had taken to their beds and lowered her voice. "Just ask her. I'll not oppose her use of your potions anymore."

"Care to seal that bargain?" Challenge lit Rem's eyes.

Kenzy glared back. "I don't shake hands with the devil."

Rem moved closer, his shoulders blocking her view of anything but his nearness.

"Another kiss was more what I had in mind."

13

The hot afternoon sun beat down upon Kenzy's back, making her wish for a slight breeze and the sight of Rem returning from Rose's. With one hand, she shielded the sun from her eyes and stared up the lane that led to the orphanage. The glance had become a habit for the last two hours, rewarding her with nothing but a growing resentment. Just when did Rem plan to return home for the day? Was it necessary for him to spend *that* much time with Rose?

He'd certainly ingratiated himself to her friend, winning the bet easily and forcing Kenzy to honor her word by not interfering with his methods. No longer bedridden, Rose felt so well today that she elected to restock her pantry and visit Euphemia at the mercantile. Kenzy had spent the past few days working alongside Noble, hoping that paying more attention to him would take her mind off how Rose seemed to thrive in Rem's company rather than hers.

Kenzy licked her lips, moistening them to prevent cracking, only to remind herself of the additional kiss she'd allowed to seal her bargain with Rem three days ago. What was it about him that she couldn't resist?

If Rose continued to favor Rem's company, then it might be the right time to finally test the power of No-

ble's kiss. After all, that was one of the reasons she'd
returned to San Augustine—to see if her feelings for him
offered a firm foundation for the future or if they'd simply been a means to imitate Rose.

Even as the thought of kissing Noble crossed her
mind, Kenzy's memory raced to the last day she'd seen
him before she'd left San Augustine. She had more than
anticipated his kiss then.

*"Kenzy, honey? Are you about dressed? That Stockton
boy came to say good-bye before he heads for school.
Said we'd be gone before he could return."*

"Be right there, Mama." Noble, here? Come to say
good-bye? *Kenzy rushed around like a dervish.* My
brush, my brush, my brush. Where's my brush? *Finding
it, she faced the mirror and glanced at her hair in horror.*

*Swatting away the image, she pinched her cheeks and
licked her lips to make them shiny. The contact of tongue
upon flesh stained her cheeks a deep crimson. What if
Noble tried to kiss her?*

*He had come to say good-bye, hadn't he? Men and
women kissed each other when they said good-bye,
didn't they? A look at her slightly rounded bodice sent
frustration coursing through Kenzy. She was only beginning to be a woman, caught in that awkward, gangly
stage of knowing what she thought was best for herself
and being too young to be taken seriously. But Noble?
A deep sigh escaped her.*

*She puckered her lips and opened one eye. Willickers!
He'd never kiss anything that looked like that! She licked
her lips again. How was it Anna captured the boys' attention so well? Oh, yes . . . Kenzy batted her lashes and
tried to appear inquisitive as she puckered. No . . . that
looked like she had a fly on her nose and was trying to
shoo it away.*

*"McKenzy Louise Dixon! The young man will be late
for school. What is keeping you?"*

"Motherrr . . ." Kenzy thought she would die of em-

barrassment. No one, positively no one but Rose, knew her middle name until now. "I'll be right out. Just one more . . ." She kissed her fist one last time for good measure.

She'd waited too long for this moment. Dreamed about it every night since she'd met him. If moving would make him finally kiss her, it was almost worth saying good-bye. Just think of what she could write about in her first letter to Rose! Then again . . . maybe she shouldn't tell Rose about it at all. It might hurt her friend's feelings. Well, there would be no need to worry whether she should or shouldn't tell, if she didn't get out there and give him a chance to kiss her.

Kenzy rushed from her room and into the parlor. Empty. Where did he go? "Mama, did he leave?" she asked as Clair Dixon came around the corner from the hallway.

"I told you, dear, he'd be late for school if you didn't hurry. The bell's already ringing."

Kenzy hurried to the front porch to see if she could still catch him. To her dismay, she saw him running hand and hand with Rose. Had she come along, too, or just joined him on the path? He never would have kissed Kenzy in front of her.

The sight of her best friend nearly stole Kenzy's voice. They'd said a private good-bye last night. Despite Kenzy's insistence that she would return someday, both feared it was the last time they would see each other. Now, the tears she had cried all night threatened again. "Rose . . . Noble. Wait!"

They turned around, still holding hands. "Sorry, Kenz," Noble yelled back. "Gotta hurry. Gonna be late. You take care now." He raised Rose's hand high over her head. "And I'll take care of Rose. Come back, Freckle Face. I'll miss you."

"Will you?" she whispered, glad he was too far away to hear her doubt. She knew she should be happy that if she couldn't marry him, Rose might. After all, hadn't they planned it that way? But Kenzy was too full of

sadness to think clearly. An overwhelming sense of loss
consumed her.

Rose chose that moment to wave hard at Kenzy and
shout, "Now and forever, always together. Sisters!"

The memory faded as Kenzy stared down at the finger
that wore the ring sealing the pledge they'd made. She
wanted them always to remember the good times they'd
had, the confidences they'd shared. Kissing Noble now
would only serve to broaden the chasm that had come
between her and Rose recently. Best to spend her time
getting reacquainted with him and talking. Trouble was,
all he seemed to want to talk about was Rose.

Kenzy pinched the white linen at her bodice and
raised the material to form a tent that allowed cool air
against her skin. What she wouldn't give to shuck her
clothes and race to the old swimming hole. Instead, she
concentrated on counting the number of boards in each
pile. "Looks like we're just about finished with this
stack."

"Won't be long before we can have a wall-raising
party. Sure is hot out here." Noble wiped a forearm
across his brow, perspiration darkening his hair to a harvest gold. He grabbed the ax again and finished shaping
the piece of lumber he'd been working on. "I hope Rose
doesn't stay at Euphemia's too long. You know how she
is. She'll try too much too soon. As soon as she's up to
it, I want to take her on a picnic."

" 'Phemia won't let her overdo, and I thought I saw
Sowboy driving Rose's buggy. He'll see she gets home
in good time." Strut slid down the large pole in front of
the orphanage where he had hung Cordell's bell on a
hook. "Well, that ought to suit the lad just fine. Guess
we ought to give it a yank and see if it works."

"Ring two times, not three." Kenzy dusted the sawdust from her hands. "Someone will think we need help,
if you use the emergency call-to-arms."

The bell pealed twice, resounding loud and clear. Strut

tied the braided cord to the pole so if the wind got up, the bell wouldn't ring on its own.

"Sounds fine to me." A loud *thwaaack* tore the air as Noble punctuated his words by burying his ax into a nearby stump. "It'll make a fine gathering bell for the children. You're really doing something special here, Kenzy."

Pleased with his compliment, she thought it might be a good time to take a break. He seemed in a talkative mood. "Thanks. I feel like it's worthwhile and not just because I'm getting to design it myself. There are so many children without homes now. Home *or* family. That's the true tragedy of the War. Something had to be done, and it might as well be us doing it. Everyone thinks we're trying to gain favor with the Unionists, but all I want is to make things comfortable for the children. Here . . ." She removed a blanket from atop the picnic basket sitting on the wagon. "I saved some of the tea Rem brewed up this morning for Rose—I thought you might get thirsty."

Noble waited until she poured both men a glass.

Strut waved her offer away. "I'm gonna head to the creek and cool myself down. Don't cotton to tea much unless it's some of that hair-growing remedy Sowboy talked about."

"No, this is plain old rosehips." Kenzy smiled when Strut's nose wrinkled in disapproval.

"You two have yourselves a tea party. I'll be back lickety-split and wetter than a bullfrog burping in a bayou."

They remained silent as their old friend wandered off toward the creek. Then Kenzy and Noble spoke at the same time.

"You first," Kenzy conceded.

"No, ladies first." Noble brought his glass up to his mouth and took a long drink.

"Not fair. You have your mouth full now."

When he nodded, she knew he'd done so deliberately. "I wondered how you feel about Rem Parker and his

remedies. Whether you think they're really curing Rose
and if his . . . uh . . . frequent visits to Rose are helpful."

"Do you mean, am I jealous of how much time he's
spending with her?"

Kenzy refused to blush. "I woudn't have stated it so
bluntly, but yes, I suppose I'm surprised you haven't
said anything by now."

"Why are you asking, Freckle Face?"

His blue eyes focused on her, demanding her gaze.
He was such a handsome man. She'd always thought so.
Everyone did. The Golden Boy. Everyone's idea of the
perfect gentleman, the perfect friend, the perfect every-
thing. Why then was he coming up short compared to
Rem?

Tell him. Now was her opportunity to approach the
subject as a friend and find out what she needed to make
an informed choice. "I assumed you and Rose had an
understanding after all these years."

"Here, let's rest for a while." Noble scooted the basket
to the middle of the wagon and wiped off the gate to
allow Kenzy to sit.

She did, and he sat next to her. Her legs dangled over
the edge of the gate, reminding her of many a time she
and Noble had sat on a cliff that jutted over their swimming hole. They'd talked about everything back then.
Though older than she, he'd never thought it too both-
ersome to spend time with a young tagalong and talk
about dreams. "Are you avoiding my question?"

Noble shrugged. "Not really. I'm just not sure how to
answer you. Rose told me she's sure you came back
home because you thought there could be something between you and me. She asked me if there could be, and
I couldn't lie to her. I said I'd always been particularly
fond of both of you. But I only said that because she
wanted to hear those words from me. And they weren't
a lie. I am, and always have been fond of you."

The thought of how his answer might have wounded
Rose was a hollow victory for Kenzy. She had to defend

her friend. "Surely, you know how much she cares for you."

"No more than I care for her."

"Why make her believe that you have any interest in me, if you're as in love with her as she is you?"

"You don't understand, do you?" He jolted to his feet, setting his tea glass down with a clank and interlocking his arms across his chest.

"I must not." Kenzy reached out and gently grabbed his arm to keep him from leaving. Perhaps she was mistaken and he only meant to stand there and brood. He didn't shirk from her touch. "Tell me, Noble. What is it?"

"She thinks I'll grow tired of loving a wife who's bound to a wheelchair. She won't say that, Kenzy, but I know it's the truth. Good Ol' Noble Stockton. Truth speaker, that's what everyone's always claimed. All knowing. All trustworthy. Truth in human form. There's never been a bigger lie. I'd be less of a man without Rose."

His voice faded as he stared into the distance. "She suggested you hire me so she could make certain you and I spend as much time together as possible. She knows that I felt slighted in the war. That I got stuck keeping books at the customs house instead of going to battle like the others. She knows I crave to do anything physical and outdoors now to prove that I'm worthy of having served."

His fist knotted, pounding his leg. "God knows I've told enough people that I wish I could have put my life on the line, just as my brother and the other heroes did."

But Noble controlled his anger, allowing his fingers to thread through the hair at his temple. "She's putting her health in jeopardy by all these visits out here and in town, and it's my fault. Rose doesn't have to prove to me she's still capable of living an active life. I already think she's the most admirable person I know. I don't see her doing less because of her circumstances. I see her trying even harder. I doubt I would be as active as she is if I'd been confined to that chair."

"Maybe she's proving something to herself, as well as to you. Maybe by continuing her life as she once knew it, she's teaching herself not to be trapped by fear. Let her work this out in her own way, Noble. And while she's doing that, you prove to her time and again that she is whole to you. That nothing has or ever will change about how much you care for her."

"She's made up her mind that you'll be my bride and she, the bridesmaid."

"When did she tell you that?"

"The first time? Before you left for Massachusetts. Once you returned as well."

"You knew about our pact?"

He nodded. "Quite a flattering prospect, especially for a fifteen-year-old boy."

"You were always so dashing. Every girl in the territory wanted to be your betrothed."

"I had eyes for only two of you."

"We both know you always favored Rose. There was never any doubt in my mind that she would be the one you chose."

"Now, you're fibbing. You wouldn't have come back to San Augustine if you believed that."

He lifted her chin to stare in her eyes. All Kenzy saw was kindness, not the searing passion that radiated back from Rem's midnight gaze. "Tell me I'm wrong then," she whispered, not understanding why she needed to know if Noble had ever felt anything more for her than affection. Had it all been one-sided, the product of a young girl's wishful thinking?

"Kenzy, Kenzy, Kenzy . . ." He rubbed his thumb across her chin. "You will always be little Freckle Face to me. A freckle-faced girl who became a boy's best friend when he wasn't even looking for one. A friend who didn't think it was silly sitting on a bank, listening to him build big dreams and analyze the universe. I knew I could tell you anything and you wouldn't laugh.

You listened and that's what I needed most—someone to listen and not run and tell anyone else about the wild future I'd envisioned for myself. Oh, no, I was too caught up in being everyone's Mr. Perfect to let anyone criticize what I hoped to become."

"I told Rose."

"Yes, Rose. She's always been a vital part of both of our happinesses, hasn't she? And now . . ." He pointed at the buggy coming up the lane. Rem commandeered the team and Rose sat beside him. "We have to make sure she maintains hers."

A deep sigh escaped Noble as he placed a chaste kiss on Kenzy's cheek. "If that means paying court to my best friend until my beloved comes to her senses, then I hope you understand that's what I intend to do. I hope it won't be too much of a burden on you."

"Burden? Of-of course not. What else are friends for?" The breath left Kenzy as surely as if she'd become a windless sail. She had never really stood a chance with Noble. His interest in her now was only out of respect for Rose's wishes.

Shouldn't the weight of having loved him all these years and learning that it was not reciprocated crush her? Shouldn't she be angry that he intended to use her to bide time until true love reached its pinnacle between him and Rose? Shouldn't she feel something other than joy that Rose was the chosen one?

But most of all . . . why didn't she feel something other than this overwhelming sense of relief that Noble had finally stated his choice and it wasn't her?

14

The sight of Stockton kissing Kenzy sent Rem's temper searing to the bone. That the kiss was given on the cheek proved irrelevant.

Jealousy ignited like a blazing sun and threatened to incinerate the marrow that guarded Rem's heart. The vow made to Brett Stockton wavered. His tolerance of Noble turned to ash, leaving him with nothing but a scalding need to slam his fist into the carpenter's mouth.

Another vow, more potent than any made to a dying ally, rose to consume Rem's thoughts. No man but himself would know the texture of Kenzy's skin, the touch of her sweet lips. No man but he would taste the depth of her passion. McKenzy would become his bride, if it took *his* dying breath to fulfill the pledge.

Rose shifted on the seat next to him, her gloved hand reaching out to calm his tight-fisted hold on the reins. She smiled and pointed her fan in the direction of the stream.

"Now, there's a sight. Strut must have fallen in." Rose's giggle seemed forced and uncommonly girlish.

The old man waved, the strand of hair he used to hide his near baldness hanging noticeably longer than the rest.

Calmed by her effort to distract him, Rem's anger

cooled a few degrees. The tenderness Noble and Kenzy
shared could not be easy for Rose to witness, either, yet
she was kind enough to consider his feelings and not
her own. When had Rose discovered how much Kenzy
meant to him?

"They've always been the best of friends." Rose
squared her shoulders and lifted her chin a notch, offering her friends a dazzling smile as they approached.

"And you're too much of one to stand in her way."
Rem's fingers unballed as he ordered the team to halt.

"No more than you will be when you let her make up
her own mind about him."

Searching Rosella's face, Rem wished he'd been allowed to get to know her better in childhood. She was
full of courage and common sense. Unselfish to a fault.
He knew beyond questioning that she was fiercely in
love with Noble. Yet she always gave Kenzy ample opportunity to accompany the man.

Did Stockton think he could continue to court both
women and not pit friend against friend at some point?
Was he arrogant enough to believe he could continue his
boorishness? Why play this childish game any longer?
Rem's mood darkened by the moment.

"What's wrong?" Noble hurried to Rose's side. "Parker looks like he could massacre someone."

"That *is* an option." Rem's words sliced as easily as
if he'd thrust a saber.

The woman beside him obviously delighted in the fe-
rocity of his words. Rose's giggle sounded more sincere
than the last. His gaze met hers for an instant, then
Rose's darted away to hide the amusement lighting her
eyes.

"Do you want your wheelchair?" Rem's feet settled
to the ground while he reached to lift the chair from the
seat behind them.

Before she could answer, Noble hurried to assist. He
grabbed the opposite corner and frowned when Rem
scooted it more his direction. Noble scooted it back.

Rem's lips curled in deliberate challenge. "Tug and

Toss is an old game I never lost . . . remember?"

"Men!" Kenzy placed her hand over Rembrandt's, saying the word as if it was the ruin of all wisdom. "Hasn't there been enough conflict around here to last you two a lifetime?"

"I won't be getting out." Rose's eyes focused on Rem, asking for permission to explain. "I think it best to ride with Rem on his way home."

She paused, awaiting his consent to tell them the rest. Rem shrugged. It was inevitable. They would learn now or once they reached town. Better it come from Rose rather than one of the less tolerant townspeople. He nodded permission.

"I felt he would be much safer if someone was with him."

Concern quickened Kenzy's pulse. Images of several men in town who'd given Rem less than a hardy welcome sprang to mind. Bitterness ran deep among the defeated Rebs. More than one grave in the Parker cemetery held the body of a soldier whose loyalty to the South had been questioned. "Who's trying to harm him?"

Rose unknotted the ribbon that held her bonnet in place, freeing her strawberry-blond curls. "There's talk of an amnesty meeting to occur in a day or two. President Johnson agrees to grant us amnesty if we take an oath of loyalty to the United States. The price to be paid by each man for this honor is two hundred dollars. A king's fortune for some!"

"My signature will never appear on any such document." Noble's tone grated like a knife against stone.

Fear etched Rose's face. "But if you don't, the carpetbaggers will take everything you own. Here, read this. Orlan said I could show you and others what it would say." She offered him the example.

"I own but one thing in this life worth keeping, and that's my honor." Noble refused to accept the parchment. "I'll not give in to their demands."

"Now's not the time to make a stand, Noble." Kenzy

took the decree. "It will only give them more cause to
penalize you . . . and Rose. Surely, they don't require so
much that we can't tolerate their demands. After all,
what good are we to them if we're left with no way to
recover?"

She began to read the missive aloud as if she were in
a hurry, tapping one slipper in time with the words.
"*Whereas, Orlan Marsdale of San Augustine County,
Texas, by taking part in the late rebellion against the
Government of the United States, has made himself li-
able to heavy pains and penalties . . .*"

"I'll show 'em heavy pain and penalties." Strut
slammed one of his fists into the other.

No one laughed, least of all Rem. He'd seen the atroc-
ities on both sides of the conflicts. Death, at times, had
been a blessing to those who would have had to live on
with their sufferings.

"*And whereas, the circumstances of his case renders
him a proper object of Executive clemency . . .*" Tap-
Tap-Tap-Tap.

"Marsdale wastes no time, does he?" Rem met
Kenzy's gaze, sensing her thoughts traveling the same
path of suspicion as his own. What did the timber baron
stand to gain from this quick amnesty? Further, *why* had
it been granted so easily?

"*Now, therefore, be it known . . .*" Kenzy sighed
heavily as her toe-tapping continued. "*That I, Andrew
Johnson, president of the United States of America, in
consideration of the promises, diverse other goods and
sufficient reasons thereunto moving, do hereby grant to
the said Orlan Marsdale a full pardon and amnesty
for all offenses by him committed, conditioned as fol-
lows . . .*"

She scanned the remainder, not reading it aloud. "The
rest just says what they consider a breaking of the oath."

"If you won't sign, neither will I." Rose's chin lifted
in defiance as she accepted the parchment again and
stored it away in the pocket of her skirt.

"The *men* were asked to take the oath and pay."

Worry creased Kenzy's brow. "You won't be required to—"

"Property owners were asked, of which I'm one." Rose replaced her bonnet and tied it beneath her chin as if to seal her conviction. "Wherever Noble stands on this issue, I stand with him."

"An admirable choice." Rem revered a woman who stood by the man she loved.

"A dangerous choice," Kenzy countered. "And speaking of danger, we all seem to be avoiding the issue here." She frowned at Rose. "Why did you feel *you* had to guarantee Rem's safety? What's happened?"

Rose started to answer but Rem interrupted her. "They might as well hear it from me." He met every gaze, then settled on the one that meant most to him. Kenzy's arms folded beneath her breasts, defining the generous swell of her bosom. She might act like her anger stemmed from his allowing Rose to put herself in jeopardy as well. But the tapping of her toe while she read verified she was impatient to know more about the danger to him.

Though her concern pleased him, he found no pleasure in worrying her. And no amount of explaining would cool the hothead. She wouldn't care that Rose had proven too persuasive to oppose. The best thing to do was tell her about the claims against him. Not that she couldn't guess if she tried hard enough.

"The lieutenant in charge of informing us about the meeting said that I didn't have to sign. All that did was convince the others that what they believe about me is true. They think I worked for the other side. That I'm a traitor to the South."

"Are you?"

Kenzy's question pierced him like no bayonet ever could. Would she ever know him well enough to know the answer without asking? "I never forsook the South."

"Did you tell them that? Did you defend yourself?"

The indignation in her eyes offered a poultice to his wounded pride. She cared more than she let on. "Why should I waste the breath? They wouldn't have believed me anyway."

"Ain't no one pure innocent in this war," Strut muttered, then glanced up. Embarrassment swept up his neck to round into two strawberry-colored cheeks. "Well . . . um . . . er . . . I mean, all of us would change a few things we done, if we had to do it over again."

Rose gently touched Rem's sleeve. "Surely there's some way to prove that you didn't defect."

Kenzy's eyes narrowed, her finger tapping against her chin as she started making suggestions. "We could . . . no, that wouldn't work. Perhaps we might . . ." She shook her head. "They wouldn't accept that either. I've got it!" Her attention shifted to the carpenter. "Noble, you were in charge of the enlistment rolls since the beginning. You told me yourself you've had to keep meticulous records of those who survived and didn't." Possibility rushed her words now. "You just might be the one person who can help him. You ought to be able to find someone to speak up for Rem. Someone who fought beside him the entire war. Surely, there's got to be someone whose word would be accepted without question."

Every eye focused on Rem, including the carpenter's. Instead of being reluctant, Noble seemed eager for Rem to speak his piece.

"Maybe Parker wants to speak for himself," Noble urged.

Rem's impatience wavered. What better to defend his honor than the words of Brett Stockton—the hero the town claimed as its own? Who better than the hero's brother to confirm the authenticity of the letter? Why then, did it matter which of them told the women that the sought-after man stood but a few feet away?

Forget the wrongful accusations. Forget Stockton's reluctance to taint his brother's legacy. All Rem could remember at the moment was Noble kissing Kenzy and the hope she'd always nurtured to marry the carpenter. He couldn't destroy her happiness, even at the loss of his own reputation. He couldn't destroy the good name of the family she wanted to marry into. Rem loved her far too much to put his needs over her dreams.

"The truth will come out in its own good time," he stated flatly, gathering a box of-dry goods from the storage trunk on the back of the buggy. It was time to head home and let them all return to their illusions. "Only two of our unit escaped the battle at Gaines Mill. Unfortunately, as you've been told, Brett died in one of our last skirmishes. Unless he can speak from the grave, it looks like there's no one to defend me. Miss Whitaker . . ." He nodded briefly to Rose. "Thank you for riding with me. I'm sure Kenzy or one of the men will be glad to see you home."

"Noble can take her back." Kenzy issued the order, then gentled her tone. "Won't you?"

"I'd be delighted."

"Strut, if you'll gather the tools, I'll try to talk some sense into Rem." One finger wagged at Rem. "Now, you know you're not going to convince anybody of your innocence by hiding away and ignoring all this. Where is that hot-blooded gypsy boy who bloodied a nose when someone called him a name? I seem to remember him looking everyone in the eye who dared demean him or his grand—"

"He was blinded by truth. Defending himself to those who'd already made up their minds proved a childish delusion." Emotional exhaustion engulfed Rem. He wasn't a man who gave up easily. He'd taken the name calling and gossip in stride for more years than he cared to remember. The desire to make anyone accept him had disappeared the day GranZeph died. All this he acknowledged. So why, then, was it critical now for everyone to know the truth about him?

"You're coming back to town with me." Kenzy linked her arm through his, her tone insistent. "I'll see that we resolve this. You can count on me."

It was then Rem knew why repairing his reputation suddenly mattered so much. Why living here would become impossible if the facts of his participation in the war were kept secret. Why isolating himself no longer seemed the answer to his dilemma.

Kenzy wanted to set things right for him with the community. Kenzy was willing to take up his banner and stand beside him. Kenzy believed in him.

15

Rem knew the exact moment the inquisitive citizens of San Augustine sensed something important was about to take place. Kenzy marched down the street, not stopping to answer an offered wave nor return a friend's greeting. She was on a mission and her proud carriage brooked no interruptions. Despite his longer gait, Rem had to step lively to keep up with her.

A line soon formed behind them, looking like goslings following in their wake. The day of reckoning Rem hoped he would never face seemed imminent. Today, he would learn if the townspeople of San Augustine would ever accept him among them. Today, Kenzy would champion him. If he lost this time, he lost more than a home and a place to rebuild his life. Today, he might possibly lose any hope of marrying the woman he loved.

She came to a halt at the bell tower that stood in the center of the town square. Loosening the anchor of rope that kept the bell stationary during a high wind, she yanked the cord three times, pealing a call-to-arms. Bentford Buchanan, the town drunk, woke from his soused sleep and promptly rolled off the spit-and-whittle bench stationed just in front of the bell tower.

"Goodgawdamighty! Sunday ain't 'til tomorrow." Bentford gripped both ears as color drained from his

face. "Warn a fella 'fore you let loose of them chimes.
Ain't no place sacred anymore for a fella wanting a little
shut-eye?"

Grateful for the release of building tension, Rem
would have laughed aloud but thought better of it.
Kenzy wouldn't appreciate anything but austerity defining his features as he stood beside her. He willed the
threatening smile into a grim line.

"I need your bench. Here..." Kenzy handed the
drunk two coins. "Go tell Marsdale, his lawyer and the
rest of the town councilmen that I'm calling a meeting.
See if you can find Anna LeGrand, as well. And *now*.
Don't stop to get a drink. Don't find someplace quiet to
sleep. Tell everyone I told you, then after you're finished, take a bath and visit the barber. There'll be
enough left for either a good hot meal or a drink when
you're done."

Her nose wrinkled at the stench of alcohol. "You
know which one I want you to choose, but I'll leave that
to your own discretion. But don't let me see you around
town dirty and unshaven or I'll never ask you to deliver
another message for me. Understand?"

The man offered a shaky salute, grimacing. "Gotcha,
Miz Dixon. Loud and ... well, really loud."

By the time the drunk sauntered away, all up and
down the boardwalk, people stopped hawking their
wares, while others left their shops. Muleskinners turned
their wagons toward the noise. Speculation grew thick
in the air, like the sound of a swarm of bees.

"What do you reckon's going on?"

Turning toward the man who'd asked, Rem saw the
questioner was one of three men who had tried to pick
a fight with him when he returned from the hunt. The
other two joined him, staring past Rem to look at Kenzy.
A leer lifted the tallest man's mouth, his gaze sweeping
over Kenzy like she was a glass of bourbon and he a
thirsty man. Rem started toward him, but Kenzy linked
her arm through Rem's, holding him back.

"Don't pay him any mind. I wouldn't wipe my boots on the likes of that scalawag."

"It's that Dixon woman," a female announced, her voice growing more shrill with each word. "Think there's something wrong at the orphanage?"

"She doesn't look like she's in any hurry, that's for certain." Another lady whipped out an ivory fan and began to cool the summer heat from her face. "I hope whatever it is, it doesn't take long. I hear she's long-winded when she sets her mind to . . ."

The woman's words faded as Rem concentrated on watching Kenzy. Determination carved her beautiful features into angles of defiance. He would have had a hard time facing her with that kind of conviction staring back at him. The fact that her resolve focused on setting things right for him only deepened his admiration for her and engulfed him with a sense of gratitude. She'd never asked him to speak of his actions in the war. She'd made her judgment on their past acquaintanceship and what she'd experienced with him since his return. She was defending him purely out of friendship—an act of kindness he thought himself incapable of experiencing. An enticement that sank the roots of his love for her even deeper.

"Gather around, everyone. I have something to say." Kenzy stood on the bench so she would be higher than the crowd. She motioned everyone closer. "I'm just waiting a moment until more of you can be here."

Not wanting her to be such a target in the event things got rough, Rem stepped up beside Kenzy. Disapproval rumbled through the crowd.

"What's he got to say?" asked the man who had eyed Kenzy with the hungry look. "I didn't come here to listen to no traitor."

Kenzy smiled sweetly at the man—offering an expression that couldn't have looked more mocking. "You won't be, Jenkins, even if he does all the talking. Rembrandt Parker isn't any more traitor than you are."

"Now, see here . . ." Jenkins shoved the people beside

him to one side. "Lady or no lady, don't be calling me
no traitor. I'll show you—"

"You best stand back, mister." Rem jumped like a
springing panther, moving to chin's length from the
troublemaker and glaring at him with feral eyes. "Make
no hasty threats unless you can back them up."

"He don't want no trouble now, Parker," said one of
Jenkin's comrades while urging Jenkins to put more distance between himself and Rem. "Besides, we'll catch
you when you're not hiding behind her petticoats."

Regardless of the berating Kenzy would give him for
losing his temper, Rem threw a punch. Kenzy somehow
managed to step between him and the instigator, causing
Rem to deflect the blow.

"Stop it." She glared at Rem. "*All* of you."

The towncouncilmen elected to show up at that moment, taking the crowd's attention away from the tension
that layered the air between Rem and his taunters. Four
of San Augustine's most respected citizens converged
on the square at the same time. One look from Orlan
Marsdale caused Jenkins and his cohorts to end the confrontation.

"Anytime, Jenkins." Rem leveled his gaze on the man.
"You *and* your partners. Makes no difference to me how
many."

"What's this all about, Miss Dixon?" Orlan Marsdale's booming voice asked the question on everyone's
mind. The crowd opened up a path to let the large councilman through. Anna LeGrand followed in his wake.

A glance at others who joined the fray—Strut and
Euphemia Jones—assured Rem that he and Kenzy were
not totally alone in their intent. But he was most surprised to see Rose and Stockton moving up for a better
view. Hadn't they been headed home?

"You all remember Rembrandt Parker." Kenzy's hand
linked arms with Rem once again. "He served with Brett
Stockton's unit and fought bravely alongside him at
Gaines Mill."

Low murmurs swept through the crowd.

"Yes, yes, we're all aware of his fighting spirit the day he left with the unit." Marsdale grabbed the lapels of his morning coat and rocked back on his heels. "What has that got to do with calling a meeting today? A meeting I might add, Miss Dixon," his gaze swept over the crowd, his voice growing haughty, "that required you to use the call-to-arms. I see no Indian attack or raiders burning our homes and businesses. In fact, you've created a threat for us all. Remember that our Union caretakers do not permit an assembly without their knowing the motivation for it beforehand."

An air of leadership about Marsdale made the timber baron stand out among the councilmen. Several people nodded agreement. Others dispersed, apparently afraid of retaliation from the carpetbaggers. Blue-coated soldiers began to line the circumference of the crowd.

"Then let them stand and listen. They'll not hear me sully their good names nor the government. Marsdale is right, however. I do speak of a threat. One that is rampant here and elsewhere in the South." Kenzy's hand unlinked from Rem's, her fists balling against her hips. "A threat graver than any we ever suffered from the Yanks."

Her voice rang loud and strong. "*We've* lost hope, not only in our way of life, but in ourselves and each other. That's why I called you here today. To remind you of faith and hope and believing in each another again. It's the only way we're going to see these troubles through. We must forget what every man, woman and child did to survive the war and go on with our lives. We need to foster brotherhood . . . comradery, where we once harbored hatred and suspicion."

"Quite eloquent, Miss Dixon." Marsdale waved the bluecoats in closer. "I'm sure these men will echo your sentiments back to Washington. But might I suggest that we stick to the real reason you called this meeting."

"That is the reason."

"I believe this speech is made for a more personal

argument than repairing the wounds between us and our conquerors."

"Leave her be, Marsdale." Rem could not abide the man's insolence any longer. There was no reason to put her on trial.

"No, Rem." Kenzy held him back. "Marsdale is right." She lifted her chin and faced the townspeople. "I did come here to defend Rem to you all. Why? Because he's one man. And we have to start somewhere in order to build the peace we all crave. He used to be one of us. He wants to be again. Why not start whatever pardoning that needs to be done with one of our own?"

Pardoning? Did she believe him guilty of something that needed forgiveness? The pride he'd taken in her speech ebbed.

"They say he fought for the Yanks," another councilman accused. "No one remembered him in the battlefield after Gaines Mill. Seems to me there should have been some kind of news about him, but it was as if he'd disappeared. If he didn't turncoat, then he must have deserted."

"What do you got to say about that, Missy?" Jenkins's voice gained strength from the growing unrest within the crowd. "You want us to forgive a man who's coward enough to let another man do his fighting for him?"

"All I know is that Rembrandt is not the kind of man to leave anyone hurt. His life's work is growing herbs to help heal people. How could someone like that harm anyone? If you don't believe me, then ask Rose Whitaker. She'll tell you how much he's helped her."

Rose wheeled closer. "Kenzy's right. He's helped me when no one else could. My legs are much better than they were."

"He's a honorable man who took his pledge to defend our community as seriously as all our men did." Kenzy stared at Anna. "As seriously as Brett Stockton had."

Every eye focused on Noble to see if he would challenge Kenzy's words in any way. He stood behind Rose's wheelchair, silent.

"Don't you dare compare him to Brett." Anger filled Anna LeGrand's tone. "If Noble won't speak up, then I will. There was no man alive braver than my cousin." She began to weep. "No one."

Kenzy's face softened with compassion. "I didn't mean to imply he was anything but the bravest, Anna. I'm sorry I've distressed you. I'm just saying that there is another measure of bravery that we forget sometimes. A bravery we all have and should do our utmost to encourage. We all have within us a shared will that could be used to pardon those whom we believe transpassed against us. A will we must use to survive so that those precious lives that meant so much to us were not lost in vain."

"All heartfelt truths, I agree, Miss Dixon. But one simple question will disturb me until you answer me adequately. Has Parker told you what really happened during the rest of his service?" The timber baron's question brought a silence to the crowd. "Can you verify that he did not desert nor join the Northern forces?"

Rem watched turmoil shadow Kenzy's features. He couldn't ask her to lie for him. He wouldn't. "I've never told her. I've never told anyone."

"Then all this is, is a young woman's fancy being defended here. You've cast some kind of spell on her, bewitched her with your gypsy sorcery." Marsdale's voice boomed like the thunder of logs rolling down-mountain to a stream. "She clearly thinks she's in love with you."

Kenzy said nothing, neither denying or confirming the baron's accusation. For the first time since arriving at the square, defeat sucked the wind out of Rem.

"Wait, everyone!" Noble shouted, moving Rose's chair through the crowd. "What Kenzy said is true. It doesn't matter what any of us did. We need to concentrate on healing the rift between ourselves before we can restore our alliance to the Union. That's what is important to remember. We all can grow stronger by offering mercy."

Rem could see Stockton's conscience working, could hear it in his word choices. Still, he wasn't man enough to put truth above family loyalties. But the letter was not Rem's concern at the moment. The important thing to remember was that Kenzy should not be made a fool of just because she'd braved the crowd on his behalf. Neither should he make a fool of himself for believing that she could fall in love with him, whether Noble was a rival or not.

"Don't worry, citizens of San Augustine." Rem faced his accusers. "Your spokesmen have made their feelings clear. Who knows, perhaps as soon as I've finished my work here, I'll move on and relieve you all of my foul stench. Then again, I might linger just so that you can always have a comparison. It's difficult to judge the quality of a fragrance unless you can smell an offending odor on occasion."

Kenzy reached out to touch him. "This won't get you anywhere."

"Won't it? They don't realize it, but they've paid me a huge courtesy." He met every eye in the crowd, refusing to be tyrannized by their presumptions. "I would have spent my time doing all that I could to become an upstanding, respected member of your community. To win approval from all of you. I tried as a boy and lost. You thought I would have learned my lesson. As a man, I hoped things might have changed. But they haven't."

He looked at them with disdain. "The Yanks didn't defeat you. You thwarted yourselves. It's easier, isn't it, to hold on to your fine standards than to question whether those standards are fair. It was easier to destroy a boy's pride in his heritage than to understand something or someone new. It's much easier to blame Kenzy for an infatuation than to hear the voice of clemency she offers to make us all whole once again."

A formidable scowl tightened Rem's forehead as he faced Noble. Rage bubbled in him. The carpenter had failed to speak up when he'd been given the perfect

chance. But love for Kenzy prevented Rem from un-
leashing the blaze to demand his due.

As if she sensed Rem's anger, Kenzy's face trans-
formed into a mask of stone. "Know this everyone . . . I
won't tolerate any sudden accidents that might befall
Rem. If he should so much as stub his toe on something
that has no reason for being there, I won't hesitate to go
to the authorities, and I don't mean the sheriff of our
fair settlement."

She hadn't been back in San Augustine so long that
she'd become an irreplaceable member of the community. Several snubbed their noses at her and turned away.

"Whatever Kenzy does, I stand behind her," a voice
familiar and dear to them all spoke up. Rose eyed everyone within her path. "If Rem's hurt, I'll take it as a
personal affront to me. I'll go to the authorities with
her."

The possible loss of support from the town's best
benefactor was enough to quiet the crowd.

Kenzy took courage in her friend's statement. "I want
to live where a man, or a woman, for that matter can be
accepted for who he is, not what others demand him to
be. I'll leave the same day he does."

With a searching look into her eyes, Rem's palm
cupped Kenzy's cheek and remained there for a moment.
"Thank you, Tadpole, but I can't let you or Rose do
that. The two of you belong here with the boys. With
Noble."

His hand wanted to linger upon her soft, warm face,
to touch the eyes now misting with unshed tears, to
stroke the lower swell of her lips and caress each inch
of her treasured beauty.

"Don't ever leave, then," she whispered.

"Staying may be impossibile."

"Help me change their minds. I'll stand beside you."

Rem's hand settled at his side. He would like nothing
more than remain here and ease the loneliness. He'd
expected nothing more than to settle down, mind his
herbs and make friends to treasure and share his bless-

ings with. He'd managed to do that to an extent. Euphemia, Strut, Rose and the boys had all become dear to him. But more than any friendship, more than any place to call home, the thing he needed most was for Kenzy to love him, not just believe in a cause he happened to represent.

"I'll stay until the new herbs can be harvested." He would keep his pledge to his grandmother, taking the new herbs and plenty of their vines and roots to start anew elsewhere. Before he left, he would see Gran-Zeph's cemetery given its proper adornment as well. Yes, he'd stay for a little longer, until his heart had accepted that Kenzy would belong to another. "Then I will do what I must."

16

The sun had barely risen the next day, slanting golden rays through the opened window to warm Rose's face and awaken her. A scattering of pebbles hit the side of the house and she heard a heavy whisper. Worthy's monster? She strained to listen.

"Rose? Are you awake? Come to the window."

She smiled, stretching her arms and feeling warmed by not only the sunlight, but the thought that it was Noble standing below, the intimacy of his tone a pleasure to her ears.

Her feet slid automatically to the floor before she realized she had shifted. Was it her imagination or had they moved separately? She glanced at her wheelchair, worrying that she might take too much time to seat herself and Noble would think she still slept. Could he hear her from here? She didn't want to yell too loudly for fear of waking the others.

"I'll be right there," she called lightly. Her and Noble's times alone came so seldom, she wanted to hoard him and let no one else intrude. Not even Kenzy.

The bottom of her feet tingled as they made contact with the coolness of the flooring. They didn't hurt like before, instead tingling as if they'd merely gone to sleep.

Rose lifted the hem of her gown and stared at her

feet. Could it be? Had Rem's potions taken effect? Had they increased her circulation or affected some sort of cure? She squealed in triumph, unable to contain her happiness at the prospect that filled her morning with promise.

"Rose? Is something wrong?" Concern filled Noble's voice.

"I'm fine. Better than I've been in a long time, I think. Just give me a minute, please." Rose willed her right leg to move. It slid forward—not quite a lift of her foot, but still enough to heighten the promise.

"Okay, so you're gaining some strength," she applauded herself, trying not to get too excited. There was still a long way to go before she could ever walk again, and patience would be needed. Rose stared at her left leg. "Now, how about you? Are you going to give it a try?"

The left proved stubborn.

"Come on." She refused to let disappointment extinguish the blaze of excitement within her. "One tiny step, that's all I ask. Take one step, then you can rest. Try as hard as you can."

The leg stood there like embedded stone, crushing the hope that made her heart race in anticipation. Rose closed her eyes and reminded herself of the instructions given during the sessions with Rem.

"Imagine your toes wiggling. Your heels lifting. Feel your calves bunching as you stride."

He spoke the words in such a low monotone, she had to listen closely to hear each word.

"Notice the flex of your thighs and how they tense then ease as you walk. This is a fluid movement, a natural motion that becomes a rhythm within you. Right, left. Right, left. Flex, bend. Flex, bend. See yourself strolling leisurely, walking confidently without pain. Your legs are healed, full of strength, whole. Walk, Rosella, walk and be made well."

Rose exhaled a cleansing breath of tension. She concentrated on her left leg and chanted Rem's instructions again and again until she completely relaxed. The tingling had gone away. There seemed to be no pain, no inflexibility. *My foot will move*, she told herself. *All I have to do is . . .*

"Rose? What's happening? Why aren't you coming to—"

"I did it!" Rose stared down at the toes of her left foot. She wiggled the big one again. The toe moved on its own, then the smaller ones shifted.

"I-I moved it," she whispered, disbelieving what she'd seen. The weight of what had just transpired settled heavily upon Rose, making her sway with sheer giddiness. Tears of awe bubbled into her eyes, streaming down her cheeks. But she didn't care. Let the flood come! For three years she'd cried over the twist of fate that had saddled her to a wheelchair. These were tears of happiness, tears that would cleanse, tears that would heal.

The power of her emotion unsteadied her. Rose grabbed for her chair, glad that it waited nearby. Better to take this new turn of events one step at a time. Yet when she sat in the chair, the cushion didn't seem quite so confining. She didn't mind that her arms must link under each knee to lift and settle her feet properly onto the footrests. She didn't care that there were calluses on her palms from having to rotate the chair's wheels. All the irritations no longer mattered. For hope whispered that this time might be one less needed to rid herself of the contraption.

Like a prisoner who'd been granted parole, she rolled over to the window. The smile that lifted her lips felt as if it might stretch from here to Fort Worth, but she couldn't help it. Her soul wanted to sing, her feet to dance. "Noble, what a glorious dawn." She stared at the cloudless sky, then down at him. "Have you ever seen such a beautiful day?"

"No, I haven't. That's why I thought you might like to ride with me out to the Sabine." He motioned to his buggy. "I took it upon myself to make us a picnic. I

thought we ought to celebrate not going to the amnesty
meeting with the others. Kenzy said she wasn't going
either, so she and the boys could do as they please."

Rose nodded. "Rembrandt's coming over sometime
this morning. It seems he promised to spend the day with
Cordell. That boy will ask a million questions, I fear,
especially with all the gossip that's circulating about
Rem. But, bless his heart, Rem never seems to tire of
the boy's curiosity."

"And Kenzy doesn't hesitate to give her opinion of
his answers, does she?"

"Of course not." The joy of the morning spilled out
as laughter. Rose wished Kenzy had been here to see
the improvement, but sharing the secret with Noble held
its own appeal. Kenzy would be envious when she
learned that Noble knew before her. "But that's what
makes her so special. There's never any doubt what
Kenzy thinks at any given moment."

"You're being kind."

"Kind? I'm rather jealous, actually." Rose didn't want
Noble to know that aspect of her friend's nature annoyed
her as much as it intrigued her. "I'm amazed that she's
knowledgeable about enough things that she feels comfortable with offering suggestions."

"Suggestions?" Noble laughed. "Now, you're being
too generous. She gives advice, Rose. Plain and simple
and whether or not anyone wants it. And since we're on
the subject of advice, would you please take this partic-
ular piece? Write a note to let them know you'll be with
me so they won't worry. I'll come up and get the lift
ready. Perhaps between the two of us, we can get you
and the wheelchair downstairs without waking the whole
household. I want to go on a picnic with you, Rosie. Not
with Kenzy. Nor the kids. Just you and me, alone.

"Oh, and Rose . . ." Dimples bracketed the smile that
radiated up to her. "The day is definitely beautiful, but
it can't compare to how lovely *you* look."

Rose realized all she had on was a thin nightdress
chosen last evening for comfort's sake. The row of but-

tons that fastened the linen from neck to breast hung open, just as she'd left them to ward off the lingering heat of her room. With her leaning over the sill this way, he must have had full view of her cleavage!

Her pulse raced, sending heat along the surface of her skin, raising fine hair in its wake. Rem's technique of helping Rose envision things she wanted to happen played havoc with her mind at the moment. She could almost see Noble's blue gaze traveling over her like an explorer seeking a new path. She could feel his strong hands encompassing her and pulling her into his embrace. Rose trembled, imagining the rough velvet of those work-hardened hands lifting the hem of her gown and caressing their way above her knees, across her thighs, cupping her breasts to test the weight and feel of them.

"G-give me a minute to collect myself," she stammered, throwing an imaginary lasso over her stampeding fancies. The points of her breasts hardened, revealing too aptly just what those fancies had been. She would have to be very careful on this picnic. More careful than any previous time she'd spent in Noble's company. The day was far too beautiful, the joy of living again no longer out of reach, and she, too ripe for the plucking.

Collecting herself and forgetting just how much she was attracted to him might be infinitely harder to do than moving her big toe. "Come to think of it," she warned, "you'd better give me a couple of minutes."

The wheelchair cut a path in the thick loam of prairie grass as Rose and Noble made their way along the bank of the Sabine River during their morning outing.

"You sure you won't let me carry you?" Noble's voice loomed overhead as he pushed the chair toward the spot where he'd spread the blanket and set the picnic basket.

"Not unless pushing is too difficult." The image of being cradled against his chest made Rose sigh. She couldn't help it. He was too close, and seduction seemed like a scent riding upon the morning breeze. "The chair is handling the ground easy enough."

As they drew closer to the swiftly moving river, Rose held up a hand to make him pause. She took in the awesome power of the Sabine as it bubbled over rocks and rushed along the easternmost boundary of San Augustine county. Pines so tall they looked like arrows pointing to the sky paralleled the riverbank, reflecting a deceptive tranquility in the surface. Rose knew the danger of the tributary, for it occasionally pooled into malignant sloughs, mired with mosquitos and the slimy backwash from the great Texas waterway that fed its current—the Red River.

The heat of summer had faded the cattails and reeds along the bank to lighter brown. Buffalo grass maintained its emerald hue thanks to the morning mists that hovered over the land until the midday sun demanded their dissipation. Rose wished she could strip off her slippers and squish the earth beneath her feet, sinking them deeply into the grass. What she wouldn't give to run to the river's edge and jump in as fearlessly as she had alongside Kenzy those many years ago.

The memory of their adventures together made Rose marvel at how indestructible they'd once thought themselves. She stared across the stream, realizing that the belief had always held firm as long as they remained in each other's company. The real danger came when they'd parted.

Movement from the west bank of the river captured Rose's attention. Two racoons scampered down a tree, spinning from one side of the trunk to the next as they chased each other.

Straining to see, Rose noticed one held something in its paws. One of the beastly bandits grabbed the treasure from the other, ran to the bank and dunked the stolen prize in the water. The second racoon raced to the bank, loudly squealing and chattering its discontent. Dunker ignored the scolding, double dipped its treasure again, then began to chew it as easily as melted butter. The protester grabbed a hunk of the feast, took a bite, then ultimately dunked it again. Dunker stood on its hind legs, looking haughty, as if saying, "I told you so."

Rose couldn't help but laugh at their antics. She glanced up at Noble and realized they had captured his attention as well. She smiled. "Do they remind you of anyone we know?"

His large hand gently squeezed her shoulder. "I was just thinking that. Now, what pair are we familiar with where one must show all she knows, and the other eventually decides it's easier just to go along?"

"I'm not sure I agree with you." She didn't want to break the spell of comraderie, squelching the irritation that flared. "We both lead," she insisted. "Just in our own ways."

"I beg to differ. She orders. You ask if someone thinks it's a good idea. There's a difference."

"Both of us mean well." Rose defended Kenzy. Though Kenzy liked to control matters, it was purely out of a wish to see that others didn't repeat a mistake she'd personally already made. "We always have the other person's best interest at heart."

Noble brought the wheelchair to a halt. "I believe that of you. With Kenzy, I'm not so sure. It's like she's driven lately. As if she is afraid of giving a wrong answer or leaving something undone. And on that same line . . ." Noble moved ahead of Rose and turned to gaze at her. "Why do you feel the need to do everything she says? Are you afraid of being different than her?"

"No more than you are of being different than your brother." The words exited so quickly from her mouth, Rose instantly regretted bringing up the comparison.

"What do you mean by that?"

His tone warned she was treading on sacred ground. Ground that didn't seem quite as stable as it had once been. Still, he'd put her on the defensive, when all she'd wanted was to enjoy his company. "After I got to know her, I realized that she wasn't afraid to experience things. She didn't care about society mores. You were there

most of the time. Neither of us could believe her daring.
Not only in the adventures we got into, but with her
challenging her parents' reasoning if it didn't make
sense. She thrived on being unconventional."

"And you wanted that for yourself?"

"I suppose it made her seem quite exciting to me in
the beginning. I was born here, just like you. Until I
suffered this crippling, I'd never gone beyond the Red
River. Even then, there were many places I couldn't
search for a doctor because of how far south the war
had stretched."

"Isn't part of the reason because you're afraid your
own life will dim in comparison?"

Rose stared into the distant horizon. "Kenzy had seen
so many places and done so many things working alongside her parents. She seemed like a ball of yarn to un-
ravel. I never knew what would color her actions at any
given moment. But I admit, that was childish fascina-
tion. Now, I tend to follow her lead because I want to
and, like those racoons there, I'm always pleased to discover there's usually a blessing at the end of it. Does
that mean taking a willing second to her lead makes me
less?"

"Only if your wants and needs wither while hers
thrive. You have a lot to give. You're a born leader
yourself. I can't think of a single person in town who
doesn't admire your strength, not just in dealing with
your affliction, but in every aspect of your life. I could
name countless folks who would like to see you take
your rightful place alongside Kenzy, instead of yielding
to her wishes all the time. Isn't that something to be
excited about . . . to know that others think of you so
highly?"

Rose met his gaze, staring fiercely into its blue depths.
Was he talking about himself? Did he believe in her that
much? "It means the world to me."

"Then why do you always step aside when Kenzy
walks into any room you're in? Why do you defer to
her as someone of more worth than yourself?"

"I don't."

"You do. Oh, you may tell yourself that you're only being a friend to her. But you can't convince me of that, somewhere deep inside you, don't you wish things could be different." He bent down in front of Rose, taking her hands into his. "You are her equal, you know. In fact, you're the most beautiful, kindhearted angel that ever existed on this earth."

Rose usually didn't let her circumstances get the best of her, but the morning's discovery about her feet coupled with his glowing words engulfed her with longing. How she craved to tell him just what he meant to her and how much his words made her dreams seem achievable.

But she couldn't. She had no right to ask him to make a choice between her and Kenzy. She could not guarantee that she wouldn't remain an invalid despite this morning's breakthrough. "I step aside for Kenzy because I want her success in everything she does, as much as I want my own."

She squeezed his hands gently, loving the calloused texture that revealed his worth ethic. The beat of his pulse thrumming against her fingertips sped up, sending a thrill of jubilation through Rose. The desire she'd fought all morning had found a willing partner. It made her decision all the more difficult.

"I'm no angel, Noble." She dared to speak her heart. "I'm flesh and bone like any woman who wants to love and be loved. I simply don't have everything to offer that Kenzy does."

"What can't you do that she can?" His face clouded with displeasure. "You don't give yourself your due. I would like any woman in town, much less Kenzy, to keep up with your schedule and with as much grace."

She pressed a palm against his cheek and smiled. He looked very much like how she imagined a knight of old would appear, donning his shining armor and seizing his sword to defend her honor. But the image of the warrior's stance only served to emphasize her reason for

seeing that Noble married Kenzy. "You forget, I'm confined to this wheelchair. Someday I hope to set it aside.
But in the meantime, the days of your life are passing
as quickly as mine. As much as it would hurt, I'd rather
see you living life to the fullest with someone instead
of harnessing yourself with . . . restrictions."

The stance eased as Noble held out one hand. "Dance
with me, Rose."

Refusing to make further contact, she lowered her
lashes and grabbed each wheel of her chair. Frustration
and the unfairness of it all welled in her eyes, stinging
them. "I c-can't."

"Do you trust me?"

His palm cupped the underside of her chin and lifted
her face. She opened her eyes to find his gaze beseech-
ing her, asking her to allay her fears. "I will until the
day I die."

"Then give me your hand, love. There, that's it. Keep
your eyes open. I want you to see the sky above you,
the color of the world around you. I want you to watch
how well we dance and know that there will never be a
restriction too difficult for us to overcome."

Noble began to whistle a lively jig, pulling her and
the wheelchair forward, then spinning it a half circle.
"That was a partial dosey-do. Now, we're going to allemande left." He grabbed both her hands and began
turning.

"I won't roll sideways." The confinement of the chair
threatened to dampen her enjoyment of his antics.

"So we allemande left, left, and left again."

She giggled at his improvisation.

"There's that's a full spin. Now, let's parley."

Their hands tented between them, bringing Noble's
knees in contact with hers. Rose looked up and felt as
if the world had been reborn, shimmering in shades of
periwinkle blue—the color of love shining from his
eyes.

"Oh, Noble . . . I *can* dance." Hope stirred inside
Rose, offering the promise of a future that could be spent

in the arms of the man she'd loved all her life.

He stepped backward, finishing the parley. "You can do whatever you set your mind to, darling. Together, there's nothing we can't overcome if you're willing to face the battle."

"I'll fight," she vowed, opening like a morning glory to the sun when his lips covered hers. Even if it meant challenging her friendship to Kenzy. Nothing or no one would ever keep her from his arms again.

17

Kenzy wiped her hands on the apron tied around her waist, then opened the front door to get the trio's attention. Supper would be ready by the time they came in and washed up. "Put away your tools, Cordell," she said to the boy bent beside Rem digging in Rose's flower bed. The man seemed bent on spending as much time with the boys as he could. She suspected it was his way of saying good-bye.

"Supper's on the table." A glance around concealed any sight of Worthy. Where had he gone? "Have you seen Little Britches lately?"

Rem rose from his knees, dusting the dirt from his pants. "Last I saw him, he had a ladder and was hammering nankeen over his windows."

"Said he didn't want the monster looking in on him in his all-together." Cordell elbowed Rem. "I told him that it wouldn't matter whether he was naked or wearing buffalo hide. If a monster aimed to eat him, it would eat him, clothes and all."

A chuckle erupted between the two males. Kenzy thought they delighted too much in Worthy's discomfort. "Cordell! I'm surprised at you, and Rem Parker, you're old enough to know better. Wipe that smile off your face and go check on him to see if—"

The smile remained. "No need to, Miss Fret. I already set the ladder up for him, put at least three braces under it so it wouldn't budge and showed him how to make the nankeen fit the windows. I assumed—and I'm sure you'll correct me if I'm wrong—that the boy needed to put up his own protection. That way, he would feel more secure knowing that *he'd* taken steps in assuring his own safety."

She couldn't fault Rem. His reasoning was sound. "Well, one of you go tell him it's time to wash up. I'd like for us to be finished with the washstand by the time Rose returns."

Cordell hastily volunteered, leaving her and Rem staring at each other. His smile deepened as his gaze examined her from head to hem. She challenged him so he wouldn't know how his perusal affected her. "Well, do I pass muster?"

"You should cook more often, Tadpole." He pointed to her chin. "And be careful how close you get to the flour sifter." He laughed when she rubbed her chin until it shone. "The heat of the stove colors your cheeks a shade of rose that's quite fetching and helps you cut a fine figure."

She stared down at herself, realizing that a sheen of moisture dampened her skin and blouse, making the material cling.

"Yes, you definitely should spend more time near the fire."

Kenzy suddenly lost her train of thought as desire rose from deep within to bask in the confection of his words. His flattery felt like warm honey oozing over her skin. "Th-thank you," she managed, unable to think of anything else more profound to say to his impertinence.

Aware that they were alone, Kenzy realized it wasn't the first time she'd wondered what it would be like to spend the day wrapped in his arms instead of having to keep the boys occupied. If only she dared . . .

Rem would find her no submissive lover. She wanted to experience lovemaking as fully as anything else she'd done in her life. And, if she were a betting woman, she'd wager he knew exactly how to conjure the magic of such a union.

Lover? When had she started contemplating such a possibility? *Every time he looks at you,* she reminded herself. *Every time you watch him move, hear the huskiness of his voice when he teases you. Every time he kisses you senseless.*

Needing to change the path of her thoughts, Kenzy shielded her eyes as if to peer into the waning afternoon sun. "Rose will be back any time, I'm sure. I can't imagine a picnic taking all day."

"Maybe she and Noble are enjoying themselves so much, they've simply forgotten the time."

"That's possible." She noticed he'd moved closer, staring at her to see the reaction his words might have upon her. Kenzy folded her arms beneath her breasts. "In fact, I hope that's exactly what they're doing."

"Would you mind too much, Kenzy, if she won his heart?"

At first, Kenzy decided to be flippant. Yet in the end, she couldn't do anything but be honest. Rem seemed to be asking her more and, from the earnestness in his tone, she sensed the importance of her answer to him. "Personally, I believe that happened long ago."

Puzzlement furrowed Rem's brow. "Yet you still allow him to court you?"

"Yes, but not for the reasons you think."

"Then tell me. Help me understand why you would hurt your friend's chance for love."

"You wouldn't understand."

"Try me."

"She'll never tell him how she feels. She thinks I came home to marry him. She's always put my needs before her own."

"Now I'm confused. Because she wants you to fulfill your dream, you feel it necessary to let him woo you?"

"I told you, you wouldn't understand. I'm not sure I do completely."

"Tell me what you think you know, Kenzy." Rem smiled patiently at her. "That's always worked for you in the past."

You enjoyed that too much, she thought. "That if I spend time with Noble, she seems happier. That if I pretend to anticipate his every visit, then she feels justified in arranging the meetings. The truth of it is that I'm not sure I ever cared for him enough to call it love. At least *adult* love. But she seems bent on matchmaking, and I know it stems from believing she isn't good enough to marry Noble."

"Not to approve or disapprove of Rose's reasoning, but the man isn't the saint everyone believes him to be." Rem's jaw tightened noticeably.

"Are any of us?" Kenzy wondered for the countless time what secret the two men shared.

"I've never professed to be one. If I was, I wouldn't do this."

He encircled her in his arms and kissed her so deeply she thought she would melt into the porch's planked flooring. Without shame, her heart followed his lead and she kissed him back with all the pent-up desire his nearness had stirred.

"Kenzy, Kenzy, Kenzy," he whispered as he brushed featherlike kisses along the curve of her lips, the lobe of her ear, nuzzling the soft velvet of her neck. "Burn for me, sweet Kenzy, and we'll blaze a path to heaven that would put the stars to shame."

"Come quick!" Worthy ran around the side of the house, his eyes full of fear. "A man's got Cordell. He's gonna tear his ear off."

Kenzy and Rem instantly broke apart. His longer legs propelled him into a dash that quickly ate up the distance. Kenzy followed as fast as she could. Worthy ran beside her, excitement making him pause to catch his breath.

"A big man . . . bigger than I ever saw. He told Cord . . . better be careful who he pays . . .'tention to. He said if Cord didn't find some other person to imitgra . . .

imi . . . you know . . . *copy*, he might get hurt. Who'd want to hurt Cord?"

A frown punctuated his anger. "I told that old bully he didn't have to worry none. Cordell don't pay a lick of 'tention to me, that's for sure. But I think he musta been talking about somebody else, 'cause he kept twisting Cord's ear and whispered real low, 'You heard what I said, boy.' "

"Is the man still there?" She turned the corner and found Rem inspecting Cordell's left ear. The menace, whoever he was, had fled. A wise decision, considering the tempest storming across Rem's face.

"Don't look like it. My Gypsy Man musta scared him off." The boy raced up to the nine-year-old and shouted, "You got any ear left? Can you hear me?"

Cordell rolled his gaze heavenward as he pushed up his spectacles from the tip of his nose. "I can lose both of them and still hear you. It's a scientific fact that outer ears are just for—"

"Gosh, I was hoping he'd tear it off." Worthy's toe dug his frustration into the dirt. "Then you'd really have something special to show everybody."

"Who did this to him?" Kenzy brushed back the carrot-colored hair at Cordell's temple to see if the bully had bruised him. The ear was redder than the soil beneath their feet.

"Worthy was the only one who seen him." Cordell pointed to the corner of the house. "When I came around there, I didn't see Worthy on the ladder, so I started looking in the bushes. I figured he was doing his usual hiding. You know how he does when he isn't finished playing and you tell me to get him to come in."

The smaller child giggled. "Worked, too, didn't it?"

The older boy punched Worthy in the arm. "I bent over a row of honeysuckle I thought he was dumb enough to wiggle into when the next thing I knew someone grabbed my ear and started twisting it. I didn't get a good look at the man, but I could tell he was big. He kind of huffed and puffed like twisting my ear was the hardest work he'd ever done. And I can sure tell you what he smelled like. His fingers stank like old tobacco."

"What did you see?" Rem stared at Worthy.

The child repeated everything he'd told her.

"Oh, yeah, and Old Mean Eyes saw what was going on and didn't even bother to yell at the man."

"Anna was here?" Wasn't she supposed to be in Nacogdoches with the rest of the townspeople? Kenzy bent and met Worthy's gaze squarely to see if he was telling the truth or embellishing the story to make it sound more exciting.

"Honest, Miz Dixon." Worthy drew an imaginary cross over his small chest, spit in his hands, rubbed them together then offered one to Kenzy. "I seen her plain as day."

"Are you thinking what I'm thinking?"

Rembrandt's question redirected her focus. Kenzy nodded.

"That the man just might have been Anna's companion of late and the one person who didn't need to attend the amnesty meeting." She accepted the child's handshake, realizing that he needed her to believe him this time. "Tell me, Worthy. Did the man have a mustache? Have you seen him here at Rose's house before?"

Worthy nodded. "I sure did. I seen him that day you caught me hiding in the coatrack. I don't know his name but he's big as a buffalo and dresses in fancy duds."

"Marsdale," Rem confirmed.

"I think we all should go inside now." Kenzy glanced around nervously, realizing that the prospect of dealing with Orlan and Anna seemed more troublesome than the edges of night forming over the horizon. "If someone is out to harm Cordell, then he shouldn't be standing here offering a prime target."

"You get the boys inside." Rem's eyes turned to black stone as he stared up the roadway that divided Rose's house from Marsdale's. "I'll go have a talk with the man."

"No," Kenzy demanded, then realized he was in no

mood to be ordered around. "Please don't. He's a powerful man. He could make trouble for you in every facet of your life. Wait till Rose returns and she'll know how to handle this situation. Marsdale won't go up against Rose, for whatever reason. Especially if Noble is at her side."

"I'll not have him harming the boy on my account."

They both knew that the man, whatever his identity, had been warning Cordell away from Rem. Was it a scare tactic or an effort to keep Cordell out of the harm intended for Rem?

"I suspect that's why Cord was warned, so he would keep his distance from you. You're the target, Rem, not Cordell. He'll be safe now."

"I'm not afraid of no bully." Cordell looked like he'd lost his calypso. "I like working with Rem. He doesn't mind letting me try different things. He could yank both my ears off, and I wouldn't quit visiting Rem."

Rem ruffled the boy's hair. "I appreciate that, Cord, but just to be safe, we'll put a little distance between us until I can verify who threatened you."

"The fastest way we can do that," Kenzy reminded, "is to find Rose. Why don't you take a ride out to the river and see if you can spot them. After this incident, and with it getting so late, I'm really worried that something might have happened to them."

"I don't want to leave you in the event he comes back." Rem grabbed the two boys' hands. "Then again, if he saw me leaving Rose's alone, I might lure him away long enough for him to try his real intent. Boys, can you take care of our Kenzy while I'm gone?"

Worthy nodded vigorously. "Sure can, Gypsy Man. Me and Cordell will wrestle up those slingshots he made out of—"

"Hey!" Anger thundered across Cordell's expression. "You weren't supposed to be looking in my trunk. I told you—"

"Boys. That's enough. Mr. Parker doesn't need to worry about the two of you squabbling while he's gone."

Kenzy grinned deliberately. "Rest assured we'll all join
forces should anything befall us during your absence.
The only concern I want you to concentrate on is finding
Rose and Noble."

Rem peered into the growing twilight and wasn't sure if
his eyes were playing tricks on him. He waited a moment, giving them time to adjust to the shadows and the
movement he'd noticed on the horizon. Something was
definitely headed his way.

The outline didn't fit what he thought a buggy's silhouette would. Instead, the silhouette was man-tall and
wider at the bottom, with an occasional flash of blue on
each side of the silhouette.

The only thing to do was meet the shadow head-on.
As Rem rode closer, the shadow defined itself, taking
on substance. It was Noble, rolling Rose's chair along
the rutted pathway.

Rem spurred his horse into a full gallop, the horse's
hooves easily eating up the remaining distance. He
reined to a halt a few feet away, trying to keep stirred
up trail dust from coating his friends' hair and clothing.

"Why are you afoot?" He dismounted and hobbled his
horse's legs, so he could examine Rose closely. "What
happened?"

"When we decided to return, the buggy was nowhere
in sight. There were signs someone took it. But it must
have just been a mischief-maker. Whoever it was didn't
disturb us." Noble looked at Rem in askance. "May I
put her on your horse? It's been quite a long walk, and
I fear she'll be feeling it in her joints for days."

"Of course."

Rem started to lift her, but Noble shook his head. "Let
me."

The carpenter wasn't asking, and Rem understood the
man's need. If this were Kenzy, he'd let no one else see
her home safely.

"I'm glad you came, Rembrandt," Rose sighed as Noble lifted her onto the saddle. The carpenter quickly

mounted behind her. "I've had a wonderful day, but home and hearth sounds very appealing at the moment."

"Kenzy and the boys have supper waiting." He elected not to tell them about what had transpired back at Rose's. The two incidents might be connected, and Rose looked too fragile to deal with anything more at the moment. "You two go on and head back to town. Tell Kenzy I have to pay a call, but I promise I'll bring in the chair as soon as I'm finished."

18

Kenzy stopped pacing the parlor floor, pulled back the curtains to look outside for the hundredth time, and frowned. The first rays of dawn shone over the forest, shedding the countryside of the shadows she had stared at all night. *Where is he? If something's happened to him, I'll . . .*

"You already up?"

Cordell stood in the doorway, his hair a tangle of red-orange curls, both fists rubbing the sleep from his eyes.

"I haven't been to bed." Kenzy stretched her arms to work out the exhaustion settling into her bones. She'd cleaned dishes, scrubbed the floors, got the dough rising to make cinnamon treats later in the day, but none of the tasks took her mind off Rem. Had he gone looking for retribution? What had he found that would keep him away this long? Was he hurt?

"You watching for Rem to come back?" The boy joined her and stared out into the dawn.

She wrapped one arm around Cord's shoulder, trying to keep her tone calm. "Yes. Something must have delayed him, but I'm sure he'll be back before Rose wakes up and needs her chair. He may have gone on home and decided to ride in this morning." *That seemed the most reasonable explanation. The least worrisome.*

"You like him, don't you?" Cordell leaned into her, wrapping his arm around her waist and hugging her. "It's okay. I do, too. Everybody thinks he's mean 'cause he's a gypsy. I do see that makes him smarter than most of us. He sure knows lots of things. Facts that could make someone lots smarter, if he'd just listen. No need to worry about Rem, Miz Kenzy. He can take care of himself."

She smiled down affectionately at the nine-year-old, grateful for the boy's effort to soothe her fears and for his defense of Rem. "You're pretty fond of him, aren't you?"

"He says I'm going to be important someday. That all these answers I want is going to make me an expert, and everybody will want me to stay around because I'll know so much."

Dear little heart. Kenzy hugged him. Cord wanted so much to belong. And Rem instinctively knew just how to appease the boy and make him feel good about himself. For a man whose own past had been full of darkness and disappointment, a light of goodness radiated from Rem to dispel the shade from others' lives.

"You're not planning on leaving us anytime soon, I hope? You do like it here, don't you?" Kenzy teased Cord to make him believe she was worried he hadn't made up his mind to stay. Cordell loved to fulfill people's wishes, if it was within his power. Doing so gave him a sense of being needed and alleviated the fear that he didn't quite belong. But the teasing only served to remind Kenzy of Rem's possible leavetaking. Her heart grew so heavy, it felt as if a cannonball now lodged there.

"I like it here, plenty, Miz Kenzy. Better than any place I've ever been." His voice turned solemn. "I'll stay around long as you think you need me."

"I can always use such a fine helper." She hugged him a little tighter. "And a good hugger comes in handy, too."

When his head bowed slightly to hide embarrassment,

Cord's glasses slipped down to the tip of his nose. "You're the first girl I ever hugged. I-I didn't know if I was doing it right."

Her gaze swept over the cherished face, filling her with affection for the boy. From what little she'd learned of his past, Kenzy suspected that Cord's mother had left him on the streets of St. Louis. She'd bet he had no clue of his father's identity.

Somehow the boy had managed to survive on his own since six, living from one offer of humanity to the next. A promise to give him more than temporary compassion became a vow within her. "You do it just fine, Cord, and I hope you continue to do so long after I've watched you grow up and get married to someone who will want those hugs for herself. Then you can bring your children around to see me and, that way, I'll still have somebody wonderful to hold."

"I ain't ever gonna get married."

He said it with such vehemence, she almost believed him. Kenzy laughed. "Sure you will, sweet. You'll find some nice girl who likes digging things up and who'll make you believe she's smart as a whip. Just the kind of girl it would take to challenge a boy on the road to becoming an expert."

"Now, you're just teasing me." His arm slid away from hers. "There isn't any such girl."

Kenzy's head bobbed. "Oh, yes there is. Just mark my words. One day you're going to find out I'm right, and it won't be because I have any magical insight into things like Rem supposedly does. It's because I believe the good Lord sends someone special to fall in love with each of us. And that special person will have all the qualities we admire."

"I don't know if I'd want someone like that. If she was everything I admired, then she'd be perfect." Cordell frowned.

His statement surprised her. "Is there something wrong with perfect?"

"If she's perfect, then I'd have to be. And I'm not. I

don't have to be a genius to figure that out."

He looked all gangly-legged and spike-haired—a paragon ready to be molded and honed into a prime example of quality.

Kenzy smiled, touched by his humility. "She'll love you because of your goodness, Cord, and because you'll try your hardest to please her. It won't matter whether you fail or succeed . . . only that you tried your best. The only imperfection in anyone is not trying to improve himself."

"I try all the time." He sounded relieved, as if that simple answer relieved the weight of years from his shoulders.

The advice she'd given him added ballast to calm the remorse she'd carried since her parents' deaths. She had attempted to save them, done everything she could think of to find them. She'd given her best effort and lost. The blame she'd cast upon herself had been unfair.

Kenzy stared past the copse of trees lining the outskirts of Rose's clearing, wishing Rem would appear with the wheelchair and she could share with him the revelation she'd just experienced.

But he was nowhere in sight.

"Why don't you wake up Worthy. We'll eat breakfast then ride out to the orphanage. I want to take a look at those holes you found the other day. I'm sure they're nothing but prairie dog tunnels, but if they've built too much of a maze, I'll have to change the floor plan slightly. Can't build on ground that isn't stable. Better to know now about necessary alterations before the walls go up."

Cord stopped halfway up the stairway. "They aren't prairie dog homes. I didn't tell Rem why I was asking, but I described what I found. He said they sounded like fissures to him. You know, holes in the ground that let off steam and kind of smell like sulpher. They definitely stink."

"Why would there be fissures on Rose's land?"

"That's why I didn't tell him where I found them. I

figured you'd want to know before anybody else did,
then you could decide if it was okay for me to tell Rem.
He said it could be that the land is close enough to the
bayou, there might be a current of swamp gas running
real low to the surface."

His interest in Rem did not rate higher than his respect
for her, touching Kenzy with a mother's pride. A deep
affection for the boy had begun since the first day she'd
met him. As the days passed, she knew he would forever
be a child of her heart.

"Thanks for the loyalty, Cord. I appreciate it. But if
that were the case, Noble, Strut or I would have noticed
it by now. With all the sawdust out at the orphanage,
we'd be aware of anything smelling of sulphur."

"I guess you're right. Rem said there are several caverns southwest of here, so there could be one here, too.
That still doesn't explain the stinky smell."

"Stench." Kenzy offered the clarification, knowing
Cord would appreciate the information.

The land around San Augustine had been full of sur-
prises to the earlier settlers, but surely Rem knew his
grandmother's property better than anyone else. "Who
knows, maybe there's a mineral spring no one's found,"
she speculated. Images of Rose reaping the benefits of
a hot spring on the land she'd so generously donated
seemed apt repayment.

"Can I tell him?" Cord's eyes widened with appeal.

"Let me take a look first, then I'll decide. Now, go
tell Worthy to get ready. I'll check with Rose before we
leave for the day and let her know that Rem's not back
yet with her chair. I may have to help her for a few
minutes so she won't be stuck upstairs until he arrives."

"I'll make sure me and Worthy eat while you do that.
Don't worry about us." Cord raced ahead of her. "I'll
even hitch up the wagon."

Grateful for the boy's willingness to help, Kenzy concentrated on the list of things she would need to do
before heading out to the construction site. *Make sure
Rose is up and had breakfast. See if she needs anything*

else for the day. Stop by Orlan Marsdale's to find out if the man is still breathing after Rem's visit.

Kenzy wanted to laugh but, with Rem's continued absence, it might be that she should worry about checking the gypsy's well-being instead. She lightly knocked on Rose's door.

"Come in."

"Don't we sound cheerful this morning?" Kenzy opened the door to discover Rose already up and dressed sitting on the edge of her bed. She moved inside, forgetting to close the door behind her.

Rose patted the coverlet. "I feel better than I have in a long, long time. Sit down and let's talk."

Talk? Kenzy had a thousand other things to do, but she'd never been able to refuse a plea in those silver-blue eyes. She sat next to Rose. "What about?"

"About life and how good it is." Rose hugged herself. "Yesterday was such a wonderful day, I can't wait to see what this one brings."

Kenzy's palm pressed over Rose's forehead. "Are you sure you aren't running some kind of fever from last night? You were out very late."

Swatting away her concern, Rose laughed. "Must I be feverish to be this happy?"

"Noooo." Kenzy's hand settled at her side. "But your eyes are all shiny, and there's a rosiness to your cheeks I haven't seen in a long time. *That* makes me wonder if you're really sick and just don't know it yet."

"Only if I'm heartsick." She grinned at Kenzy.

"You look like you've got a secret to tell." Kenzy's eyes narrowed as she stared intently at her friend. Rose's blush heightened. "It's about Noble, isn't it?"

"Ummmhmm." Rose's strawberry-blonde curls bobbed.

"And . . . ?" Possibilities raced through Kenzy's mind. Rose and Noble had been gone all day. Her concern over making sure the townspeople quit badgering Rem had delayed questions Kenzy wanted to ask Rose last night about how she and Noble spent the day. But there was a lot riding on what transpired between them. A lot that could change, not only their lives, but her own. How should she broach the subject? "What did . . . I mean . . . the two of you didn't—?"

"Of course not!" Rose's fingers splayed against the collar of her blouse. "Not without a pledge of marriage."

A strange sense of disappointment swept through Kenzy, surprising her. She should be glad her friend's passion had not swept her into Noble's arms. Instead, Kenzy wished the opposite. She wanted Rose to experience love to its fullest, not just the promise of it.

The strangest aspect of what Kenzy considered was that if she had spent the day alone with Rem, she wasn't sure she would have returned with her principles so intact. "Of course not," Kenzy echoed Rose, reminding herself that the kind of contemplation she'd been doing could lead nowhere but to trouble. "Then he must have kissed you."

"Like there was no one else on this earth but the two of us." Worship radiated from Rose's face.

"I'm glad, Whit. You two should have been together long ago." She gripped Rose's hands and gently squeezed them. "I've been meaning to tell you for a while now that I'd be thrilled to stand as your bridesmaid. You'll make a lovely bride for him."

"You mean you don't plan to marry Noble? You're not here to win his heart?"

Kenzy stared at the rings they'd traded long ago. "At first, I did. I always thought that he would make a wonderful husband and a loving father to our children. I enjoy visiting with him, and he makes me feel good about myself. But I had to ask myself if I hung on to that hope because it was what I really wanted or I just didn't want to fail again. I can't honestly say I do or don't love Noble the way a woman should for the man she wants to spend the rest of her life with. Things have changed."

My opinion's been changed lately, she admitted without wanting to express more to Rose. Kenzy had never been uncertain how she felt about anything or anyone in her life until now, and that frightened her most of all. But this discussion wasn't about her. She wanted to make sure Rose knew her own mind and heart before she committed herself to Noble. "How do you feel about him?"

A soft glow radiated from Rose's face as she began to describe her feelings for Noble. "When I'm without him, I have trouble breathing. It's as if I'm searching for something I can't find . . . yet I know I'll never truly be happy until I do."

"And when he's near?" Kenzy remembered her own loss of breathing. It occurred every time Rem touched her, as if his breath demanded her own.

"I feel as if I'm more than myself, more than I dreamed possible." A whimsical smile curved Rose's lips. "I don't know how to describe the feeling adequately enough, but perhaps it's that I'm unafraid when I'm with him. Yes, that's it. I believe that nothing can wound me when he's at my side. I feel complete . . . indestructible." Rose paused, her head bowing as the room filled with silence. Finally, she whispered, "But that's a lie. I *am* breakable."

"Stop that, Whit. Stop it now." Fear leaped into Kenzy's heart, giving rise to her true concern for Rose. It wasn't that her friend didn't believe she was whole enough for Noble. It wasn't that Rose would always allow their friendship to take precedence over her own dreams. The true fear stemmed from Rose losing hope in finding a cure. If she lost that belief, then there would be nothing left to help her overcome the other two. "You're going to walk down that church aisle on your own, Rosella Whitaker, if it takes the rest of both our lives and a river full of Rem's potions to see that you do."

"You mean that, don't you?" Rose's chin lifted as she stared at Kenzy. "You promise, Kenz?"

Raising the hand that wore Rose's braided ring, Kenzy waited until Rose understood and pressed her palm against it. Years of growth had demanded a transfer of the rings to smaller fingers, but the vow to always be there for each other had never altered. Yes, she meant it—both the promise made to Rose and the newfound respect for Rem's efforts. "Now and forever . . ." she began, pleased when Rose's voice joined hers to complete the vow. "Always together. Sisters."

Kenzy's hand slipped first, compelled by a need to hug her friend. They cried and carried on like the day they'd made the promise at eight years old.

A throat cleared at the doorway. Kenzy spun halfway around and saw Rem leaning against the door frame, with one boot crossed over the other. The relaxed position hinted that he'd been there long enough to get comfortable and only served to remind Kenzy how well he held his power and raw sexuality in check . . . when it suited him.

"How long have you been standing there?" Kenzy ran through the last few minutes of conversation, trying to determine if she'd said anything that might reveal her growing attraction to him.

"Long enough," came his reply. "Would you like this now?" He turned and grabbed the wheelchair from the hallway.

Rose nodded. "Of course. I've been dressed for a while."

He rolled it toward them. "I hope you haven't waited on me too long."

"Not at all. In fact, Kenzy and I were just talking."

"Forgive me, but I happened to walk up and hear part of what you said. That sweet little pledge was too precious for me to interrupt."

Kenzy bolted to her feet. "Don't you dare poke fun at something you know nothing about."

His hands raised from the wheelchair as if someone had pointed a gun at his back. "Sorry. I didn't know it was such a sore spot for you." Amusement danced in the abyss of his eyes. "I was just thinking that if Rose now intends to make good her plan to become Stockton's bride, that you might want to consider setting *your* sights to something higher than being someone's bridesmaid."

"Are you proposing?" Kenzy's head tossed back haughtily as she met his gaze. His palm pressed against her cheek, the touch so warm it sent ripples of desire coursing through her.

"Eventually."

She didn't care for his certainty. He acted as if she had already agreed! "Excuse me, but you didn't ask, and I'm not at all sure I'll even consider it." Then her heart spoke what her pride refused to ignore. "What do you mean . . . eventually?"

"Just that. There's something I have to tell you that may change how you'll answer."

19

"*I*s it time yet?" Rem untied the kerchief from his neck and wiped the perspiration from his brow. He'd worked silently with Kenzy for most of the afternoon. Noble had taken the day off to stay with Rose, and Rem took his place wanting a moment alone with Kenzy. But Worthy and Cordell were having another of those days where they were all boy and less intellect. Kenzy had her hands full dealing with them so Rem had felt compelled to take up the slack of her to-do list.

Sun beat down upon him so intensely, Rem's shirt clung to him like ticks on new blood. He laid down the maul and stripped himself of the soaked garment. The skin itched beneath the thick band of silver he wore on his left forearm like a cuff, but he didn't remove the jewelry. GranZeph had placed the prize there the last time he'd seen her alive and, there it would remain.

"Time for what?" Kenzy asked.

Without a backward glance, she barely acknowledged his question. Shading her eyes, she seemed intent upon studying the two orphans crawling around in the grass as if they were searching for buried treasure. Probably looking to see if there were any of those fissures Cordell had questioned him about a few days ago. "Are you ready to hear what I have to tell you?" Rem demanded.

"It depends on what you have to say and why you wanted to wait until we were alone to do so."

She faced him as her fingers delved into the hair at her temples. The simple act stretched the white muslin that defined the generous swell of her breasts, igniting his imagination and pushing the exhaustion of a sleepless night behind other needs.

He was surprised by her insolent attitude and thought he deserved a little more courtesy for having replaced Stockton on the spur of the moment. Tired muscles slowly bunched and tightened as anger threatened to spoil his patience with her.

"You're bruised." She took a step closer then seemed to think better of it.

Rem's hand pressed over the yellowish bruise discoloring a lower left rib. Her eyes were keen, considering his swarthy skin tone made it more difficult to see an injury. "It's nothing."

"It's new." Her gaze swept up to his face. "How new?"

"Doesn't matter. It will go away in a few days." He fought the urge to yell what he knew she was thinking. *Yes, I got it sometime during the night, but believe me when I say Marsdale suffered far worse.* But she'd learn that soon enough.

"Put one of your potions on it."

"You know . . . I hadn't thought of that." He chuckled, relieved to find something to lighten the mood.

"Quit mocking me. The injury is nothing to laugh about."

"Then quit bossing me, Kenzy. I've taken care of myself for years now." Wanting to see just how much she cared, he purposely added, "I'm surprised to see you so concerned about it."

"You're hurt and won't tell me why. God knows who in town is out to make sure you leave San Augustine, so we don't know from which direction the danger will come. I'm not supposed to be concerned?"

He was being unfair. "Not really. I have a pretty good

guess who the guilty party is. The one thing I'm uncertain about is the reason why it's so important to run me out of town."

"Guessing isn't good enough. We need to find out for sure. In the meantime, everyone knows you're spending a good deal of time with Rose, so that puts her in danger. The boys, too. Noble can't sit with her every day, and neither can I if we're going to get this orphanage built. You should take the threat against you more seriously, Rem. This isn't something you can simply dismiss and hide behind your silence."

"Hide behind my silence? Isn't that what you're doing?" He didn't want to fight with her, but exhaustion and hot sun played havoc with his better judgment. "First, you demanded that I ride out here with you. No problem. I wanted to see you all safely to the site. Then you tell me if I don't have anything better to do, you'd pay me a day's wage if I could replace Noble. I seldom turn down an honest wage, because I like to have a few coins in my pocket like the next man. Why, if you feel that I'm such a threat to all of you, did you ask me to work with you?"

"I needed an extra set of hands." Her architectual voice of authority set in.

"You could have hired anyone in town."

"I didn't have time."

"You wanted to hear what I had to tell you, and it made things easier if you didn't have to go looking for me at the alcove. That way you could choose when we talked. Well, hours have gone by, Kenzy, and you've deliberately ignored me for most of the day. You've dismissed me as if I were nothing but a day hand. Your cold manner makes me wonder if you even want to know what I have to say."

He took a step toward her but she moved away. "Somebody is trying to run you out." She sighed in exasperation. "I've thought about it all afternoon. If they see you with me, they'll use me against you. You're not safe in my company. I've been trying to find a way to tell you all afternoon that it doesn't matter what you think you have to tell me. I'm not going to put you in any more danger. The boys won't be visiting your camp for a while, and I'll . . . I'll keep my distance. Maybe then whoever is after you—"

"It's too late for that. Anyone with the ability to see will know that I can't stay away from you." He moved closer. "I want you in my sight until this thing is over. To make sure you're protected."

"Stop it. You act like I'm a defenseless damsel in need of an avenging knight." Her chin raised slightly. "I can take care of myself. I always have."

"That's right. McKenzy Dixon knows exactly what to do in any given situation. She doesn't need anyone, does she?"

Her emerald eyes frosted with anger. "I learned to count on myself a long time ago."

Stubbornness was one of her strongest traits, but he planned on cultivating that attitude for himself. Damn her for pitting them against each other. "Fine. I'll get the hell out of your life, but I'm not leaving San Augustine until *I'm* ready."

Her voice lost an ounce of control. "Good. Th-then we agree on something."

The moisture brimming in her eyes twisted at his gut, making him want to shatter the wall her fear for his safety had erected between them. No matter what else she said, her motivation for separating her and the orphans from him was to protect Rem. How could an act so caring become such an obstacle between them? There seemed to be only one solution. "I'll go right now, Tadpole. I'll leave GranZeph's land and find some place new to settle, if you and the boys will go with me."

"No, someone has to stay with Rose. I won't leave her until I'm certain she's no longer alone in that big old house."

"There's Noble to care for her."

"You and I both know that until her legs are better, she'll never accept his proposal. Rose is my responsibility, Rem. She's my dearest friend, and I'm not leaving her as long as I have the power to make even one of her days easier."

He'd never wanted to hold Kenzy as much as he did right now with her standing there, fists on hips, looking like she was facing an army of accusers. "What is it that you've done, Kenzy? This is more than a need to protect a friend. You're acting as if I've told you to put a rope around Rose's neck and hang her."

"You might as well have, if you expect me to leave her now. I won't leave her, Rem. I *can't* leave another person and not know what will happen to them . . . I just can't fail her when she needs me most." She paused, struggling for words. Finally, she met his gaze. "I want you to understand why I can't. But it's hard for me to talk about this. I don't quite know where to begin."

"Begin where you want, Kenzy. I'm no judge and jury. Just an ear that's willing to listen."

She took a deep breath, then exhaled it in a rush of words. "About a year before I returned, I lost my parents to a flood." Her voice was low, the words deliberate as if she was repeating a newspaper report. "I'm sure you heard about it. More people's lives were lost than at any other time in Massachusetts history."

Rem nodded. "I remember some of the reports."

"What they didn't say was that my parents and I had a falling out earlier that afternoon. I'd told them I was returning to San Augustine to live near Rose, and they were adamantly opposed to my going. They'd thought I would waste all the architectural studies I'd done if I returned South where women were expected to marry, have children and further their husband's ambitions."

She motioned to the orphanage. "They wouldn't listen that, North or South, I was facing resistance to my choice of livelihood. That the South, particularly Texas, was a prime opportunity for me. With the transcontinental railroad being built that could bring thousands of people to all corners of the Union, the need for builders of every kind would overcome the prejudices against me.

But they wouldn't listen and believe that the logging being done in this area and the Piney Woods would give me plenty of opportunity for building."

Tears streamed down her face unchecked. "I'd stormed out of the boardinghouse that night with little more than my tools and a few coins to pay for the stage. I told them I was never going back to the boardinghouse again, that I would make my home near Rose." Her hands flew to her face as she sobbed. "I didn't know that I'd never have the chance to change my mind. That they would die that very night."

She sobbed uncontrollably. Rem stepped up beside her and gently urged her to turn. She pressed her face into his chest, her shoulders shaking so hard that he feared they would break away from her neck. When her sobs finally softened to hiccups and the shaking became an occasional tremble, Rem encouraged her to go on. To cleanse herself of all the blame she'd stored against herself. "They came after you, didn't they?"

Her head bobbed beneath his chin.

"They were swept away by the flood?" Compassion gripped him.

Her body tensed as she struggled with the past. "Yes," she hissed. "My father had just called to me to wait as I finished crossing the bridge. I was startled to see him and Mother, glad for one last opportunity to tell them I didn't want to leave angry, but that my mind could not be changed. No matter how long I'd planned to return to San Augustine, I never meant to leave them under angry circumstances."

Rem's hand caressed her back, trying to soothe the hurt she'd carried for so long. "They wanted the same, Tadpole. Otherwise, they would have never tried to find you before you left."

"None of us saw the wall of water roaring down the riverbed until it was too late. I was told later that a cloud had burst upriver, pouring buckets of rain so fast no one could have prepared for the disaster." Her tear-filled eyes met Rem's, desperate for his understanding. "Mother and Father had just started across the bridge when the force hit their buggy and catapulted it into the torrent."

The shock of what she remembered registered in her eyes. "I was so dumbstruck, so disbelieving of what I saw that I didn't see the wave that pelted my side of the bank. The next thing I knew, I was being swept downstream at a speed so agonizing I didn't have time to do anything but fight for something to hold on to. I went under several times. Driftwood, shattered sections of trees, and what must have been shacks that had broken up rode the current with me. They hurdled at me with such force, I feared I would be knocked unconscious and drown. But ironically, I managed to latch on to a large enough piece of debris, I was able to keep afloat. My salvation was my parents' overturned wagon."

Pain flooded her cheeks with new tears. "I shouted for Mother and Father every time a wave lifted me. I pushed with all my might hoping I could shift the wagon toward them. It was too heavy and the current too swift. The force of the water started shredding it into slivers."

Grief etched Kenzy's face. "I heard my mother's screams, Rem, and I couldn't save her. I yelled as hard as I could for them to fight to reach shore. That I would get to the bank and find something to pull them out. But I didn't, Rem. I failed them."

Rem wiped the tears streaming uncontrollably down her cheeks. "You didn't fail, Kenzy. You cannot do the impossible. You tried your best."

"But my best wasn't good enough!" She spun away, angry with herself rather than his words. "That's the whole point. I wasn't strong enough to save their lives." Her hands cupped both ears as she whispered, "I still hear their screams every night in my nightmares."

"The flood happened after dark, didn't it?" The pretense had been stripped away, revealing the truth he'd begun to suspect days ago. Her fear of the night had begun with the loss of her parents. For a long moment he looked at her, not seeing the stubborn woman before

him, but only the frightened young lady who believed
she'd failed someone she loved.

Her need to control now made sense. Her constant list
making simply assured she covered every aspect. Behind
all that bossiness lay an apprehensive heart that wanted
nothing more than to keep someone else from suffering
as she did. He loved her at this moment more than he
ever thought possible.

"Yes, just at sunset. If I had left earlier in the day, I
might have been able to see better, run faster, once I
reached the bank. I could have found something to throw
to them that would have allowed me to pull them ashore.
I wouldn't have kept stumbling over everything in my
path."

"That's why you light lamps wherever you go, isn't
it? You're afraid you won't see something you need to."

"Yes, and because I sense that the shadows feel
cheated that I lived." She shivered and rubbed her hands
up and down her arms. "They lie in wait to claim their
due."

Rem gripped her arms, giving her a gentle shake. "No,
Kenzy. That's nonsense. The shadows are not your enemy. Your inability to forgive yourself for something
you couldn't control is your true foe. You don't need
forgiveness, Tadpole. You did nothing that needs for-
giving. You tried to save them, with every ounce of your
will, but sometimes there are things beyond anyone's
control."

Kenzy looked as if he'd offered a sinner her first taste
of salvation. "I d-did. I spent days going up and down
the river to see if they'd washed ashore. I spent months
checking with survivors I'd heard about in towns all
along the waterway. Finally, I realized there was nothing
more I could do."

A shout from Cordell shattered the haunting misery
that echoed in her tone.

"The boys are in trouble!" Kenzy yelled, the past
she'd revealed adding intensity to the fear that widened
her eyes. "I can't see them!"

"They'll be all right, Kenzy," Rem assured her as they broke into a run. "It won't be anything you can't handle."

Please don't make me a liar, he prayed. *Don't let us be too late.*

20

*B*lood pulsed in Kenzy's ears, streamed like wagon spokes from her abdomen to every muscle in her body, pumping power to the calves of her legs. She ran like a demon chased her, her eyes searching for sign of the boys. "Worthy, Cord! Where are you?"

"Over here, Miz Dixon!" Worthy rose from a prone position in the knee-high grass. "Come look what happened to Cord."

"Is he all right?" she shouted, the encumbrance of her petticoats making running difficult. If she managed to live through this scare, she would see that she wore men's trousers while she worked. To hell with anyone's criticism.

"He's stuck." The seven-year-old giggled. "Like an ol' badger in a prairie dog hole. A four-eyed badger at that."

"Will you shut up and get me out of here. I don't know how long this is going to hold me, and I sure don't know how far I'll drop."

Kenzy almost ran over Cord before she could see him. Her heart felt as if it leaped into her throat. "My heavens, how did you manage that?"

Rem was seconds behind her but unaware of Cord's

position. Kenzy screamed as he barreled past her, certain he would trample the child.

"What in the name of—" Rem managed to hurdle Cord's head as if it were a fence but lost his balance and went down on his knees. "Great moons, what is that devil of a smell?"

"Sulphur," Cordell informed as his glasses slid down his nose, but he was unable to reposition them. His arms were pressed against his side, his body lodged in the ground below them, buried past his elbows. "I think we found a couple of your fissures."

"I think you're mistaken. A fissure is a *small* break in the surface." Rem regained his balance. "You're stuck in something else."

Kenzy grabbed Cord. "We'll get you out, don't you worry. But you need to tell me if I start hurting you." She began to yank.

"Don't, Kenzy." Rem placed a hand over hers to remove it. "Take Worthy and stand back."

"I'll do no such thing. I can—"

Rem shoved her away, then apologized for his abruptness. "We don't have time to argue, and we don't know how stable the ground is beneath our feet. If he fell in what I think he did, this could easily give way . . . especially when he's pulled out. You and Worthy need to stand back." He noticed Worthy was not backing up. "I said both of you, son." His tone brooked no argument from the seven-year-old, who did exactly as instructed. "He may need your help afterward."

"Hurry." Frustration that she could do nothing more soured Kenzy's stomach.

"You trust me now, don't you, Cord?" Rem bent on one knee so the boy didn't have to strain to look up. He pushed Cord's glasses upward.

"Yessir."

"Then I want you to listen to me carefully. Imagine me putting my hands on you, counting to three, then lifting you with one clean motion."

"Okay."

"More importantly, concentrate all the power in your body to your arms. Feel the strength surging there, waiting for you to call upon it whenever you need it. Feel it?"

Kenzy recognized the techniques he had used on Rose recently. Though she'd been skeptical at first, she could do nothing but trust them now.

"Yeah. It doesn't feel like much."

Worthy snickered. Kenzy wanted to pinch his ornery ear off, but refrained from showing her ire.

Rem shot Worthy a frown, but he kept a monotone as he continued instructing Cord. "It will be enough. And you can claim it anytime you need to call upon it. It's there and will remain there for you to demand forth at any moment you choose. But you won't need it yet. It's simply a reserve. For now, your arms are growing soft like after you've taken a hot bath. It's as if you've been asleep and just awakened. Your body is relaxed, supple. Your arms feel light; your skin as soft as a baby's blanket."

Cord's eyes blinked, then blinked again.

"That's the way. Relax, Cord. Let your arms go limp. On the count of three, you're going to slide. One. Two." Rem gripped the child's shoulders and, with a grunt of exertion, yanked.

"Three!" Worthy yelled with Rem.

Cord's body launched into Rem's, hurtling him backward. A deep rumble shook the earth beneath them, making Kenzy rush to them and help them scramble backward to solid ground.

She grabbed Worthy's hand and, to her dismay, realized Rem was shirtless. There was nothing to grab on to but his bare flesh. She linked her hand through the pit of his arm and pulled with all her might. The backward momentum tangled Rem and Cord in her legs. How she managed to remain upright seemed a miracle.

The rumbling stopped. The gangly nine-year-old raised on his palms, staring at Rem and Kenzy. "Y'all okay?"

Kenzy wasn't. The heat of Rem's bare back radiated through the muslin to blister her thoughts.

Rem exhaled a stream of tension before he could answer. He offered a quick apology to Kenzy for nearly knocking her down, smiled at her quick step backward, then grinned at Cord. "Never better. How about you?"

The child stood and brushed the sides of his arms where his shirt had been ripped. "Nothing's broken, but I won't be able to save the shirt."

Kenzy threw her arms around the boy and hugged Cord fiercely. "You nearly scared me into the next lifetime."

"Ow. That hurts!"

"I imagine that would," Rem teased, staring at Kenzy with amusement. "I didn't know you believed in reincarnation."

"This is no time to talk religion. Save it for another day." Kenzy instantly made Cord strip off his shirt so she could see how much injury he'd suffered. "There's going to be some bruises and you'll be sore for a few days, but it looks like you were only scraped hard. After Rem takes a look at you, we better get you home. I sure don't want us working out here when we can't see where we're stepping."

Rising, Rem found it surprising that she had not insisted Jubal be sent for. Was she changing her mind about his herbal treatments?

A quick check of the boy confirmed Kenzy's assessment. "You pretty much summed it up, Kenzy." Rem ruffled the boy's hair. "Cord's going to be really sore tomorrow and the next day. The blood you see is just surface scratches. I'll get some liniment, after we get the boys settled. That will keep the scrapes from getting infected. He's really lucky he didn't get hurt worse."

"You reckon there's a cavern down there, Rem?" Cordell's concern was not for his health but for the new discovery he'd made. "My legs weren't touching ground. They were dangling, and I felt cool air around me. When the ground shook, I heard pebbles and things falling a ways."

"It just might be." Rem eyed the boy carefully. "You sure you can walk back to the team?"

"No problem. I'm just a little shook up."

Kenzy refused to let go of Worthy's hand, despite the child tugging on it to race ahead. "Stop it, Worthy. I want you right here with me in the event there's another one of those holes nearby." They headed toward the construction site, the ground becoming firmer as they proceeded.

"It seems if you'd built a few yards the other direction, you'd have to alter your foundation."

Rem's words echoed her own thoughts. "I was just thinking that very thing. I had hoped that the sulphur the boys told me about was a product of a hot spring or something I could put to use for Rose and the other orphans who will come to live with us. Now, I'm not so sure the place is safe enough for children to live here."

"Don't make any hasty decisions. Give me time to check this out." Rem motioned Cord toward the back of the wagon. "Why don't you two climb in and have your fill of that water jug. Kenzy and I need to talk for a minute or two alone."

"Last one in is a swamp slug," Worthy challenged, Rem's coaching giving him impetus to break away from Kenzy's hold.

Kenzy allowed them time to climb inside, but still made certain they were both securely within her sights. Satisfied, she turned her attention to Rem. "Yes?"

"Over here by the sawhorse. You'll be able to see them but they won't be able to hear us if we keep our voices low."

"What don't you want them to hear?" Kenzy followed his instruction and realized he was right. She could still see the children well.

"Cord probably found an entrance to a huge cavern lying beneath this land. GranZeph told me about the place once, but I never quite believed it existed. After all, she never took me there. But she said she'd hidden the entrance so no one else could find it but her. She grew special herbs there that thrived only in the darkness. Apparently there were two entrances, and she didn't know about the second. The location of the first, I thought had died with her. But I suspect someone else has found it by now."

"Why would you think that?" Kenzy didn't see the logic.

"The smell of sulphur. GranZeph would never grow herbs in a place reeking of sulphur. So that tells me someone has used the cavern for other purposes."

Realization dawned within Kenzy. "I heard the gunpowder made for the Confederacy was made in one of the caverns near Austin. Do you think that could be happening here?"

Rem nodded. "Whatever is going on, it's something that the instigator doesn't want anyone to know about. Now who has bent over backward to run not only me out of town, but you out of building the orphanage?"

"Marsdale." The picture began to form for Kenzy. "He would believe that you might be the only possible person to know about the cavern. And I might discover it by accident. And I would have, if I'd not chosen the exact location I had." She checked on the boys and saw that they were both fine. "But where does that lead us?"

"I don't know all the repercussions yet. But I do know that I need to do some investigating. I plan on making a big production of leaving. Then Marsdale will feel he's run me off and there's one less reason to be careful concerning his business."

"You're leaving?" Kenzy had asked him to earlier, even demanded that he do so, but the prospect of his actual leaving made her realize how much she wished things could be different.

"Not really," he whispered, "but we've got to convince everyone else. Are you ready to start the convincing?"

Her gaze swept the area and found only the children. "Who? The boys?"

"From the mouth of babes. No one will question them. Children don't lie . . ." One of Rem's brows winged upward. "Well, at least Cord won't."

She could see the sense of it, but didn't like fooling the boys. "What must I do?"

"Just say whatever you think you would say after I yell at you. Let it flow naturally."

That ought to be easy. Kenzy couldn't imagine what he had in mind.

"You always got your way in the past by bullying everyone around here, but I'm not giving in no matter how far you stick out that proud chin of yours."

Surprised by the vehemence of his tone, Kenzy took a step backward. Her chin lifted instinctively. Amusement stared back at her as she realized Rem anticipated the reaction. Was she that predictable to him? Then again, wasn't he a fortune-teller by ancestry?

"No, I want you to leave now and don't ever come back." There, that sounded pretty convincing. A glance at the boys told her they'd heard, too. They'd moved over to the edge of the wagon, remaining inside as they had been told.

"Why do you have to be so stubborn?" He grabbed Kenzy and spun her into his embrace. "All I want to do is take care of you, and you act like I've committed some crime I should be horsewhipped for."

She felt his muscles tense beneath her touch. Her breath caught in her throat. It had been too long since he'd kissed her. Too many daydreams about him repeated the act. She knew he felt the jolt of attraction sparking between them.

"I'm not leaving you, Kenzy. You know the feelings between us run too deep. You belong to me, and I don't give a damn what anyone else says. You're mine. No promise you made years ago to Stockton will change that."

There was truth behind his storm of words, almost convincing Kenzy he meant them. "Don't bad talk Noble to get your way. I don't want you or need you!"

The boys were discussing what they heard, she could tell it by how fast Cord shook his head. Kenzy struggled in Rem's arms. "I can manage for myself," she said a little louder.

He moved closer. "You mean too much to me."

For the first time since they began the farce, Kenzy realized she had put herself in further danger by allowing herself this close to Rem. He felt so wonderful beneath her touch, sounded so sincere. Her senses reeled as she realized he had either practiced the words at some point or was speaking from his heart. "There can't be anything between us, Rem. Don't you see?" Her eyes slanted to the direction of the wagon, hoping she could remind him of the purpose for this display. "Rosc's welfare will always be my first concern."

"I can't stop feeling the way I do about you just because you have some misguided notion that she can't make her own life work without you."

She ground her hands into fists at her sides, the accusation touching too close to the truth. She wanted to hurt him in return. "You want me only because I stood up for you in front of the others," she taunted.

"I'll not have you questioning how I feel about you."

Before she could reply, Rem's mouth covered hers with a fire that burned Kenzy to her core. His kiss was savage but it tasted of need and desire. He locked her in his arms, demanding her response. She tried to break the captivation weaving its way through her, but her hands had a will of their own and threaded through the hair at the base of his neck, pulling him closer. The kiss deepened.

He pressed his body against her. As she molded to his demand, his grip tightened and he moaned. Kenzy had never felt so pliant, so needful to be touched. She wanted him like she'd never desired Noble. The realization only served to frustrate her more.

He moved his open palm along her back, spreading over one hip to pull her against his need. Somewhere along the way, the sham had ended, replaced by sincere arousal.

The children are watching, her mind recalled. Her eyes flew open to find Cordell's palms cupped over his eyes, and Worthy standing up higher so he could see more.

With one violent shove, Kenzy broke free of his arms. She tried to calm the hunger he'd awakened within her. "No, I'll not let this happen." She shouted at him as though he were deaf. "You must go."

He grabbed her hand. "Is it because of my past?"

Kenzy saw where he led. He'd been waiting to tell her something all day, and she hadn't wanted to hear it. His patience had apparently run thin. What if what he told her demanded she not accept his proposal? The prospect of that happening had more effect than when she hadn't realized whose arms she belonged in. "You forget, you haven't shared that bit of history with me."

"I'm no traitor, no matter what everyone says."

When Rem let her hand go, Kenzy decided he wanted her to stay and listen because she wanted to, not because of some role they played.

"Right after Gaines Mill, one of the field doctors came to me and said that most of the other medics had been killed and he needed my assistance." Rem's sigh was deep. "I warned him I had no institutional education, but I knew my grandmother's remedies and could find herbs in the field that might be used in place of diminishing supplies."

"You became a doctor?" Kenzy should have guessed, but wondered why she found the prospect so surprising.

"I worked as an assistant to Dr. Daniel Williams."

"This Dr. Williams allowed you to practice your cures on the soldiers?"

"He had studied the writings of St. Hildegard of Bingen's about folk medicine. She was a German mystic of the twelfth century whose writing integrated natural medicine with spiritual and educational enlightenment."

"Which means?"

"That he didn't scoff at my remedies. He understood the value of my knowledge."

"So why haven't you told anyone that you worked the war under his tutelage? From what I've heard, every medic available spent twenty-one out of every twenty-four-hour shift up to their elbows in trying to save lives. There would have been no time for you to have fought battles."

A weariness settled over Rem's face. "Oh I fought plenty of battles, Kenzy. For every life that depended on me—Yank or Reb. Yes, you heard me. I was no respecter of uniform. If the Great Power of this Universe sent a man into my tent, then I did my best to preserve him. If he was wearing blue or gray made me a traitor or disloyal to the South, then I am guilty as charged. Surely you can understand that and not judge me too harshly."

He was asking her to understand, not just letting them all know the truth.

"You spoke up for me in front of the crowd. That was because you believed in the need for us all to heal the wounds of this war. Now, I'm asking you to believe that I'm not guilty of anything but the very act you want us all to take . . . to heal one another."

"I do believe you. I think I always did." So many words raced to mind. Kenzy realized she could speak them, and he might believe they were only meant to carry out the scheme. But it seemed the exact time to tell him the truth and see its effect on him. "I'm afraid the price of loving you might warrant a higher cost than facing the years ahead alone. Loneliness is a prison I've lived in most of my life. The foundation is deep and the walls barred with sorrow, but it's a place where I knew I could retreat and never have to worry about being uprooted."

"I once lived there myself," Rem's voice lowered so only she could hear. "Until you came back into my life."

"End this farce," she demanded loudly, resisting the seduction that whispered for ner to throw caution to the wind and follow where his admission led her. "And leave me in peace."

21

Kenzy paced the floor, staring at the varnished wood as if its shine were a window to view the world. The petticoats beneath her white muslin dress rustled as she walked, adding a rhythm to the pacing. Though she normally enjoyed the hour Rose requested their agendas be set aside to enjoy nurturing more creative pursuits, the parlor walls seemed to be closing in on Kenzy. Worthy wouldn't be still. Cordell had his nose stuck in a book and hadn't said a single word for the last half hour. Rose embroidered and hummed a tune that Kenzy heard Noble whistle yesterday. The day was just too idyllic, making Kenzy want to scream.

If only she were a gyspy like Rem. She would look into one of the crystal decanters on the sideboy or stir up the leaves at the bottom of the near-empty teapot gleaming on the service table in front of her. Perhaps she could trace the patterns in the wooden flooring and the configurations would instantly divine Rem's whereabouts.

That seemed appropriate, considering she made her livelihood as an architect. But all she saw were whirls of dark grain blending with the golden gleam of oak, much like the disquiet spinning through her thoughts. He had been gone for three days without word. Plenty

of time to investigate and let her know *something*! The
fear that some mishap had befallen him grew like a rampant vine in the pit of her stomach.

"You're going to wear the soles out of those shoes.
All the pacing in the world won't bring him back,
Kenzy." Rose set aside her embroidery needle and the
pillowcase she'd been stitching.

To satisfy her friend, Kenzy lowered herself into the
plush cushion of the settee adjacent Rose's chair. Weighing whether to be honest with Rose or protect her from
any danger that knowledge might cause had taken its
toll, too. In the end, she'd elected to protect Rose and
not share her uneasiness about Rem.

She had to stop this worrying and *do* something, or
she would give away his ploy. That is, if Marsdale didn't
already know about it and had taken measures to ensure
Rem didn't return. "You mean Rem?" she evaded her
friend's statement. "I'm glad he left."

Silver-blue eyes leveled on Kenzy. "McKenzy Dixon,
do you think I don't know you better than that? I have
no clue what game the two of you are playing. But you
can't tell me that every time you look out these windows
and every time you've taken a break from work to stroll
down the hill to the graveyard, you haven't been trying
to catch sight of him."

"She don't like Gypsy Man." Worthy tumbled head
over bottom on the braided rug he used for a castle.
"She's just trying to make sure he don't come back."
He got on his knees and swung the rug around a full
circle. "Like I do. This is my castle and I'm the king.
Out there is one of those lake things—"

"It's called a moat," Cord informed without looking
up from his book.

"A moat with alligators big as Mrs. Campbell's barn.
Nobody can reach me, 'cause if they try, the alligators
will gobble 'em up."

Kenzy suspected that pronouncement was to keep him
safe from a quick pinch from Cord. The nine-year-old
rarely lost his temper but, when he did, it was always

because Worthy had pestered him so long he couldn't take any more persecution. Cord usually retaliated with a quick punch. And when Cord read, like he had been since entering the parlor, Worthy tended to get bored and demand the older boy's attention.

It seemed prudent to agree with Worthy's terms. At least, it kept her mind off Rem. "Alligators, huh?" Kenzy glanced at the tips of Worthy's boots. "That means you have to keep your feet and hands on the rug, or the alligators will bite yours off, too."

Worthy's knees instantly tented to his body. Realization that he'd narrowed his own boundaries made his lower lip pout in response. Kenzy waited, knowing it wouldn't take long for his sense of adventure to set in and bring a new challenge. Sure enough, his brown eyes began to sparkle with mischief. One chubby leg slid out. His boot arched as the tip tried to touch the farthest edge of the rug. It was hard to maintain a straight face or criticize his daring. She'd been just like him at that age.

"Rem's kind of like that." Cordell looked up and closed the book, careful to save his place with the ribbon Rose had given him for that purpose. "He isn't a bad sort, but he hides so nobody can hurt him. He's like me in ways. Some people don't like being around me 'cause I'm too quiet most of the time. But I like to study things. That way, I can learn things so they'll like me. Now you, on the other hand, enjoy talking and want people to pay attention to you right now."

Kenzy's brow arched. "Very astute of you."

"Astute. I'll have to remember that word." Cordell looked relieved that she wasn't offended. "It's not that Rem isn't paying attention to you," Cord continued his defense, " 'cause I seen him do it a lot of times when you're not looking. But I think he's afraid you'll find out there's something he knows that'll make you not like him. That's why he really went away."

"I'm already aware of his past. He shared that with me on the day he left." *Was the boy right? Did Rem have other reasons he felt the need to leave? Was telling her he would search for the cavern just an excuse?*

"I don't mean him working for that doctor. I mean something else he doesn't want you to know."

"It's the letter, brainbump." Worthy did a cartwheel, definitely trespassing past the established boundaries. He nearly knocked over the lamp on the reading table next to Rose.

"Worthy, you promised to keep your tumbling on the rug." Rose grabbed the tilting lamp and set it back on its base. "If you can't, you'll have to go upstairs and play in your room."

"The alligators are biting." Worthy managed to regain his balance and started backing away from Rose.

"What letter?" Kenzy gently grabbed the boy around the waist and made him stand still in front of her.

"The one I fou—the one that blew out of Gypsy Man's hat."

"Look at me." Kenzy's tone demanded him to stop squirming. Apprehensive brown eyes peered back at her.

"Yes, ma'am."

She wanted to laugh. He could suspend any mother's wrath with that angelic expression and obedient tone, but she was in no mood to be misled. Pilfering someone else's property was no laughing matter. "Did you take Mr. Parker's hat?"

"I kinda borrowed it." For a second, he looked like a man doomed to hang, then suddenly pointed his finger at Cordell. "But Cord told me if I put things back once I looked at 'em, nobody could call me a stealer. He does it all the time."

Horror etched Cord's face. "I didn't know you took his hat! I thought you was asking me about studying things in general." He shook his head vehemently. "Honest, Miz Kenzy, I didn't know he was asking me for that reason."

"I didn't say you did." Worthy's finger lost its aim as his cherubic cheeks puffed up like a squirrel with a full meal in its mouth. Finally, he blew out a rapid breath of justification. "Strut paid me a whole dollar to get the

letter and copy the words for him. Said he'd been wanting to know what was in it for a long time."

Cordell's frown switched directions. He began to
laugh so hard the freckles over his nose wrinkled into
one blotch. His hawklike beak snorted, sounding like a
goose flying south. The honk doubled him over in a fit
of laughter as he gripped his torso to keep from sliding
out of the reading chair.

"Strut should know better than that." Despite Rose's
recrimination, the edge of her lips quivered ever so
slightly.

"That . . . that ain't why I'm laughing." Cord straightened, wiping tears from his gray eyes. He pointed at the
seven-year-old. "It's because of what he done to Strut."
Cord's shoulders shook all the harder. "Strut doesn't
know it, but Worthy pulled one over on him. Worthy
can't read a lick."

Worthy's cheeks blistered red as he hotly defended
himself, "Well, it was a *whole* dollar."

Kenzy lost all semblance of control. She and Rose
shared a glance and both burst into laughter. All the
tension that had mounted during the past three days
vented itself and left her gratefully free of any other
feeling but amusement at the little con man. "Just how
did you expect," she giggled one last time despite her
best effort to offer him a stern expression, "to honor
your debt to Mr. Cuthbert?"

She watched him think and could just imagine what
whopper of a tale the boy was formulating to convince
her of foregoing any punishment. "I'm waiting," she increased the impatience of her tone. Kenzy had learned
not to give the child too much room to hang himself.

Worthy glanced around the parlor until his attention
focused on the secretary that filled one wall. Rose's ex-
tensive business ledgers and household accounts were
stored in the desk's dark mahogany drawers and shelves.

He rushed over and grabbed the inkwell, pen, and a
piece of the parchment that lay ready for Rose's next

transaction. "Here, I can show you how. Write your name."

"My first or my full name?" Kenzy accepted the material.

"Both."

She scooted over the tea service and laid the instruments on the table in front of her. After lifting the cap off the inkwell, she dipped the feather pen into the ink and wrote her name on the parchment as directed.

"Now let me have it." Worthy took the pen and began to slowly trace the letters of Kenzy's name. He then moved down a few spaces and copied the first letter of her name almost perfectly. "That's what I did."

Interest brought Cordell to the smaller boy's side. "Show me again. If you can do that, Worthy, I can teach you to read."

"Huh-uh. Words on a page don't look the same way they feel when I write 'em. One time one of them do-good church ladies decided I needed to go see a doctor. When he told her that I mixed letters up, she decided maybe I was too much trouble to fix. But I don't mix 'em up if I draw them first."

The pride in Worthy's voice tugged at Kenzy's heart, putting a new promise in the growing list of vows she'd made since returning to San Augustine. She would find that doctor, the *right* doctor, and she would make certain Worthy learned how to read.

"Were you able to copy it all?" Rose asked the question germinating in Kenzy's mind.

Worthy shook his head. "No, just part of it. Gypsy Man came back sooner than I expected. We'd all gone swimming, and him and Cordell wanted to dig around in that old garden of his. Cord started asking him a thousand million questions, so I figured I had plenty of time to copy the letter."

"Did Strut happen to mention what it said?" Rose leaned forward, her eyes staring intently at the child.

Kenzy was as curious as the next person, but Rose seemed too absorbed in the question. What gain would she have in knowing the contents? Even if Brett Stockton had authored it, why did that interest Rose so suddenly? Wouldn't that just prove her right about Noble lying the night he'd helped carry Rem to a sickbed? If true, wouldn't that make her wonder how many other times he'd lied to her?

Rose's faith in him had carried her through the trials and tribulations of the war, the death of her parents and Kenzy's long absence. No matter what else may have happened to her, she'd always been able to count on the rock-solidness of Noble's integrity. Kenzy wanted to warn her friend to proceed carefully. To make certain whether she wanted to push this issue.

"Strut said that people around here were going to be mighty surprised. I asked him what he meant, but he just rubbed his head and said, 'Mighty surprised,' again." Worthy shrugged his shoulders. "I told him I'd make another grab at it for another dollar, but he looked kind of sad and said no. Strange thing, though, he still gave me a second dollar."

A knock sounded on the front door. Kenzy glanced at the clock on the fireplace mantel, then back at Rose. "That must be Noble. He said he'd be coming by to see if you're up to a buggy ride along the river."

Cordell hurried to the door and greeted the carpenter, taking his hat and hanging it on the coatrack standing to one side of the entryway. "Afternoon, Noble."

"Good afternoon to you, Cord." He entered the parlor and smiled at them. "My, but don't you all look like a happy little group."

"Kenzy ain't," Worthy announced. "She's too worried about my Gypsy Man not coming back."

The seven-year-old might be precocious, but he was a perceptive imp as well.

"Didn't you tell him to leave town in the first place? A surprise, I'll warrant, since you told everybody else in town to let him stay. What did you find out about him to make you change your mind?"

Kenzy's anger flared at Noble. She wouldn't share

Rem's past to satisfy Noble's curiosity. "The reason I
told him to leave has nothing to do with what kind of
man he is. And I—" A plan formed in her mind. If she
could find Rem, she could use this discussion with Noble
as a seed to explain Rem's return. "I have too much on
my hands already that keeps me busy. I grew tired of
him implying that the two of you were secretly in love,
and for whatever reasons, refuse to tell me to back off.
I told him I know the both of you far better than he ever
would and that if he couldn't mind his own business
then he could just leave town. I guess he thought he'd
lost the one person on his side, so he took me at my
word."

Puzzlement furrowed Cord's brow. "That's not what
you and he said out at the orphanage. At least, that's not
the part I heard."

"Sometimes you shouldn't listen in on big people's
conversations." Worthy wagged a finger at his friend,
echoing words he'd obviously been told himself.

The need to find Rem became an urgency within
Kenzy. All of this talking about him and the speculation
behind his leavetaking was too much to quiet the
thoughts that he might be laying out somewhere hurt . . .
or worse. Marsdale was ruthless in his business dealings.
She couldn't imagine him being any less if he felt threatened.

"It'll be sunset soon." Kenzy stood and moved to the
window. "I think I'll saddle up and see if he's at the
alcove or his grandmother's cemetery. I've had time to
think and I probably owe him an apology. It's not right
to be angry with him because he had the gumption to
say out loud what I'd been thinking myself for several
weeks now."

Rose gasped. Noble moved to stand beside her.

After spending most of her time creating harmony in
Rose's life, Kenzy wished there was some other way
than confrontation to bring the truth out into the open.
She hadn't known she resented her friend in any manner,
but the resentment rose to give impetus to her demand.

"Quit sacrificing your dreams for my sake, Whit. You know you want to marry Noble. Stop using those legs as an excuse to salvage our friendship. I am a survivor ... remember?"

"But only one of us will see our dream fulfilled," Rose reminded miserably as Noble's hand pressed against her shoulder.

"That was a given the minute we made the pact, and that's where you're wrong now." Kenzy recalled the shrewdness of Rem's grandmother. She allowed the advice to seep into her, felt it warm the shell of her heart until it shattered the loneliness and disillusionment of years. She'd deluded herself into thinking she loved Noble enough to become his bride. By doing so, she may have lost the one man whose love meant more than her commitment to appease Rose. "We've just got to be strong and wise enough to admit our true heart wishes."

Rose half-turned and looked up at Noble, hope shimmering in her eyes. "I'll try my best to be wise."

Noble's gaze swept over her features, his knuckle reaching out to catch the tear that trickled down one of her cheeks. "And I'll be strong for the both of us."

Feeling as if she and the boys were intruding, Kenzy shooed the orphans out of the parlor. "Cord, you and Worthy, play outside for a while. I'll be back before you know it. In the meantime, you two," Kenzy took one last glance at her best friend and beau, "have some talking to do. And when I come back, I want to know what colors and style you want the master bedroom. It will be my wedding present to you."

"Let Noble saddle up the team for you, at least." Rose motioned upstairs. "Cord, will you bring down some extra lamps for her while she changes into riding clothes?"

Kenzy countered her request. "No, I can be halfway there before the team is hitched and the lanterns lit. I'll just wear what I have on and take a horse."

"I ain't never seen you go nowhere without them lanterns." Worthy ran up to her, his arms wrapping around her hips. "Ain't you scared of the dark no more?"

Kenzy ruffled his coffee-colored hair as she bent down to look at him eye-to-eye. "Not anymore, love. I found out there's a darkness deeper than night, and I have the power within me to make it go away."

22

Edges of twilight crept into the horizon, cooling the last hot breath of afternoon sun upon Kenzy's flesh. She was too close to the cemetery to turn back now, and if worse came to worse, she had left a lantern or two at the building site.

Her plan was simple; she'd find Rem and make him take her home. They'd discuss whatever he'd found out about the cavern, decide how they would proceed with the information, then . . . Then what? For the first time in her life, Kenzy was unsure how she wanted to proceed.

"A fine to do, isn't it, horse?" She patted the animal's neck and realized she was speaking to the creature as Rem often did his own mount. She leaned over and whispered, "You don't happen to have any idea where I can find him, do you?"

The animal veered to the left, as if he knew her destination. Spooked, she told herself it was just a coincidence. Something in her body movement had probably triggered his reaction.

As she rode past the orphanage and headed downhill toward the cemetery, a breeze lifted her skirt slightly and rippled the prairie grass like a banner of green fire. The wind winnowing over the blades sounded as if someone

raced alongside Kenzy, whispering. The rustle of leaves
overhead suddenly broke the spell, making her aware
that her already vivid imagination was running amok in
the growing twilight.

"*Kenzy.*" Her name echoed on the wind.

Seeing nothing in front of her, she reined to a halt,
looking to the right and left. Nothing. Kenzy shifted in
the saddle so she could see if someone had followed her.
Still, no one.

"*I need you, Kenzy.*"

The wind rushed past her face, whipped her hair and
billowed the ebony strands of the horse's mane. The
animal snorted, bobbing his head as his muscles tensed
beneath her.

"This was a stupid, stupid thing to do." Kenzy realized how vulnerable she was out in the open. Sitting atop
a horse stopped dead still would make her a prime target
for a would-be robber. Or worse . . . Marsdale. But she
saw no one, and she'd looked hard.

Swallowing back a lump of fear, Kenzy lightly
nudged her mount into a trot. *Keep your calm. You
didn't really hear anything. It's just your imagination.*

Concentrating on the path, Kenzy pretended that it
was broad daylight and she could see for miles. She'd
almost bridged the distance between the cemetery and
orphanage when suddenly the fine hairs on the back of
her neck rose.

Kenzy glanced up. A figure clad in black stood amid
the stark tombstones and crosses. A dark lock of hair
waved against his forehead. The red bandanna knotted
at his neck fluttered in the breeze. His broad shoulders
and ready stance had braced to defend him against a
trespasser. *Rem.*

Relief coursed through Kenzy, warming the chill of
dread that had settled into her bones the past three days.
She reined the horse to a halt. "You're alive."

"Not really. Why are you out here this late?" He
walked up to the horse and stroked the beast's neck.
"And alone?"

She couldn't hear the words he spoke to her mount but experienced a moment of envy. Rem stroked the animal's forelegs, traced the length of its nose, then shifted to where he could meet the horse eye-to-eye. He thanked the beast for the safe journey given Kenzy. The horseflesh beneath her legs eased, but Kenzy's whole body was alert to Rem's every move. "Wh-what do you mean . . . not really?"

"Is anyone really alive if they walk this world alone? Life is to be shared, or where is the joy? Let me help you down."

Rem's hands encompassed her waist just as she swung one leg over to dismount. If Rose saw her, she'd never hear the end of not having ridden sidesaddle. Kenzy tried the ladylike way and found it too confining for a true horsewoman.

Rem urged Kenzy down into the hard wall of his chest. She closed her eyes, taking in the scent of him, the strength of his arms, the mesmerizing essence that could rob her of breath with the slightest touch.

"Are you all right?"

His whisper rustled the top of her hair, sending a hot stream of desire racing from her crown to the nether regions of her desire. *Never better*, she sighed inwardly. "Just dizzy," she answered truthfully. Dizzy with the countless sensations his nearness evoked.

"Then don't move. I'll be your strength."

Kenzy leaned back and knew the moment she became the subject of his intimate perusal. His hand caressed her shoulder, then gently traced the side of her breast to linger at her waist before splaying his fingers over her left hip. Yearning surged within her, so raw it became an ache, so magnificent she thought only the taste of his lips would satisfy its obsession.

"Did you say my name?" She half-turned in his embrace, certain he had murmured it.

"Not just now, but I did a moment or two before you rode up."

That wasn't possible. "But I-I couldn't have heard you that far away."

Rem brushed back a wisp of hair that fluttered against her cheek. "You heard me? I was screaming it silently." His hand pressed over his heart. "From here."

Sincerity shone in the depths of his piercing gaze. How could she have possibly heard what he'd not spoken aloud? Was she to believe they had some sort of secret connection?

"I don't believe in such things." Kenzy anchored the wayward strand of hair behind her ear and stepped away from him. She had to get control of herself or be forever lost to the man and his mesmerizing will. "At least . . . I never used to."

It was then she noticed the changes within the graveyard. White flowers formed a border around the patch of purple flowers where she'd found Rem that day. The crosses had been painted and new letters carved into the wood. A fence of shrubbery that had been transplanted now enclosed the burial grounds. "It's lovely, Rem. Your grandmother would be pleased."

He glanced up at the treetops and smiled. "She is. She's been singing all evening."

Puzzled, Kenzy looked at him askance.

"The wind. My grandmother's name was Zephyr. Her spirit rides the wind."

Gooseflesh pebbled in the wake of Rem's words. She'd thought it all her imagination, but now Kenzy began to wonder if it were possible she'd actually heard the woman's laughter and felt her racing alongside the horse. She *knew* she'd heard *something*. The man could weave a convincing spell.

She needed to concentrate on why she'd come out here. To see him safe. He didn't look hurt in any way. She should ask him about the cavern. "Don't you have other things you should be doing instead of beautifying the graveyard?"

"If you mean finding the cavern, I already have. About a mile and a half up the creek, there's an entrance.

Someone hid it well by stacking a couple of lightning-struck trees over it so if you passed by you would think they fell where they once grew. Lots of thistle had been stacked around the deadwood, too, making it appear as if the wind had blown them up against the trees. I've already shown it to the authorities."

Surprise made her spin around to face him. "I haven't heard any news about it in town."

"A Texas Ranger happened to be in the vicinity. I thought with the possible connection to Marsdale, an impartial authority was called for. He said he'd let me know when he finds out more, but it seems he agrees with you about it being used to make gunpowder. None of GranZeph's herbs survived, I'm afraid."

"Why didn't you come back and tell me any of this? Why did you let me worry all this time about whether something had happened to you?"

"Were you really worried, Kenzy?" He reached out to touch her but she shirked away.

She lifted her chin. "Despite what you may think, a heart does beat inside me. Shouldn't I care whether you're hurt trying to find out why the land I'm building on could cause danger for us all?"

"Is that all it was . . . a sense of obligation?"

"Isn't that what drives us both?" She motioned to the tombstones. "Engrossing ourselves in duty so we can tolerate the crosses we bear?"

"Accountability is not a sin, Kenzy, and making a resting place for men like myself is a worthy task. I like the thought of building a place where men"—he motioned to the patch of purple flowers—"and women who chose not to live by others' standards, but what they personally believed in, can be laid to rest."

He read the question in her eyes. "Yes, that's GranZeph's grave. Euphemia and the others believe she's buried under the live oak, but I returned home four days after she died and reburied her here so no one would disturb her grave."

"But we all thought you'd—"

"She needed a proper burial. We gypsies . . ." Rem dismissed the tombstones with a wave, "have customs that must be followed. Daniel didn't like my leaving, but he understood. He managed to keep my superiors from knowing I had left, long enough to allow me to put my grandmother properly to rest."

"But moving her body must have been—"

"Don't look so taken aback. You have no idea how many gypsy graves are robbed because we bury our gold and silver with us."

Rem walked over to his grandmother's grave and picked a weed that had taken root there. "No man or woman deserves to be forgotten, McKenzy. No matter how a life has been lived, everybody is somebody's hero. Each of us deserve a special place to sleep . . . to be remembered. I promised GranZeph that this would always be a place where any kind of hero could sleep."

The sadness in Rem's voice blended with the need to show him how much *he* had come to mean to her. A man who'd done nothing but tried to help her and Rose and the boys since his return. A man who kept promises to a loved one no matter what the personal danger to himself. A man whose one desire was to belong somewhere. "You've become my hero, Rem."

His hands were suddenly around her waist, pulling her into the shelter of his arms. The dark stubble of three days' growth of whiskers only served to emphasize the brooding intensity of his eyes and the heavy blackness of his brows and hair.

"Be careful what you say, Tadpole. I warn you this is a place meant for only the truest of hearts."

She stared at his mouth and thought he had the most sensual lips she'd ever seen.

He swore an oath. "Don't look at me like that unless you mean it."

Suddenly she was aware of a hundred things about him. The pulse beating frantically at the base of his throat. The unfastened button of his shirt that allowed her to see tiny fine hairs curling downward to who knew where. A sheen of perspiration sparkled at his hairline, sending a tiny bead of sweat streaming past his temple. She watched with envy as the drop left a wet trail beneath his ear and continued on. Kenzy lifted one finger and caught the moisture on the tip of her nail. The pulse beating in Rem's neck quickened, sending a thrill of triumph through Kenzy.

No longer was her future a clouded jumble. Here in the shadows of night, she saw what she clearly wanted. A kiss would never be enough of Rem. Like a child looking in the window at the biggest piece of candy in the store, Kenzy discovered she wanted all of Rem, not just the flavors of his kisses. She tasted anger in his first kiss, relished the challenge that had inspired the second. What she needed and wanted now was to savor the taste of his passion and shed the pretense that had kept her from realizing her love for him.

But she wouldn't give herself without knowing he wanted her equally, that he was willing to fight his own demons for the right to love her. "I never say what I don't mean, Rem. You know that. Now show me why I shouldn't look at you this way."

His control shattered. The moment he took her face in his hands, his palms urging her lips up to his, Kenzy knew there would be no turning back now. She'd known from the moment he left her days ago, that if he returned she would never let him go again.

"Beloved fool," he whispered just before covering her mouth with his own, completely, possessively, hungrily.

He cradled her in his arms, carrying her a few steps to lower her to the ground. The fragrant scent of meadowsweet drifted all around her as she realized he had lain her down near his grandmother's grave. His full length pressed against her, defining his desire and enflaming her own.

In desperation, Kenzy's hands gripped his shirt and tried to pull it over his head. He braced himself on his palms to help the momentum, then raised first one, then the other arm to rid himself of the garment.

He looked as if he wanted to devour her. Kenzy wanted to be closer and wasn't sure how to make that more possible. Her fingers began to unfasten the buttons that closed the bodice of her dress, but they trembled and made the task tormentingly slow.

A masculine growl wrenched the air as Rem's patience shredded. With one yank, he ripped the bodice open and stared at her with no apology. "Let nothing ever come between us again, beloved." He pressed a gentle kiss upon her cheek, the tip of her chin, then lower.

She watched his dark head nuzzle the valley of her breasts and knew when he raised his head, Rem was not asking but demanding her to be his and his alone. She would not deny him. Could not. For to deny him would be a denial of herself and the love she'd waited all her life to experience. This was the depth of feeling Rose could not express the other day, and Kenzy had not understood truly until this very moment. How did one express a happiness no words ever created could define?

"Nothing . . ." she promised, her fingers lacing through the petal-soft thatch of hair that adorned Rem's chest. She thrilled at the quiver of desire that followed in their wake. "Nothing will ever come between us."

His lips sealed the promise as his chest pressed provocatively against her. Passion lit like a thousand suns within her. This kiss was like no other, shaking Kenzy to the core of her existence, changing how she would forever speak of love, demanding eternal devotion from her soul. In return, she knew he pledged a love that would never know boundaries, love that accepted all that she was and all she dreamed of being, love that would stand beside her no matter how many times she failed.

The rumble of approaching hoof beats penetrated her brain. Kenzy blinked away the haze of enchantment.

Rem cursed, lifting the pressure of his body from hers. "Rider coming."

Kenzy was too consumed with the feel of him to think clearly. "I c-can't just—"

"You can't be seen like this either." Rem grabbed his shirt and hurriedly redressed. He shoved her behind him, "Stand behind me as if you moved there for protection. I'll make sure whoever it is won't see your state of dress."

She gathered the torn material of her bodice and held it closely together, watching as Rem braced himself for the rider's approach.

Thank goodness for the shadows. If the man had come any earlier, he would have to be blind not to notice her slightly swollen lips and the abrasion Rem's stubble had inflicted on her cheeks.

If she were really in danger, she would never hide behind Rem's back. But prudence warned she should obey Rem's instructions and give her body time to calm the pulse beat of desire still drumming in every vein.

"Don't bring that horse past the outer shrubs," Rem warned. "This is holy ground."

"All right. I thought you'd be here, Parker." The rider halted a few yards away. "Found your horse cropping grass back there, Kenzy."

Kenzy recognized Noble's voice, no matter that she hadn't yet braved looking at him. "He likes to nibble on that patch of wintergreen on top of the hill."

"Rose asked me to come get you. She doesn't want you out here in the dark."

"Tell her that I'm fine." Kenzy looked over Rem's shoulder. "Tell her I found Rem, and he's . . . he's showing me a few changes he's made to his property."

"It's getting a little dark for that, isn't it?" The saddle creaked as Noble shifted. "No, I don't think it's a good idea, and you know she won't rest if I go back without you. You don't want to upset Rose, do you?"

Kenzy pressed her palms against Rem's back. She couldn't worry Rose. She didn't want to leave Rem. "I have to go," she sighed. Every muscle in his body stiffened.

"Go then."

"I'll come back tomorrow," she promised, knowing he didn't believe her.

"The wall-raising is tomorrow," Noble reminded, gently pulling on the reins of her horse and moving it closer to his own. "Better saddle up now. Everyone is expecting you to be bright-eyed and ready to tell us all what to do."

"I promised to be there." Kenzy's fingers traced the broad expanse of Rem's shirt, but he stepped away. She grabbed her ripped bodice in order to maintain her modesty. "I'm supposed to be in charge of—"

Rem shrugged. "No need to explain your choice. There's obviously something more compelling to do than traipsing along with me in the family plot."

Traipsing? Was that what she was doing? "I'll hurry as fast as I can. I'll not linger at any of the festivities afterward. Rose and Noble can fill in for me as host."

"That's unfair, Parker. She planned the wall-raising weeks ago."

"Unfair, Stockton? You dare accuse *me* of being unfair?" Rem marched up to him and jerked the reins of Kenzy's horse from his hands and held them out to her. "How about you?" he challenged.

Kenzy dashed to mount the animal, realizing that Rem was deliberately distracting Noble so she could have both hands free for a moment.

Rem glared at Noble. "When do you intend to tell the others about that letter?"

Rem's voice echoed over the tombs so adamantly, Kenzy thought he might wake the dead.

"Or, better yet, do you ever intend to tell them?"

"Shut up, man." Noble reined his horse halfway. "If you're coming with me, Kenzy, I'm leaving now." True to his word, he tapped the horse with his heels and took off toward home.

Kenzy had no choice but to go with him. The gathering tomorrow might prove more necessary than she first believed. With that many friends and townspeople in attendance, the wall-raising party just might provide the prime opportunity for Noble to read the letter. At least, many of his friends would be there to shore up his courage. "I have some things I have to take care of, Rem. Some obligations I need to see to their end. Then I promise . . . I'll be back after I finish them."

"Another promise so soon, Kenzy? Why should I believe this one any more than I did the one you made a moment ago?"

His gaze swept over her, deliberately halting at the material clutched tightly in her hand. She could feel the intensity of his thoughts, was certain she heard him speak, but his lips remained closed.

"*Let nothing come between us again, beloved.*"

His words echoed through her brain as she realized the promise he spoke of.

He swatted her horse's flank, making the animal burst into a gallop beneath her. Kenzy raced like the wind toward Rose's house, no longer able to call it home. For home now meant being wherever Rem dwelled.

Persuading Noble to read the letter tomorrow was a necessary goal, but convincing Rem she would keep both promises became her driving purpose.

23

The ride to Rose's was the most difficult Kenzy had ever made. She refused to catch up with Noble completely, so she would not have to ride side-by-side. Instead, she lingered a horse-length behind, grateful for the shadows that did not permit a closer look at her appearance.

Noble was not so easily fooled and lived up to his name. He halted long enough to remove his frock coat and held it out beside him. "The night's turned cool."

She lightly nudged her mount and moved just close enough to accept the offering. "Thank you."

Donning the garment, Kenzy appreciated the heat of his body that still lingered in its folds. She fastened the coat's single line of buttons as fast as possible, hoping he would continue to contain his curiosity.

"There." She knew he was waiting for some word that she had finished. "Nice and snug. I didn't realize how cold it was getting. I hope it's sunny for tomorrow."

"You might bring a shawl with you next time. That way you'll be prepared . . . when you find yourself in need."

He knew. She was sure of it. He knew and criticized her actions in the only way he would—without rancor.

Kenzy spurred her pony into an easy trot. She rode

beside him now, wondering if she should broach the
subject of what had transpired between him and Rose
while she was gone. Hearing Rose's account was a must,
but listening to his account was equally important.

"Do you know what you're doing, Kenzy?"

Noble's question was almost inaudible. She wasn't
sure she had truly heard it. She pressed a hand to her
ear. After the business with Rem earlier, she wondered
if she didn't need to have Jubal examine her. "Did you
say something?"

The bobbing of the horses's heads as they trotted
seemed to answer for him.

"I asked if you know what you're doing by offering
a man like Rem Parker your affections."

Anger welled inside her so powerful that her thighs
tightened around the horse and she sat straighter in the
saddle. "What do you mean 'like Rem Parker?' He's a
fine man with a caring heart."

"Giving your affections to *any* man would be seen as
scandal." Noble grabbed her reins. "Hold up. I want to
have my say before we get back to Rose's."

She stopped out of respect for their longtime friendship. "I'm in love with him. That's all that matters. Be
careful what you say."

"That's fine for now, but what about when you walk
down a street and they call you Gypsy Woman, or call
any child you have a halfbreed? What about the first
time you're hired to build something and the contract is
retracted because you're married to a gypsy? What about
the first time he sees frustration or even resentment in
your eyes for being labeled such?"

Kenzy didn't recognize this aspect of Noble. The boy
she'd befriended championed those of less position than
himself. Was his bias only for Rem or for all gypsies?
"And you're not prejudiced?"

"What I'm saying has nothing to do with how I feel.
I'm simply warning you about the intolerance you're
going to receive from others. If you truly love him, then
that love has to be strong enough to overcome all those

trials. If you have any doubts, any second thoughts that he's the right man for you, then now is the time to end this before you both get hurt."

Anger fled as the reality of his words sank in. Noble had never been anything but a friend to her. He said these things to make sure she knew her own mind. It was a friend's concern she heard now. "I love him, Noble. With everything that I am. There are no doubts, no second thoughts, no obstacle too large to endure . . . if it means I get to spend eternity in Rem's arms."

A heavy sigh escaped him. "Good. That makes what I have to tell you a lot easier."

"You persuaded Rose to marry you." Moonlight bathed his face, revealing his surprise that she had guessed. Kenzy laughed. "Even a too-busy-for-her-own-good architect can see the love both of you tried so desperately to hide. It's so sweet to watch you, it's almost sickening sometimes. I expect to find your first child to be born grinning from ear to ear. A grin bracketed by those dimples of yours . . . and, knowing Rose, it'll be wearing a halo, too."

Noble's dimples dented as his laughter joined with hers.

The night seemed tranquil now, the stars a little brighter. No longer was there the unspoken challenge of which of them would win Noble's heart. No longer would she have to second-guess why Noble felt more like a brother to her than a possible lover. Now, there would be an abiding friendship and joy that each had found her true love.

"I'm curious." Kenzy's tone sobered. "How did you manage to convince Rose to accept your proposal?"

"Well, after you *demanded* that we come to some sort of decision, that helped. I'd tried to be patient and understand her fear that she would never leave the wheelchair behind. I went along with every attempt she made to matchmake you and me, because that was an easy concession. Personally, I've always enjoyed your company. But deep down I think we both knew that neither

you nor I loved each other enough to become man and
wife."

"And?" Kenzy rolled her hand as if it were a wagon
wheel, impatient to hear the rest.

"And, I might add, she was slightly more patient than
you, Freckle Face. Tolerance can be a powerful persuasion."

Though she laughed, Kenzy's hand continued its encouragement. "Too late to change me now. You had
your chance."

Noble's face beamed, his voice filling with anticipation. "I told her she was the one who has to deal with
whatever she deems are her physical flaws. In my eyes
she's whole. I fell in love with the beauty of her soul,
not the body that will grow old one day like all the rest
of ours. I want love that will last beyond the ravages of
time."

"You're a fine man, Noble. Rose is lucky to have
you." Kenzy couldn't wait to get home and congratulate
Rose as well. They could start planning the pattern of
her wedding gown and trousseau.

"I have my faults."

He'd opened the door to discussion, so Kenzy took it.
Tomorrow would bring the perfect opportunity to tell
everyone about the letter and to set right whatever was
wrong between him and Rem. "I listened to your piece
of advice a few minutes ago, and it was sound. But as
I told you, I know *my* choice is the right one. I heard
about the letter Rem brought to you . . ." She waved
away his objection. "No, he didn't tell me its contents.
For some reason, he's set on letting *you* tell everyone
what it says. I don't even know his reasoning behind
that."

Noble's gaze averted to the horizon. "First, because
Brett asked him to. Later, because he knew if the truth
were told, the Stockton name will be tarnished."

"Why would he concern himself with that? There's
never been anything more than a casual acquaintance
between you and Rem, has there? I don't remember him

being overly friendly with Brett in his youth, but I suppose war could have changed that. Still, it doesn't make sense why he would sacrifice his own good name to salvage yours."

"It does if you're a man protecting a woman who believed she would marry into that family."

Everything fell into place—Rem's secretiveness about the letter, his refusal to accept Noble's goading to speak up so he wouldn't have to. Most of all, she realized how much Rem had sacrificed for the sake of maintaining the respect for the Stockton name.

Rem was not a destroyer; he was a healer. He was trying to help Rose recover from strife. If . . . *when* . . . Rose married Noble, she would become a Stockton. Rem was too much a gentleman to increase Rose's burden.

He could have done it for you, her heart whispered. *He believed you wanted to marry Noble.* The moment she speculated on the possibility, Kenzy knew it to be fact. Rem had given up rescuing his reputation for *her* future happiness.

A long heart-to-heart talk with Rose was in order. If Rem's motives had been to protect Kenzy, she now found herself rowing the same canoe. The contents of the letter would help Rem or there wouldn't be such a controversy over its reading. Now that Rose had agreed to marry into the Stockton family, the same topic might bring trouble for Rose. How could she choose between her best friend and Rem?

"I hope Rose is in the mood for talking." Kenzy's thoughts raced ahead. "We've got a lot to discuss before tomorrow."

"I told her we would celebrate our engagement when we announced it to the community. She looked too tired to do anything much this evening."

The selfishness of her thoughts made Kenzy apologize. "I'm so caught up in making sure everything's ready for the gathering that I forgot the two of you had gotten yourselves engaged tonight. Congratulations, Noble."

"Thanks, Freckle Face. I hope you still plan on being her maid of honor."

"I wish Rose and the others would get here." Kenzy shielded her eyes against the morning sun. The steady sound of hammers echoed over the building site, beating a rampant tom-tom at her temples.

There had been no opportunity to talk to Rose last night. When Kenzy arrived back at the house, one look at her friend's ashen face stopped any discussion other than insisting Rose go to bed. What if she didn't feel well enough to ride out to the wall-raising? The decision to encourage Noble to read the letter would become solely Kenzy's, and that was a troublesome prospect.

"It's going on ten o'clock, and my Strut's been working since dawn. That little darling could use some vittles. He's worn himself to a nub." Euphemia's difficulty with hearing urged her to be even louder when being drowned out by too much noise. "I'll go ahead and set the kettles to boiling and the tables spread. We're going to have some mighty hungry wall-raisers in about an hour or two. Those gals better come on with the grub."

Kenzy stared at the line of stakes she'd hammered into the ground near the hole in the earth. A yellow ribbon linked the stakes to form a protective boundary she'd told everyone about the first thing this morning. She hadn't mentioned the cave, just about the sulphuric fissures weakening the ground.

"Make sure you don't set them up anywhere near that ribbon," she reminded Euphemia. "The odor coming up from the ground is fairly strong, and I imagine it's quite flammable."

"I heard tell there's a bandit's cave under there. Somebody's using it to make gunpowder and shipping it down to Mexico and Brazil. Said they're selling it to the Rebs who fled there after the Yanks won. The Loyal Order of the White Camillias, they call them. I always think of 'em as the cowards with the white hoods myself. But whoever's doing it is gonna make a fortune. Those Cam-

illia fellas are paying in pure gold, they say. Gold stolen
from Jeff Davis's vault itself."

Did Rem know all this? Kenzy looked at the store
owner in astonishment. "Where did you learn that information?"

Her chubby cheeks beamed and her ample bosom
swelled, stretching her shirtwaist to its seams. "Where
else?" She nodded toward the bald man standing at one
of the two chimneys and bragging to an interested
townswoman about his handiwork. "Ol' Gossip Garter,
there, spoke to some Texas Ranger who's been hanging
around the past few days."

Strut was good if he could get a Ranger to talk. Kenzy
said as much.

"Pshaw!" Euphemia's nose wrinkled, forming parallel
creases down her cheeks. "Not so hard when he used to
be a Ranger himself. Just gotta talk the right lingo."

Kenzy couldn't imagine Strut as one of the breed of
Texas peacekeepers whose rugged justice kept the laws
of the Republic obeyed.

"It takes all kinds, you know."

Kenzy laughed at Euphemia's questionable compliment, grateful for the reprieve from her worry about
Rose. But her laughter didn't last long. All of a sudden,
a dozen other people said they had details that needed
her attention. "Keep a lookout, will you, Miss Euphemia? I'd like to talk with Rose before you get her
too busy."

"Go on about your business, Sugar. I'll get the cook
fires stirred up."

An hour later, a shrill whistle jerked Kenzy's head
around.

"Food's coming!" Worthy pointed to the band of buggies moving up the path toward the orphanage. "Boy,
am I getting hungry." He rose from bended knees behind
a pile of two-by-fours someone had stacked in what
would become the orphanage's business office.

"Worthy, you need to stay out of the workers' way
or somebody's going to board you up and not even know

you're there." Exasperated at having given him the same warning several times already, Kenzy forced her temper not to flare. After all, it wasn't his fault she couldn't go to Rem, and that was the true frustration here.

"But there could be a million zillion hiding places, if you want them." Worthy's eyes rounded like chocolate-filled saucers. "Wouldn't it be fun to build a passageway nobody but us knew about? Then we could sneak up on . . . I mean then you could look in on us children and make sure we was behaving like you asked us. We wouldn't even know you's there."

"You forgot one thing, Brainrot." Cordell pulled the boy out from behind the stack.

"Oww! Let me go." When Cord released him, Worthy glared back. "I didn't forget nothing."

"Yes, you did." Cord laced his thumbs under his suspenders and looked to see how much of an audience he had. "You forgot everybody here knows the floor plans now. Not much of a secret if everybody in the territory knows about it."

"You just wait and see." Worthy's jaw set, his chin lifting. "I'm gonna build me a house someday and it's gonna have a whole buncha secret places. Maybe I'll have one in this one, too."

"That can be decided another day." Kenzy bent and looked at Worthy eye-to-eye. "But for today, I want you to stay out of the men's way. Promise?"

"I'll try."

"And Cord?" She waited until he straightened his glasses. "Will you keep watch over Worthy for me?"

"I ain't no baby." Worthy folded his arms beneath his chest and pouted. "I don't need no watchdog."

"I don't think you do either. I just thought he might help you *try* a little harder." She attempted not to smile. "Unless, of course, you want to give me that promise I asked for."

The child shook his head. "Better not. I might just have to tell a fib. I'll just try to promise . . . okay?"

He started to spit in his hand and offer a pledge, but she told him his word would do.

"Don't worry," Cord assured her. "I'll make sure he stays in sight."

Cord took his responsibilities seriously. Kenzy had no doubt assigning him the task of patroling the smaller boy's antics the rest of the afternoon was a wise decision. She should have been concentrating on the construction, but she needed to talk to Rose first.

Waiting until Noble lifted Rose down from the driver's box and sat her in the wheelchair, Kenzy wiggled her finger at Rose. "Can I see you for a minute?"

"I'm sorry I'm late. Noble and I—we ..." A blush stained Rose's cheeks. "Were delayed."

Kenzy looked from one friend to the other, noticing the shared glance between them, the slightly disheveled state of Rose's curls, the vest Noble had put on inside out.

"Oh." No doubt their engagement would be a short one. "I understand. But now that I have you here, I need to speak to you alone, if you don't mind."

"I believe that was actually a request I heard exiting your lips." Noble laughed. "This is a rare day."

"Don't get insolent with me, Mr. Head Carpenter. Remember I was the one who let you arrive late," she teased, tapping the incriminating vest. "I'm not the one who needs to change around here."

Noble's eyes focused on her meaning, then glanced up to find her smiling back at him. His shoulders shrugged. "Oh well. I've never been much for subtlety."

"Stockton, quit flirting with that petticoat and get your broad back over here!" One of the men took off his slouch hat and waved it at Noble. "We're about to divide up in teams."

"Good, he'll be busy for a few minutes." Kenzy's smile disappeared as Noble walked away. "We've got some serious business to discuss, Rose. Let's go over there so we can have some privacy. Would you like me

to roll the chair for you?" Kenzy always asked her friend
so as not to offend her. Often, lately, Rose wanted to
commandeer it herself.

"I will." After she followed Kenzy a good ways from
the others, Rose halted. "That ought to be far enough.
Now what's so secretive that no one else can hear?"

"That's not it at all. I think everyone needs to hear
what I'm going to tell you. But I want to know how you
feel about it first." Kenzy quickly relayed all the facts
she knew so far about the letter Rem brought. "According to Worthy, Rem still has possession of the letter.
Even if Noble agrees to read it, we'll have to get it back
from Rem somehow. What do you think, Rose? My natural instinct says to force the issue. My love for Rem
and my concern for you says to leave it up to the men."

"Trust your heart, Kenzy, and do what it compels you
to do. Whatever the outcome, I'll stand by Noble." Rose
shared her own concern. "I'm just not sure he'll be willing to forgive me if the letter says what I think it does."

Kenzy didn't understand. "What could it possibly say
to make you think that?"

Rose's lower lip quivered. "Before Brett left for the
war, I told him that whatever choices he had to make,
to always choose life." Anguish filled her tone. "I
wanted him to take care and come back safe. You know
how much he meant to Noble. He practically worshipped
his older brother. When the news of Brett's death came,
it nearly destroyed Noble inside."

Squeezing Rose's shoulder gently in compassion,
Kenzy tried to understand her friend's concern. "So you
think Noble will be angry because you told his brother
to choose life? That doesn't seem any reason for him to
be angry."

"Doesn't it? What if the letter reveals what I told him
had caused his death? What if in encouraging him to
choose life, it had cost his instead? Would Noble ever
be able to forget that, much less forgive me?"

"No one can blame you for offering such sound advice." Kenzy thought back to all her hastily given guid-

ance, wondering if she had ever caused problems for others by giving it. *No . . . I always knew what I was doing at the time.*

Realizing what she'd just thought, Kenzy bit back a smile. She might be in love and not afraid of the dark anymore. But one thing remained the same—it would take her a bit longer to quit telling people how to do things.

"It looks like the teams are about to start." Rose pointed to Noble. "I told him I would be there to watch him win."

"I need to ask a favor of you, Whit." Kenzy knew Rose's attention now focused on Noble. She had to hurry or she'd never get this said.

"Name it."

"Once the contest is well under way, I'll like to go to Rem. You don't mind seeing that everyone eats and is kept busy, do you? Euphemia has a host of activities planned. I'm going to do my best to see if Rem will return with me, but if he won't . . . then I'm spending some time with him. I hurt him last night by leaving the way I did."

"Take your time, Kenzy. Noble and I can handle things here. And when you get back, I'll show you the surprise I've been keeping from you."

"A surprise?"

Rose nodded, anticipation shining in her eyes. "A wonderful surprise that I waited for just this day to share with you." She winked. "But I'll understand if you don't come back very soon. Just remember that everyone's going to take a hayride and have a sing-along by the creek later this evening. I hope the two of you will join us by then. After all, the architect should be here to celebrate the framework once it's standing."

"I'll try to get Rem to give me the letter." She didn't want Rose to think she was deserting her for selfish reasons.

"In the meantime, I'll discuss what we've talked about

with Noble. Personally, I'd rather get everything out in the open and get on with our lives."

"That's exactly what I intend to do right now." Kenzy waved at Rose as she headed for the cemetery. "Get on with my life. Wish me luck."

Rose raised the hand adorned with the braided ring. "Now and forever . . ."

24

She found him at the creek, swimming. Kenzy moved silently, slowly unfastening a button with each step closer to the bank. She shrugged out of her blouse and let it glide to the ground. Her skirt came next, left in a puddle around her ankles. As she stepped out of it, with her heart pounding so wildly she could scarcely breathe, she feared he might not welcome her into his private world. That he might refuse her.

She wanted Rem Parker so desperately that nothing would keep her from showing him that she trusted him implicitly and loved him with every beat of her heart and belief in her soul. Her heart sang as he turned and those wondrous black eyes stared at her intensely. Her toes curled when his lips twitched, sending gooseflesh racing across the surface of her skin.

It was then she noticed his trousers and shirt flung over a low hanging branch. Just the thought of his nakedness beneath the surface flooded her with anticipation. Her body responded by igniting passion in its every pulse point.

Kenzy's knees felt like they had become the water she was about to enter, forcing her to reach out and grab the branch where his clothes lay.

"Rembrandt," she whispered, her gaze drifting over

the broad expanse of his shoulders to the thick black
hair that framed his face.

"You've come."

The husky groan that exited after his statement went
through her like lightning, fusing every nerve ending
throughout her body. Desire—bold, overwhelming, un-
restrained—compelled Kenzy to shed her shoes and
reach for the ribbon that secured her pantaloons.

"Don't. Let me."

Slowly, he moved toward her, inch by aching inch.
Beads of water slid down the washboard plane of his
abdomen. Kenzy's throat dried. Her lips felt hot and in
need of moistening. Her tongue darted out, just as the
water level delved below his navel.

She stared at him, afraid to blink, afraid that if she
shut her eyes even for a second, he would disappear like
a mist conjured to bind her in its spell. She couldn't
breathe.

Her gaze riveted on the swarthy skin that veed wondrously from muscular shoulders to slim hips and the
trail of dark hair that plunged even lower. "You're beautiful," she whispered in awe.

"Come here, Kenzy."

The invitation in his voice went through her senses
like ripples on the creek, touching the banked passion
smouldering within her. She swayed under the impact
of the deep timbre.

Shimmering light filtered through the arbor of fushia,
blue, purple and white flowers that rose behind the alcove to shield the delicate herbs from the western sun.
The golden aura illuminated Rem, reflecting the healthy
strength of his shoulders and glistened the moisture
beading over the dark matte of his skin. The effect was
breathtakingly seductive, robbing her of anything but the
desire to touch him and be touched.

Gone were the brooding shadows of their lives. Gone
was the need to control lest she fail. All that remained
was her necessity to tell him how she felt about him and
what she intended to do about it. Yet she couldn't speak.

"Stockton is no longer the man you intend to marry."

His directness unnerved her. It was as if he could read her thoughts. Then again . . . perhaps he had. Battling for her dream, she waded into the water. "He and Rose plan to announce their engagement in a few hours."

The distant sound of countless hammers carried on the wind. "And so that freed you to come to me now?"

He circled her. She felt him staring at her shoulder blades, trembled at his touch upon one of the straps of her chemise as he lowered it. Kenzy shook her head. "I'd already decided last night before I ever rode out to the cemetery to find you." She shut her eyes and let the wave of passion soak her senses.

"Then you don't love him."

"I never did." Kenzy shook her head, sending her auburn hair shimmying to her waist. "I can't."

"Tell me why I should believe you, Kenzy."

"Because I love you." Her confession came without a moment's hesitation. "I love *you*," Kenzy repeated, needing him to hear the truth it had taken her so long to understand.

His fingers threaded through her hair, coiling the reddish-brown mass. He kissed her then with sweet abandon. She turned, her arms flying around his neck so she could arch her body against his. His breath was moist, demanding, hotter still as he rained kisses over her eyes, her chin, the hollow of her neck.

She wanted him to imprint his taste, the way he felt, the rhythm of his heart upon her memory. But he pulled away.

"What's wrong?" She felt suddenly bereft, uncommonly alone.

"It can't be easy to let go of a dream you've nurtured all your life."

In that instant she understood his hesitation and knew that if she could not convince Rem now, she would forever lose him to doubt. "Noble was a part of my fantasies, Rem. I'd be foolish to deny that. But the truth is,

my affection for him never became the reality of love I
feel for you."

The shift in his emotions surged through Rem's rigid
body and flamed in his eyes.

She touched his face. "Remember when we played
leapfrog?"

"It was the first moment I began to love—"

Their bodies collided. Hands, mouths, thighs touched.
The intensity of his ardor pressed hotly against her, forcing Rem to sweep Kenzy up into his arms and carry her
past the bank to the seclusion of the alcove.

Laying her down in the soft scattering of herbs, he
quickly rid her of the offending clothing that remained
between them. She shivered as he stood above her, magnificent in his maleness. The hunger in his eyes only
served to increase her willingness to satisfy it.

His mouth plundered hers, his tongue demanding a
kiss so intense it threatened to take her breath. As she
tasted the inner sanctuary of his lips, she moaned with
anticipation.

"Kenzy."

Her name was a prayer, a reverent, worshipful whisper that beckoned her to press kisses from the stubbled
underside of his chin to his ear, then down the muscular
sweep of his shoulder.

In turn, he scattered hot, wet kisses over her eyes,
down her neck, to the valley of her breasts. Her pulse
kept rhythm with the tune singing through her senses.
"Rem. My darling, Rembrandt."

She almost wept the sweetness of his name and the
love he was awakening with her. She wanted him, all of
him. Her body arched toward his, offering her breasts to
his intimate caress. He wrapped his hot tongue around
one peak and suckled it as if he were a child searching
for nourishment. Softly she cried out at the ecstastic pain
of it all.

Her fingers slid through his hair, tightened over his
nape and pressed him more closely to her breast. He
lavished it thoroughly, then paid homage to the other.

His breath grew ragged, and the muscles in his arms quivered from restraint. When his head came up, his eyes were fathomless pools of black that reflected the fiery passion burning within him.

"Before your God," he rasped in a passion-induced voice, "swear to me, Kenzy, that your love will be mine alone, not only through this life, but all those to come."

The beat of her heart threatened to break through her ribs. Kenzy touched his face and vowed never again to be part of any disappointment or disillusionment that might mar the beloved features. "I would rather spend eternity in hell before I did."

Rem began to explore her. His thumb traced the wet trail of her nipples, honoring them as his tongue had. Running lightly down the plane of her abdomen, his fingers splayed to test the width of her waist then hesitated over the downy softness between her legs. She arched toward him, wanting more.

Rem slid down the length of her slowly, the hot shaft of his desire mounting pressure inside her as he led them to the brink of ecstasy. She opened herself to him without shame, without thought of what society, or even Rose, might remind her of later. Kenzy gave him her heart and her body without stipulation.

"Easy," he told her. "A moment more, so the pain will be slight and the joy worth waiting for."

"Oh, Rem." His thoughtfulness hummed in her veins.

He caught her hand, and as he shifted, Kenzy became aware of his intent.

"Touch me."

Her eyes widened as his hand closed over hers and gently guided it to the smooth hot skin of his burgeoning desire. Her breath left her in an unsteady exhalation of surprise at the length of him and pleasurable sound rumbling from deep within his throat. His head dropped, causing his dark hair to tickle her chin. How incredibly hot he was in her fingers. How magnificent he felt to her touch.

He trembled and groaned again as her exploration

commenced. Her fingertips lightly tested the curvature of his knee, the swell of buttocks, the span of muscle that protected the gift of his heart.

Their bodies had started a rhythm between them—a motion so natural, it was as if they'd practiced the tempo all their lives. The strange dance wasn't enough. A hunger was building inside her, a painful craving that only the closest intimacy could satisfy. "I want to be closer," she murmured. "Show me how to be closer."

Rem lifted his head, the love in his eyes bonding her to him more inexplicably than any manner their bodies desired. Rem smiled, and the promise in that smile opened Kenzy to him forever.

He entered, slowly. She thought she would explode with the sheer pleasure of feeling him deep inside her, but suddenly he breeched the barrier of her maidenhead. Pain, unlike any she'd ever known, assailed her. She froze.

"This will be the last time I hurt you," he promised.

The obvious control it took him not to move echoed in his raspy tone. Closing her eyes, Kenzy willed herself the courage to withstand whatever pain remained. She wanted this, regardless of the discomfort inside her. She ached to be as close to him as their bodies allowed. Drawing her legs around his buttocks, she arched her hips to offer him further access to what he would not take if she were unwilling. He covered her cry with his lips, sinking against her, driving deeply, so their bodies joined completely.

Liquid fire raced through Kenzy's veins as her tender threshold yielded to his love. He filled her to the point of bursting, allowing her body to adjust to the sweet torture. Laughter bubbled up inside her—pure joy singing wondrously from her soul. "So, this is your magic!" she cried in his ear.

His own laughter was husky and deeply thrilling. "No . . . this is *our* magic, and now we shall have the eons to master this spell."

The tantalizing prospect of spending such a future in his arms must have shone in her eyes, for a savage growl emanated from deep within him and he began to move slowly. With a rhythm that demanded she join him in the dance, he rocked her. Her body responded to his every whisper, to his every thrust.

Gone was the sharp pain of their earlier joining. Now there was only rapture in his touch, pleasure in his possession. With each met thrust, Kenzy welcomed the intense ache building inside her. Sensation upon sensation enveloped her, compelling Kenzy to vie for something just beyond her reach. Something so majestic she would die if she could not touch it soon.

Then it happened. His gaze locked with hers, and she saw eternity reflected in its depths. Rem's hands braced to each side of her, his hips twisting against hers. Her fingers traced hotly over the taunt, bunching cords of his chest. The urgency that consumed her body sent Kenzy spiraling up, up, up.

The mounting, heart-stopping pleasure shattered into a million shards of blinding-white ecstasy. Her soul cried out his name as Kenzy clutched at his arms, his back, his hips to glory in the euphoria of their love.

She drifted back to reality, basking in his deep caress and the sweet murmurs of his ancestral language. He rolled to his side, carrying her with him. Her fingers absently trailed through the soft hair on his chest as she peered into his beloved face.

He smiled. Kenzy couldn't help but return an even bolder one back to him. "I had no idea it could be so wonderful."

She kissed his cheek, suddenly conscious of stubble of his beard against her her tender lips that hadn't mattered a minute ago. "Thank you," she whispered, feeling seductive and beautiful and, oh so womanly.

Rem closed his eyes. but a smile still lingered on his lips. "No shy wanton, my Tadpole."

"Too much time has been wasted already, and I'm sure it's no surprise to you that I'm not shy. I am perfectly willing to discover how much of a wild woman you've made me." She winked at him. "But first, I'd like a list of what you have in mind for us."

"Let's see, I can kiss you right here." He nibbled on her earlobe.

"Ummhumm. That will do for starters."

"And I can taste you there." He lavished the tip of one nipple with his tongue, then raised to see her expression. "Liked that, did you?"

"What else? I need to make sure . . . Oh!" She cooed her pleasure as he ground his hips against her. "I definitely liked that. I think I'm going to enjoy you enlightening mc to your ways."

"There's countless measures of my magic. Are you ready to experience more?"

Adventure—wild and wickedly seductive—called to Kenzy. She was ready for anything Rem had to offer her.

He slid down her body and didn't stop where she expected him to. Rem's dark head bent. His mouth laid claim. And she lost every semblance of sanity.

25

For a long while, Rem pretended to sleep, telling himself that if he waited there long enough, Kenzy would have to return to the wall-raising party and he could gather all his belongings and leave.

He'd awakened from the haunting thoughts of his nightmare still whispering in his head. When Rem reached for Kenzy to assure himself the turmoil was sleep-induced, she was absent from the bed they'd made in the alcove. He'd wanted to make love to her again, reassure himself that she'd come to him today out of love alone.

But he found her pilfering Brett's letter from the inner fold of his hat. She obviously had another purpose for making him delirious with ecstasy. She'd done her job well, he'd give her that. He could not fault her enthusiasm for the role she played.

From the way she held the letter in her hand, he couldn't determine if she'd already read it and was attempting to put it back, or if he'd caught her in the initial act. Whatever the case, her actions were intolerable and unexcusable, giving him just the excuse he needed to make her go.

All afternoon he'd gloried in the way her skin felt to his touch. The way her body boldly claimed and gave in equal measures. The way she had filled him with light and love and laughter. For a short time, he'd basked in the brilliance of her love, believed that together they could dispel any darkness that stalked them. But reality cast a long shadow and claimed its due, as Kenzy predicted it would last night. It seemed he couldn't trust her, and she didn't need to be saddled with the constraints of being a gypsy's woman.

"What are you doing?" Rem sat up, burying the disappointment in the deepest recess of his heart.

Startled, she turned and smiled at him. "Getting the letter for Noble. I believe he plans to read it to the others today "

"It's too late." *Too late for us, Kenzy.* "I don't want it read."

Puzzlement creased her brow. "But why? You have a right to be vindicated."

She'd read enough to understand its implications. "Good people will be hurt by it. I came back to San Augustine to repair my name. I stayed here because I hoped you might share my name and my life. Now, I don't care to live my life anymore worrying what other people think of me. I could change in a thousand different ways, and I'll always be considered an outcast. No letter will ever alter that."

"It's what you think of yourself that counts."

"I've learned that, but it's equally important to remember *how* you think of others . . . not *what* you think of them. I've made a decision not to force the reading of that letter. I don't need its confirmation anymore. And Noble and Rose don't need its trouble." He hadn't really decided how he felt completely until this moment when she'd almost stolen the choice from him. "I'd appreciate if you'd put that back where you found it and leave me."

"I'll only have to go for a little while." She shrugged and lay the letter inside the hat, not taking the time to fold it neatly nor place it within the liner. She started combing her fingers through her hair to tidy the auburn mass. "Better yet, you can go with me. They're having a sing-along tonight."

He stood, shaking his head. "No, Kenzy. I mean you must leave me forever."

Dismay carved her features. "I don't understand. Days ago you made me worry when you intended to leave, then you actually do go and I'm not sure where you are for days. Last night, you make me feel that I have to prove myself to you all over again because of my return with Noble to see about Rose. Now, after we've had what I consider the most beautiful day of my life, you stand there and tell me I have to leave you forever. Why, for God's or whoever's sake you believe in, do you ask that of me?"

"I'm not asking, Kenzy. I'm telling you. What you feel for me is only an attraction to danger. I'm the forbidden. A new adventure for you. If you think about it, that's why you're not in love with Noble. He was the boy every girl wanted in their youth. He was the boy who made you feel good about yourself and let you test your wiles upon him. He was the young man who captured Rose's heart . . . which made him the forbidden to you. You've known since you came back that Rose and Noble loved each other so deeply you couldn't possibly come between them."

"And you think that my feelings for you are because I've moved on to something new? Something a little more daring? Something I felt I could control?"

He couldn't bear the hurt in her eyes, the anger in her voice. *Better anger than tears, love,* he offered silently. His heart would mourn her long after he lay for eternity beside GranZeph in the meadowsweet.

Kenzy whirled and started pinning her hair up. "I'm angry because you're being unfair and couldn't be more wrong."

Had she heard his very thoughts? If so, their bond was greater than he imagined. A gust of wind whistled through the hunter-green vines that threaded the kaleidoscope of flowers shielding the alcove. "I'm trying to save us both pain. When your physical attraction to me wears thin, you'll yearn for the goodness of your golden boy or someone like him."

"I was wrong about you, and I thank you for letting me see that before I waded in too deep." Kenzy walked over to Rem and stared him straight in the eyes. "You are the most prejudiced person I know, and do you know why that is?"

He half expected her to slap him. Her hands opened and closed into fists as she clearly fought the urge. "I know you won't leave here until you tell me," he said.

She executed his expectation, slapping him. "Don't pretend to know what I will and won't do, Rembrandt Parker. You may have played me for a fool, but at least I'm no coward. That's what you are, Rem, the coward everyone thought you were, but not for the reason they believed it of you."

Her chin lifted. "You're afraid to belong to me, even though you've wanted to belong to someone all your life. Afraid to believe I'm willing to go up against all the injustices that could possibly be inflicted upon us. You'd rather consider yourself some strange breed of man forever doomed to spend your nights alone than fight for me and the right for us to make a life together. Why? Because *you* don't know if you're strong enough to deal with it."

He started to protest, but she would have none of it.

"You can stand there and talk all you want, but that's the truth of it, Rem. Love is about taking risks. Offering all you are and all you feel, no matter what anyone else in the world says."

Her gaze averted his, turning to look uphill to the orphanage. Tears shimmered in her eyes but did not fall. "I'll leave. You bet I will. And I'll take every ounce of love I ever had to offer you with me."

Anger, frustration and despair battled within her in equal measure. "Someday when you're old and lonely, remember that it didn't have to be this way, Rem. Together, we could have shed light on the darkness that haunts us both."

26

$\mathcal{K}$enzy ran blindly toward the orphanage, miserable and feeling betrayed. She rubbed at the haze of tears stinging her eyes.

The closer she drew to the top of the hill, the more she realized that her eyes were affected by something more than the heartbreak she'd just experienced. Her nostrils flared. A stench filled the air. Her throat convulsed in reaction to an acrid taste assailing its sensitive lining. Shades of gray billowed over the top of the hill. Smoke!

She shouted and broke into a run. In seconds her eyes focused on her worst fear. Her dreams were on fire! The orphanage was cast in a sickly orange glow. A scan of the countryside showed everyone must be on the hayride. Only a handful of empty buggies remained to prove there had been people here earlier. The newly erected framework of the house looked like a blazing sun rising from the earth. Firebrands leaped from every corner of the building's skeleton, consuming the tender wood until it blackened and shriveled. Thank God, everyone had left and was at a safe distance.

The sight of Rose's empty wheelchair, sent a tingling up Kenzy's scalp. *She's safe*, she assured herself. *Your imagination is running away with itself again. Noble*

*probably just set her on the haywagon and didn't bother
with the chair.* But Kenzy had to be certain. Her presumptions lately had cost her too much. *Please don't be
in there, Whit. Especially not without your chair.*

The bell! Kenzy needed to reach Cord's bell and ring
the distress call. God bless the child for demanding one
be stationed in the orphanage's foreyard. Battling the
intense heat proved a more daunting task than envisioned. Every time she won a few inches closer, the
flames licked out fiery tongues to test her tenacity.

The sound of wood splintering erupted into a blazing
inferno. Kenzy screamed Rose's name. Frantically, she
covered her mouth with her sleeve and barrelled into the
rolling smoke.

The fire at the entrance to the orphanage burned white
hot, but Kenzy pressed closer, praying that the bell rope
had not been consumed in the flames's fury. Her eyes
watered as smoke filled her lungs.

She reached where the bell pole should have stood,
but her fingers grasped only liquid heat. The smoke must
have misdirected her. *Calm down. You know this land
like the blueprints you've made of it. Look at the ground
where you step.* Yes, she could see a sawhorse amid the
occasional break in the cloud of smoke to the left of her.
She'd last seen Cord standing on it to adjust something
about the bell. Kenzy rushed to the sawhorse, started
making a semicircle until she was rewarded with her
goal.

The rope was so hot it blistered her gloveless fingers.
Gritting back the pain, she pulled on its weakened rawhide and rejoiced when three peals rang out loud and
clear.

"Kenzy! Help us!"

Kenzy spun around scrutinizing the ghostly specter of
the entrance knowing that somewhere in that darkening
pit of smoke and flame Rose was trapped. "Call to me
Rose! I can't see you! Your voice will have to direct
me. The smoke is too thick. Just keep calling to me. I'll

find you." Kenzy hesitated only as long as it took her friend to call out.

"Find Worthy first." Rose choked out horrifying words. "He was hiding somewhere inside the building when the fire broke out. Noble and I haven't been able to find him. Hurry, Kenzy. We've got to find him."

Kenzy followed the desperation in Rose's voice, keeping low since the boy would probably be hunkered down somewhere to get more air. And Rose? Did she lay prone unable to rescue herself? Suddenly another flare, outlining a woman's form. A woman moving with a cane! The shadowy figure teetered, almost fell.

"Whit!" Kenzy cried out her name, rushing through the black abyss to reach her. Her hands touched precious flesh. Rose gripped her as if Kenzy were a lifeline and, Rose, about to be swallowed by quicksand. Kenzy clutched her, wrapping her arms around Rose to steady her. "We're going to get you out first, Whit. We've got to." On occasion, she thought she saw a shadowy form highlighted by the licking flames. She prayed for Noble's presence whether or not he had already succumbed to the blaze. "Noble will keep looking. Lean on me as well as the cane."

Rose jerked away. "No, I'm not leaving Noble, and he won't leave the boy. You'll stay just to see me safe. If we die, then we die together."

"No one's going to die while there's still breath in my body. You are leaving this place, the both of you, and there's no time for more argument."

The command came from a cherished voice Kenzy thought she'd conjured up at will. But to her relief and great fear Rem was no figment of her imagination. His two strong arms lifted Rose off the ground and barrelled through the flaming specter of death threatening to seal off any retreat.

Despite Rose's protest, he managed to position them far enough away to assure their safety. As he placed Rose back into the security of her wheelchair, Kenzy collapsed to her knees. She sucked in deep breaths of fresh air to loosen her lungs that were tight and painful from inhaling too much smoke.

Rose began to weep, her voice a raspy plea. "You've got to save them, Rem." A fireball rolled heavenward, nearly jolting her from the chair. "Noble! Oh, my precious love. Don't die. Don't die!"

"Stay here with Rose, Kenzy."

Kenzy breathed out a steady stream, all the while shaking her head. "You'll need help."

"I need you to make sure Rose doesn't try to go back in. I'll be back soon. I have to be."

His black eyes swept over her, examined her as if he were commiting Kenzy to memory. "Don't you dare, Rem Parker! Don't you dare say good-bye to me or, I swear, I'll haunt you for a hundred lifetimes."

"How touching." The sarcasm of Anna LeGrand's remark focused all their attention in the direction of the bell. "You just won't go away, will you, gypsy? Well, when I tell everyone you set this holocaust, you'll be driven out."

"Move away from the door, Anna. I'm just gypsy enough to have no qualms about shoving you aside."

"You'll never get past me . . . alive." Anna's hand reached from inside her pocket and pulled out a gun. "You didn't think I was stupid enough not to bring a weapon?"

Kenzy moved in front of Rem, making her body a target for the woman's wrath. "You've got to let him pass, Anna. Noble and Worthy are still in there and this is the only section that isn't entirely engulfed in flames."

She shrugged. "I'm sorry about the boy, but if I can't convince Noble not to marry that cripple, I'd rather see him dead."

The heat of Rem's body shifted behind Kenzy. He was about to try something. How could she help? Possibilities raced like a wind-driven prairie fire through her thoughts. *Redirect Anna's anger toward you.* It wasn't much of a plan, but it was all Kenzy could think of. Maybe it would be enough to give Rem an opportunity.

She had to take the chance that Noble and Rose had waited on her return from the alcove so Kenzy could be in attendance when they made the announcement of their coming marriage.

"He's your cousin, Anna." Kenzy took a few steps forward, but the gun signaled her back. "You know if Rose doesn't marry him, I plan to."

"I'm not stupid, McKenzy. What were you doing all day when you should have been here watching the walls go up?" Her laughter echoed with demonic glee. "Come to think of it, they are going up now, aren't they? Just not in the manner you expected."

"I knew someone was spying on me."

Rem should have refrained from talking, for it only served to infuriate Anna more.

"I had to think quick when you started setting all those little traps for me. I lost a good roan over it. His hooves tangled in the ginseng you used to fence in that fancy-colored wagon you call home. The fall broke both his front legs. Do you know how hard it was to get that animal out of sight with two broken legs?"

"You must have had a conspirator. An awfully large one at that."

"You're a smarter man that I thought. Marsdale was right about you. Oh, now, there I've gone and given it all away, haven't I? It's a real shame, none of you will live to repeat any of this."

Anger fused Kenzy. She wasn't going to stand there and do nothing. Kenzy took a running leap, intent upon making only one body the madwoman's target.

"Kenzy," Rose screamed.

"Overhead. Look out!"

Rem's warning came too late. The timber that formed the bell pole snapped, crashing toward Anna. Anna's howl of disbelief echoed eerily in Kenzy's ears. Kenzy reacted instinctively as the bell and its tower toppled on Noble's cousin. She rushed to the woman and began to roll her over and over to stamp out the fire eating away at the woman's clothes and hair.

"Find them, Rem! Find them now." There was nothing to do but encourage him. A man like Rem would never break his word. He'd promised to save them all or die trying.

Kenzy whispered a hurried prayer for his and the others' safety, adding a thank you for having saved her from Anna's bullet. But for the grace of seconds, *she* would have become the tower's victim. The flames had grown so intense now, the countryside lit with an unholy light. It might have appeared to be a waning sunset to some, but to Kenzy it was a reminder that courage must be taken no matter what the hour.

Silhouettes of the crosses dotting the makeshift cemetery down the hill loomed like dark sentinels forever standing watch for new prey. She suppressed a shudder, wondering if this terrifying night would claim its due after all, by adding another more beloved hero to its midst . . . her hero.

A rasping fit of coughs awarded Rem the sight of Noble carrying Worthy in his arms, stumbling through the smoke. By his labored walk, Rem knew the smoke had all but overcome the carpenter. Rem raced to reach the man and tugged the child from his arms. "Hang on to my back, Noble. I'll help you out."

"Worthy," Noble gasped, bracing his hands on his knees to steady himself. "He's unconscious."

"He'll be more than that if we don't get out of here. Hang on."

Noble gripped Rem's shoulders, and Rem literally dragged Noble through the blistering heat.

When he finally cleared the flames, he discovered a riot of motion in front of him. The hayriders had apparently heard Kenzy's initial signal for help and had just arrived. A bucket brigade had formed, using the cooking utensils from the day's meal preparation. A line of men, women and children transferred each bucket hand-over-hand to the last person throwing the creek water in attempt to stop the fire from raging out of control.

Men were already digging a firebreak around the house so that if the water wouldn't stop the fire, the lack of burnable fuel might.

"They're out!" Kenzy shouted hysterically. "Thank God, they're all alive!"

Cordell rushed up to Worthy, tears streaming down his face. He looked up at Rem, whispering over and over, "I'm sorry. I'm so sorry."

Rem asked one of the larger men to take Noble to Rose so she could check him for injury.

"Worthy's the only family I have, and I let him down. I failed him," Cord muttered miserably.

"You didn't, Cordell." Kenzy motioned them to come closer, putting more distance between them and the men forming the first line of defense against the fire. "You didn't fail anyone. This was not your fault, do you understand me. Not your fault."

Rem put his mouth over the seven-year-old's and blew methodically, trying to breathe fresh air into his lungs. Worthy whimpered.

"But I was supposed to be keeping watch over him." Apology etched Cord's features. "I got distracted studying the nightshade growing on the downslope of the hill. Then I wondered why Miz LeGrand was moving through the trees like she didn't want to be seen. I thought she might be spying on you and Rem, but come to find out she was meeting with Mr. Marsdale."

"I crept a little closer when I heard her say something about the sulphur and how easy it would be to make it look like an accident. That's when I saw that other fellow. The one everybody says is a Ranger. I had to hide or they would have seen me. I saw him talking to them, kind of playing with his handcuffs. I sure didn't want him to think I was any part of Anna and Mr. Marsdale's scheme, if he decided to arrest them."

His breath blew out in ever-quickening puffs. "I ran to your wagon, but you weren't there. Then I thought you might be working in the garden, but you weren't. That's about the time my bell rang and I knew exactly

what they decided to set afire." He clutched at Worthy's
hand. "If only I'd paid more attention to him. If only I
could help him . . ."

"You can. Go to my alcove and grab a handful of the
aloe plant and the stinkweed I showed you. We need
something to soothe his burns and revive his senses."
His eyes focused on Anna's prone body. "Get enough
for two."

"I know exactly which ones you mean." Cord took
off with the speed of a lightning strike.

"Thanks for giving him a way to forgive himself."
Kenzy took Worthy from Rem's arms.

"We all make mistakes. Forgiveness is a salve that
costs little to offer."

"I agree." Noble rolled Rose's chair forward. "Brett
once said something similar, only I was too ignorant to
listen to the wisdom of my brother's words. I'll explain,
but first things first . . . Kenzy, turn around here and let
Rose see you. She's not convinced that you're entirely
unharmed."

Kenzy showed her palms. "Just some burns. Nothing
that won't heal easy. I'm fine. It's Worthy who got the
worst of it." Kenzy lay the boy in the grass gently,
kneeling to tilt his head upon her lap. "But he'll be all
right once Cord returns with the herbs."

"The break is holding!" someone shouted.

All attention focused on the swatch of upturned earth
that held the fire's wrath at bay. A loud cheer went up.

Cordell raced up with the plants, thrusting them at
Rem. Rem immediately set the stinkweed beneath Worthy's nose. The seven-year-old's forehead wrinkled. His
nostrils flared and his mouth screwed up like he'd eaten
a persimmon. "Goodgawdamighty!"

Everyone laughed, relieved that the boy still had
enough breath within him to complain.

"Rub this aloe on Anna's burns and get someone to
help you put her in one of the wagons. And be careful
with her. She'll be pricklier than a porcupine if she
keeps yelling like that." Rem placed a hand on Cordell's

slim shoulder. "Think you can handle that?"

Cord pushed up his glasses as he nodded. "Yessir."

The sizzle and crack of dying wood punctuated the silence that consumed the party. The orphanage was completely lost. Burned to its foundation. Only the two chimneys Strut had fireproofed remained, the stone of their outer surfaces charred with black.

"Some other healing needs to take place, Rem." Noble stared at the top of Rem's head. "I hope you didn't lose your hat in the fire."

"It's back at the wagon. I didn't take time . . ." His gaze swept over Kenzy. "I heard the bell and came running."

"Then you still have the letter?"

"What letter?" Rem evaded. There was no need for this. What good would it do?

"The one he gave me the day Rose took Rem in to nurse back to health." Noble addressed the townsfolk rather than Rem. Curiosity made the group move closer. "The one that Brett dictated to Rem just before he died."

"This is not necessary, Stockton." Rem wanted no part of this. It was a hollow victory, at best. "I'll not give you the letter."

"This *is* necessary and I can recite it word for word if I have to. Brett's words have echoed over and over in my mind every day since the first I read them."

"What does it say, Stockton?" someone yelled.

Noble told of his brother's defection to the Union, illiciting gasps and recriminations through the crowd. Still he continued on, "One of his fellow officers found him exchanging information with the bluecoats for food and warm clothing."

Noble faced those who might enjoy seeing him and his brother disgraced. Rose reached out and threaded her fingers through his. He smiled at her gently. "Brett didn't die charging up that hill. He was shot for fraternizing with the enemy, then taken to one of our field hospitals. He'd asked a fellow San Augustinian to write his last words, a medic who didn't care if a hero or a traitor lay dying . . . only that he must grant a human being's last request, if it was within his power." Noble's shoulder shook as grief overcame him.

Rose stood from her chair, causing people around her to gasp in surprise. She wrapped her arms around Noble, urged him to bury his face in her shoulder, then held him as his body shook with silent sobs.

"Brett said something more that day," Rem defended the brother of the man who had been his arch rival until this afternoon. "He said a man's worth should not be measured by his willingness to fight but his belief in what he fights for. A very wise and caring woman once told him to fight for life, not death." Rem knew the minute Rose pulled away from Noble he had guessed the woman's identity correctly.

"Noble," Rose began. "I—I feared you would—"

Noble touched his forefinger to her lips. "There's no need, love. Your wisdom let Brett die in peace."

Kenzy waited impatiently as Rem made sure Worthy was properly settled into the wagon in Rose and Noble's care, and Strut had been sent to see if the Ranger needed any help corraling Marsdale. It seemed Cordell had witnessed Marsdale's capture, but Anna had somehow gotten away.

Kenzy gently squeezed Rose's hand as she looked up to her best friend. "Everything will be all right, Rose. You'll see."

"Everything already is." Rose leaned her head into Noble's shoulder. "I have all I need to be happy now."

Under Noble's commands, the team swung the wagon around, giving Kenzy one last glimpse of Cord and his pale-faced but still very much alive, patient. Somehow, Anna had managed to survive, too. Kenzy matched the wave Rem offered the children.

When the wagon formed the last of a long line heading back to town, Kenzy linked her arm through Rem's. "Okay, Mr. Wait-and-See-That-Everybody-in-Sight has been checked for burns or lung fever. Do you have enough magic to soothe one more wound?"

His eyes examined her so thoroughly, she thought he possessed the power to see through what remained of her once-white dress.

"Where do you hurt?"

"Here." She took his hand and pressed it warmly over the beat of her heart. "A deep wound that only one kind of medicine will heal. *Your* kind of medicine."

"I warn you . . ." Passion darkened his eyes to midnight. "Once I take you under my spell, you will be mine for all the eternities."

"That will never be long enough," she sighed in anticipation.

He branded her lips with forever.

Epilogue

*K*enzy and Rose watched the children playing in the yard of the year-old orphanage. Rose tapped her cane against the porch railing and motioned toward the two men heading up the path. "Noble says Rem would finish the carving of your tombstones this morning. He said to give them an hour, then come see what he's done. Guess we sat here gossiping too long."

"Or they got in too big of a hurry." Kenzy struggled to her feet, feeling the baby shift inside her, whether at the sudden movement or the thrill Kenzy experienced every time she saw the man to whom she'd given her heart so completely.

"You're shameless, Kenz. At least look like you can wait to see him. He's only been gone an hour."

"Does it show that much?"

"Wonderfully so." Rose laughed, reaching out to touch the tiny soul that would soon become her god-child. "I can't imagine why Rem is so insistent upon preparing for eternity when you've obviously got much more life to live here."

"Don't blame him. It's my fault. Remember I told you why he landscaped the place? Well, I made him promise to make sure that my own personal hero sleeps

beside me now and for all eternity. He said I always
know best." Kenzy giggled. "Which is true, of course,
but the real reason he agreed is because that man is
always in a hurry to get me to lie down with him somewhere."

"Kenzy!"

"Whit!" Both women laughed like twelve-year-olds
sharing their first introduction to boys.

The two men waved to Cordell and Worthy who raced
to join their elders. Worthy took up a stride alongside
Rem, his small legs working quadruple-time to keep up.

Cordell glanced up at Noble, receiving a gentle punch
on the arm. The boy pushed up his glasses and beamed,
punching the carpenter back and matching Noble stride
for long-legged stride.

It was in that moment Kenzy realized Noble's special
calling. He could be anybody's friend. He had a quality
about him that you couldn't help but respect. He made
a person feel special and cared for. And that's what he
would always be to Kenzy . . . a special friend married
to her best friend.

But love came calling under a different name . . . and
that name was Rembrandt Parker.

Rose's hand reached out and locked with Kenzy's.
"Will you look at that." She sighed. "Do you always
think we'll be this happy?"

Kenzy squeezed her hand in return. "Now and forever . . ." she began to chant.

"Always together," Rose finished their pledge.

"Family," their voices echoed in unison.

DeWanna Pace enjoys hearing from her readers.

DeWanna Pace
c/o The Berkley Publishing Group
a division of Penguin Putnam Inc.
375 Hudson Street
New York, NY 10014

DeWannaP@juno.com
www.angelfire.com/tx/dpace

FRIENDS ROMANCE

Can a man come between friends?

❑ **A TASTE OF HONEY**

by DeWanna Pace   0-515-12387-0

❑ **WHERE THE HEART IS**

by Sheridon Smythe   0-515-12412-5

❑ **LONG WAY HOME**

by Wendy Corsi Staub   0-515-12440-0

All books $5.99